Chrysostom P Donahoe

Life of Daniel O'Connell

Chrysostom P Donahoe

Life of Daniel O'Connell

ISBN/EAN: 9783744789479

Printed in Europe, USA, Canada, Australia, Japan

Cover: Foto ©Andreas Hilbeck / pixelio.de

More available books at **www.hansebooks.com**

PREFACE.

THIS volume, now presented to the admirers of the great Irish Liberator in America, has been compiled from the most authentic sources, with the object of placing in the hands of the people the simple story of his life, at a price fully within the reach of everybody.

THE COMPILER.

BOSTON, OCTOBER, 1875.

LIFE OF O'CONNELL.

CHAPTER I.

DANIEL O'CONNELL, the Irish Liberator, was born at Carhen, near Cahirciveen, August 6th, 1775.

Seventeen hundred and seventy-five was a memorable year in the annals of Ireland and America. In that year began the war for American Independence, which was the birth of the United States, whilst the advent of O'Connell was a new era in the destinies of Catholic Ireland. It is a singular fact that these two events, so vital to the existence of both countries, should have occurred so nearly together.

The struggle which began at Lexington created a profound impression on all classes of the Irish people. The grievances of both countries were in many respects identical. The commerce between them was already considerable, creating a bond of mutual interest, whilst the Catholics, who formed the great bulk of the Irish nation, saw in the issue of the unequal contest the only possible hope of terminating their grievances. At this period the Irish Catholics were still suffering under the brutal torture of the Penal Laws. "An execrable, infamous code," says the lamented Wolfe Tone, "framed with the art and malice of demons, to plunder, degrade, and brutalize the Catholics of Ireland." It was, indeed, an execrable code, as may be seen from the following summary:

"The Catholic peers were deprived of their right to sit in Parliament. Catholic gentlemen were forbidden to be elected as members of Parliament. All Catholics were denied the liberty of voting, and excluded from all offices of trust and emolument. They were fined £60 a month for absence from the Protestant form of worship. They were forbidden to travel *five miles* from their houses, *to keep arms*, to maintain *suits at law*, or to be guardians or executors. Any four justices of the peace could, without further trial, banish any man for life if he refused to attend the Protestant service. Any two justices of the peace could call any man over sixteen before them, and if he refused to abjure the Catholic religion, they could bestow his property to the next of kin. No Catholic could employ a Catholic schoolmaster to educate his children; and if he sent his child abroad for education, he was subject to a fine of £100, and the child could not inherit any property either in England or Ireland. Any Catholic priest who came to the country should be hanged. Any Protestant suspecting any other Protestant of holding property in trust for any Catholic, might file a bill against the suspected trustee, and take the estate or property from him. Any Protestant seeing a Catholic tenant-at-will on a farm which, in his opinion, yielded one-third more than the yearly rent, might enter on that farm, and by *simply swearing to the fact*, take possession. Any Protestant might take away the horse of a Catholic, no matter how valuable, by simply paying him £5. Horses and wagons belonging to Catholics were in all cases to be seized for the use of militia. Any Catholic gentleman's child who became a Protestant could at once take possession of his father's property."

It is not surprising, then, that the operation of such a code of legalized robbery and oppression for nearly a century should, at the period of O'Connell's birth, have reduced the Catholics of Ireland to a state of absolute degradation. No nation ever maintained its faith and traditions with greater fidelity and loyalty, no nation has ever made greater sacrifices to perpetuate them. There were found individuals, however, during that period of trial, who were willing, Judas-like, to barter their faith to preserve their property. The following incident, which was told by O'Connell himself, proves that such conversions were neither lasting nor sincere.

"There was a Mr. Myers, of the County of Roscommon, who was threatened that a Bill of Discovery should be filed against him. He instantly galloped off to Dublin in a terrible fright, and sought out the Protestant archbishop. The archbishop examined him upon the points of difference between the two churches, and found that he knew nothing at all about the matter. He accordingly said he could not receive him into the Anglican Church unless he should get some previous instruction; and politely offered to commit him to the care of the Rector of Castlerea, who chanced to be in Dublin at the time. This proposal delighted Mr. Myers, for the rector had long been a hunting and drinking companion of his own in the country. The pious convert arranged to dine every day with the rector until the ensuing Sunday, upon which day it was absolutely necessary the recantation should be publicly made. Myers and the rector had a jovial booze — six bottles each at the least — and their jollification was repeated each day until Sunday; when the archbishop, on receiving an assurance from the jovial rector that Myers was *au fait* at the theology of the case, permitted him to make his solemn public abjuration of the errors of Popery, and to receive the Protestant sacrament. In order to celebrate the happy event the prelate invited Myers and several zealous Protestant friends to dinner. When the cloth was removed, his grace thus addressed the convert: 'Mr. Myers, you have this day been received into the true Protestant Church. For this you should thank God. I learn with pleasure from the Rector of Castlerea, that you have acquired an excellent knowledge of the basis of the Protestant religion. Will you be so kind as to state, for the edification of the company, the grounds upon which you have cast aside Popery and embraced the Church of England.' 'Faith, my lord,' replied Myers, 'I can easily do that; the grounds of my conversion to the Protestant religion are two thousand five hundred of the best *grounds* in the County Roscommon.' "

The population of Ireland was up made of three classes. The first class, though comprising only one-tenth of the inhabitants, controlled the government and possessed the greater portion of the landed property. It monopolized church and state, the law, the revenues, army and navy, magistracy and corporations, — in short, the entire patronage of Ireland.

The second class, the Dissenters, residing principally in the north, and forming a body double the size of the Established Church party, were mostly engaged in trade and manufactures. This class was largely in sympathy with Catholics, whose privations they materially shared.

The Catholics, numbering four-fifths of the population, formed the third class. They were the natural heirs to the broad acres of Ireland — the custodians of her faith and traditions — and yet they found no representation in her national council, not even a mediator before the throne. Denied the right of appeal, their one alternative was submission. Unarmed and undisciplined, without leadership, an appeal to force would have resulted, as was proven in '98, in indiscriminate slaughter. As we have already seen, the laws excluded the priesthood from the land, and those religious consolations so dear and necessary to the fervor of the Irish Catholic, were denied.

Such was the state of Ireland in 1775, when God sent to that devoted country the immortal O'Connell.

The surname of O'Connell emanated from an ancient prince of the royal line of Heber, who immigrated from Connelloe, in Limerick, to Iveragh, in Kerry,

long before the English invasion.   The direct ances-
tor of the Liberator was Hugh O'Connell, who held a
commission issued by Edward III., in the year 1337.
Hugh O'Connell was succeeded by a son of the same
name, who married Marguerita, daughter of the
Prince of Thomond, and from this union proceeded a
long line of illustrious descendants.

The O'Connell's were a prolific race.   "My grandmother," said O'Connell, "had twenty-two children,
and half of them lived beyond the age of ninety.
Old Maurice O'Connell, of Derrynane, pitched upon
an oak tree to make his own coffin, and mentioned
his purpose to a carpenter.   In the evening, the butler entered, after dinner, to say that the carpenter
wanted to speak to him.   'For what?' asked my
uncle.   'To talk about your honor's coffin,' said the
carpenter, putting his head inside the door, over the
butler's shoulder.   I wanted to get the fellow out,
but my uncle said: 'O! let him in, by all means.
Well, friend, what do you want to say to me about
my coffin?'   'Only, sir, that I'll saw the oak tree
your honor was speaking of into seven-foot plank.'
'That would be wasteful,' said my uncle.   'I never
was more than six feet and an inch in my vamps, the
best day I ever saw.'   'But your honor will stretch
after death,' said the carpenter.   'Not eleven inches,
I am sure, you blockhead! But I'll stretch, no doubt;
perhaps a couple of inches or so.   Well, make my
coffin six feet six, and I'll warrant that will give me
room enough.'"

Of the uncles of O'Connell the most remarkable
was General Count O'Connell, who served in the

Irish Brigade. At the tender age of fourteen he entered the military service of France, and was made colonel before he had attained his fortieth year, which appointment came of his gallantry at the siege of Gibraltar. In time he was commissioned Inspector-General of the French Infantry, and the discipline of his command was the admiration of all Europe. He afterwards invented a manual of tactics which was accepted by Napoleon I., and adopted by the armies of Russia, Prussia, Austria, and England.

Morgan O'Connell, in 1774, married Catherine, daughter of John Mullane, Esq., by whom he had ten children, the first of whom was Daniel O'Connell, the subject of this biography.

The scenes in which we are brought up impress their character upon our souls. Cromwell, so great a scourge to Ireland, grew up amid the stagnant marshes of the Ouse, whilst O'Connell reflected in his after life the inspiration of his own beloved Kerry. But the Kerry of 1775 was not the Kerry of to-day. At that time smuggling was carried on extensively by many leading traders of that county, and there is reason to believe that one of the O'Connell family owed his prosperity to this practice. The smugglers drove a thriving silk and cloth trade with France, and landed their cargoes in the dangerous coves of the coast, their knowledge of the various harbors and inlets giving them a superiority over the revenue officers, who dared not pursue them.

The mountains of Glencara were infested by a daring band of robbers who alternately pillaged the plains of Clare and Kerry. On one occasion, O'Connell's father came near losing his life at their hands. Riding home alone one evening, he was set upon by these desperadoes, determined to revenge on his friendless head the injuries which, when surrounded by companions, he had inflicted on them. Rushing down the slope of a mountain they called on him with threats to stop, and fired on him as he continued his course. His horse at this moment, terrified by the discharge of the musket, became unmanageable, and he was flung heavily to the ground. While thus prostrate he was again fired at, but fortunately without effect. Regaining his feet, he succeeded in recovering his horse, and, springing upon its back, he was speedily beyond the reach of the banditti, who pursued, and fired at him as he fled.

Thus the childhood of Daniel O'Connell developed itself amid stirring scenes of adventure, and the mournful traditions of an oppressed people. In 1777, the Catholics were permitted to purchase and hold property for the term of 999 years, but education, so necessary to the future statesman, was still vetoed by Penal Laws. Yet there were men to be found, in the face of these restrictions, in whom the love of learning was greater than the fear of punishment, who went about the country instructing the few fortunate youths happy enough to secure their services. The better to evade the law, their classes assembled behind the friendly shelter of a hedge, from which they received the well-known appellation of " Hedge Schoolmasters." The home of O'Connell, from its isolation, offered a rare opportunity for such instructors to ply their calling unmolested. When our young

hero had attained his third year, one of these itiner-
ant teachers came by chance to Carhen, where he
was installed as tutor.

John Burke, for such was his name, had been in-
structed at the Sorbonne, in Paris, and had received
a very superior education. His young pupil was by
no means dull, for it is said that he mastered the English alphabet in one hour. Having once learned to
read, a passion for study seized him, and whilst his
companions were romping in their games, he was
poring over his books.

On one occasion, some friends were discussing the
merits of Flood and Grattan around the hospitable
board of O'Connell's father. A warm debate ensued,
during which the young Liberator, then but nine years
of age, was noticed sitting dreamily in an arm chair,
lost in thought. A lady, observing his abstracted air,
was curious to learn the boy's thoughts.

"What ails you, Dan? what are you thinking of?"
He turned, and looking at her said: "I'll make a stir
in the world yet."

Was the curtain of the future raised for an instant
before the mental gaze of the young dreamer?

O'Connell's uncle, Maurice, being childless, adopted
his young nephew, and at his expense he was sent to
Rev. Mr. Harrington's school, near Cork. O'Connell
had reached his thirteenth year, and the good Father
O'Grady, whose presence in Ireland was at the risk
of his life, had prepared him for the sacraments.
With what tender piety he received the "Bread of
Life" may be judged from the tenor of his after life.
At his new school he worked hard; and he has said

himself, "I was the only boy at Harrington's school who was not beaten. I owed this to my attention." After having spent some three years at the Harrington school, O'Connell and his younger brother were sent by their uncle to Liege, in Flanders; as Catholics, in 1791, were still denied the right of education. They sailed from Ireland in a vessel bound for London. The captain undertook to land them at Dover, from which they could embark for Ostend. Approaching the shore from the vessel in a small boat, they were capsized, and O'Connell landed on the shores of England, for the first time, thoroughly drenched. A few days after they arrived in Liege, where it was discovered that the boys had passed the age at which students were admitted.

Having acquainted their uncle with this fact, the brothers were ordered by him to St. Omer, in France. The hard work at Father Harrington's school was not without its good results. The young tribune pursued his studies with such ardor, that in a short time he was at the head of his class. This honor was no sinecure. The Munster students, his rivals, were famous for their proficiency in Latin and Mathematics, and his success was due to that untiring perseverance, which, in later days, proved so effective in the great work of agitation.

The President of St. Omer, in a letter to his uncle, thus alludes to him:

"With respect to the elder, Daniel, I have but one sentence to write about *him*, and that is, that I never was so much mistaken in my life as I shall be, unless

replied made an ineffaceable impression on the mind of O'Connell — gazing on him in astonishment. He said, " From love of ·the cause." The strangers were the two Sheareses.

These two brave but rash patriots afterwards offered up their lives on the altar of their country.

CHAPTER II.

AN act of Parliament, passed in 1792, threw the bar
open to the Catholics of Ireland. This was a long
and eagerly coveted concession. It gave rank and
status to its members, and, above all, it offered to the
poor and friendless Catholic a chance of justice in
the courts. Candidates for legal honors were obliged
to study in London. O'Connell, whose talents were
of a forensic character, determined to enter that profession.

Accordingly, in 1794, we find the Liberator lo-
cated in what he considered comfortable apartments,
in a small court on the north side of Coventry St.,
London. Soon after arriving, he became a law student at the celebrated Lincoln's Inn. Although
O'Connell worked hard, he seems to have enjoyed
his leisure hours in boating on the Thames. It was
necessary to preserve that vigor of body which he
had acquired in the noble field sports of his native
Kerry, and when not engaged at the Inn or in row-
ing, he took long walks in and about the great city.

During one of these rambles his life was placed in

imminent peril. The doings in France had not failed to make a deep impression upon the democracy of England, and riots in London, at this period, were both frequent and bloody.

Strolling through St. James's Park, with a young Irish friend, on the afternoon of October 29, 1795, O'Connell came upon a great gathering of people, whose intention, he shortly learned, was to attack their king. The carriage bearing his majesty soon after slowly hove in sight, surrounded by a mob of excited men. A penny, thrown in bitter irony by some one in the crowd, broke the window of the royal equipage. Immediately the dragoons, who formed the royal escort, encircled his carriage, and, drawing their sabres, charged upon the people. O'Connell, eager to catch a glimpse of the oppressor of his country, had already approached too near. His temerity attracted one of the guard, who aimed a most deadly blow at his head. Fortunately, the arm of a tree, two inches above his head, received the descending steel, and thus averted a danger which would have unquestionably cost O'Connell his life. The monarch escaped as by a miracle, and, palsied with fear, was driven off to Buckingham House at a gallop.

In 1795, O'Connell wrote to his uncle Maurice, of Derrynane, as follows:

"I am now only four miles from town. I pay the same price for board and lodging as I should in London; but I enjoy many advantages here (in Chiswick) besides air and retirement. The society in the house is mixed; I mean, composed of men and women, all of whom are people of rank and knowledge of the world; so their conversation and manners are perfectly well adapted to rub off the rust of scholastic education; nor is there any danger of riot or dissipation, as they are all advanced in life, another student of law and I being the only young persons in the house.

He further adds: "I have now two objects to pursue, — the one, the attainment of knowledge, the other, the acquisition of those qualities which constitute the polite gentleman." It may be seen from this, the young law student was not losing sight of his future, nor was he neglecting those means calculated to make it illustrious.

Whilst O'Connell was enjoying the quiet of Chiswick, there arose in Ireland a murderous institution, which has maintained its organization, even to the present day. This was the Orange society. At the small town of Armagh, called "The Diamond," in September 21st, of this year, the Protestants and Catholics came into deadly collision. Forty Catholics were killed in this fratricidal encounter, and the better armed Protestants, though inferior in numbers, supported by the magistrates, were victorious. Maddened with their success, in an evil hour they resolved to call themselves "Orangemen," in honor of William III., Prince of Orange. This illegal and inhuman body swore its members in under the following oath: "I do swear that I will be true to king and country, and that *I will exterminate the Catholics of Ireland, as far as in my power lies.*"

Apart from the disgraceful event which brought into being this outrage upon public tranquility, there never was a period when men of all religions were better disposed to amalgamate; but the interests, nay, the existence, of autocracy required that it should be otherwise; and the ignominy attached to Orangeism must forever rest upon the British ministry, who fostered and encouraged its progress. Some estimate may be formed of the fiendish character of this society from the fact that in a single year, 7,000 people were killed or driven from their homes by its members, in one county alone. They posted on the cabins of their victims this pithy notice, "To Hell or Connaught;" and notified them to leave on a certain day. When the period prescribed had elapsed, the Orangemen assembled, and burned the furniture and dwellings of the proscribed, and forced the ruined families to fly.

There was another society organized in 1791, whose constitution had a far nobler object in view. This society was called the United Irishmen. Theobald Wolfe Tone, a name dear to Irish patriots, conceived the noble project of uniting in one patriotic body the Catholics and Protestants of Ireland.

At that time he was a rising lawyer in Dublin, and, strange to say, *did not know personally a single Catholic.* The first clubs of "United Irishmen" were perfectly legal and constitutional in their structure, aims, and action; and so they continued until the new organization was adopted in 1795. Both in Dublin and in Belfast, they were composed chiefly of Protestants, though from the first they were joined by many eminent Catholics. Mark the first sentence of their constitution. How far more loyal than the Orangemen's oath; how far more Christian in its spirit:

"This society is constituted for the purpose of forwarding a brotherhood of *affection*, a communion of rights, and a union of power among Irishmen of *every religious persuasion*, and thereby to obtain a complete reform in the legislature, founded on principles of civil, political, and religious liberty."

This organization, having at heart the welfare of Ireland, strove hard to better her condition and aid the Catholics in obtaining justice. All their efforts, however, proved useless, and in 1796 they opened negotiations with the French government. The delegates were Lord Edward Fitzgerald, Arthur O'Connor, a gentleman of property in the county of Cork, and Theobald Wolfe Tone.

The state of affairs grew daily more critical, until, finally, the Insurrection of '98, fomented in a great measure by the government for its own satanic purposes, burst forth with terrible violence. Wexford was the first to strike a blow, and the whole island was soon convulsed by a struggle in which 70,000 of her citizens fell, and £18,000,000 of treasure were squandered.

O'Connell returned to Dublin in 1797, and in the following year was admitted to the bar   Soon after his arrival he joined the "Lawyer's Artillery," which was at that time the best equipped corps among the volunteers. Many of the United Irishmen belonged to this organization, and O'Connell, it would appear, was induced to join them. "I had," said O'Connell, "many good opportunities of acquiring valuable information, upon which I very soon formed my own judgment. It was a terrible time. The political leaders of the period could not conceive such a thing as a perfectly open and above-board political machinery. My friend, Richard Newton Bennett, was an adjunct to the Directory of United Irishmen. *I was myself a United Irishman.* As I saw how matters worked, I soon learned to have no secrets in politics."

At this period, he resided in Trinity Place, in Dublin, and at the house of a certain Mr. Murray, a respectable grocer, who, though a thorough rebel at heart, had the prudence to control both himself and his young and enthusiastic friend. A rising was hourly expected. One evening, Mr. Murray found O'Connell, under the fever of patriotic excitement, about to attend a meeting of the United Irishmen. He felt O'Connell's presence at this meeting would greatly endanger his liberty, and accordingly led him to the canal bridge, at Leeson St., and induced him to embark on a turf boat, bound for Cork. That very night his friend's house was searched by the notorious Major Sirr, showing how narrow had been his escape. This was in June, of the memorable year of '98. Landing at the Cove, he paid the boatman half a guinea, and was soon after enjoying the breezy heights of his native Kerry, "within the sound of the everlasting wave."

The Irish gentry were hard riders and hard drinkers in those days. His uncle Maurice was always known by the soubriquet of "Old Hunting Cap," and his "Cousin Kane," who appears to have been a thorough "character," could drink any man in the county under the table. O'Connell, however, seems to have been the first to break through that long-standing rule, that the door should be locked and the key thrown out of the window after dinner, until every guest present was thoroughly intoxicated. The young barrister rose early, and consequently retired early. This Cousin Kane spent his time in visiting one family after another, claiming kindred with them all. Wherever he went, his two horses and twelve dogs went also; and thus he passed the greater portion of the year in "droping in" upon his friends. His potations could not always have agreed with him, for at one time no less than seventy-six actions for assault and battery were pending against him at the Tralee assizes.

Once more in Carhen, O'Connell gave himself up, during the summer months, to his absorbing passion for field sports. During one of his rambles he was exposed to a drenching rain, which brought on a fever, well nigh proving fatal to him. He thus describes it: "My illness was occasioned," said he, "by sleeping in wet clothes. I had dried them upon me at a peasant's fire, and drank three glasses of whiskey, after which I fell asleep. The next day I hunted, was soon weary, and fell asleep in a ditch under sunshine. I became much worse; I spent a fortnight in great discomfort, wandering about and unable to eat. At last, when I could no longer battle it out, I gave up and went to bed. Old Dr. Moriarty was sent for; he pronounced me in a high fever. I was in such pain that I wished to die. In my ravings, I fancied that I was in the middle of a wood, and that the branches were on fire around me. I felt my backbone stiffening for death, and I positively declare that I think what saved me was the effort I made to rise up, and show my father, who was at my bedside, that I knew him. I verily believe that effort of Nature averted death. During my illness I used to quote from the Tragedy of Douglas these lines —

'Unknown I die ; no tongue shall speak of me ;
Some noble spirits, judging by themselves,
May yet conjecture what I might have proved,
And think life only wanting to my fame.'

I used to quote those lines under the full belief that my illness would end fatally. Indeed, long before that period — when I was seven years old — yes, indeed, as long as ever I can recollect, I always felt a presentiment that I should write my name on the page of history. I hated Saxon domination. I detested the tyrants of Ireland. During the latter part of my illness, Dr. Moriarty told me that Buonaparte had got his whole army to Alexandria, across the desert. 'That is impossible,' said I, 'he cannot have done so; they would have starved.' 'Oh, no,' replied the doctor, they had a quantity of portable soup with them, sufficient to feed the whole army for four days.' 'Ay,' rejoined I, 'but had they portable water? For their portable soup would have been of little use if they had not water to dissolve it in.' My father looked at the attendants with an air of hope. Doctor Moriarty said to my mother, 'His intellect, at any rate, is untouched.'"

CHAPTER III.

O'CONNELL'S professional labors now began in
earnest. His wonted vigor had returned, and upon
the opening of the Circuit, in September, he eagerly
started forth on his first circuit. We may form some
idea of O'Connell's immense energy at this period,
from his having ridden sixty Irish miles in one day,
starting at four in the morning. This was not all:
a friend persuaded him to attend a ball the same
evening, where he remained dancing until two o'clock
the following morning.

The young barrister early developed that wonderful faculty of his for cross-examining, which in after
times was the terror of the wiliest witness. There
was no shelter behind which the struggling witness
could retreat; the victim, first thrown off his guard,
next confused, was finally, in his desperation, forced
to acknowledge what he had endeavored to conceal,
or fatally contradict his former evidence. A case
of this kind occurred in Tralee. O'Connell had to
examine a witness, of whose sobriety there was
some question. To all his inquiries as to *how much*
he drank, the witness replied, "his share of the

pint." "On the virtue of your oath," said O'Connell, "did not your share consist of *all except the pewter.*" The witness finally muttered, "It did," much to the amusement of the Court.

Travelling from Cork to Dublin, in company with a certain Judge Grady, O'Connell stopped over night at Fermoy Inn. Shortly after their arrival, four dragoons entered the tap-room where they were sitting. This reminded the travellers of the dangers of the next morning's journey. On examining their arms they found themselves short of ammunition. The judge approached the corporal, and asked for some powder, but made the mistake of addressing him as "soldier," thus ignoring his rank. The corporal replied, "he did not sell powder," and seemed insulted. O'Connell, perceiving the error of his friend, thus mended matters :

"Grady," said O'Connell, in a low tone, "you have made a great mistake. Did you not see by the mark on his sleeve that the man is a corporal? You mortified his pride in calling him a soldier, especially before his own men, amongst whom he doubtless plays the officer."

Having suffered a few minutes to elapse, O'Connell entered into conversation with the dragoon.

"Did you ever see such rain as we had to-day, *sergeant?* I was very glad to find that the regulars had not the trouble of escorting the judges. It was very suitable work for those awkward yeomen."

"Yes, indeed, sir," returned the corporal, evidently flattered at being mistaken for a sergeant; "we were very lucky in escaping those torrents of rain."

"Perhaps, sergeant, you will have the kindness," continued Dan, "to buy me some powder and ball in town. We are to pass the Kilworth mountains, and shall want ammunition. *You*, of course, can find no difficulty in buying it; but it is not to every one they sell these matters."

"Sir," said the corporal, "I shall have great pleasure in requesting your acceptance of a small supply of powder and ball. My balls will, I think, just fit your pistols. You'll stand in need of ammunition, for there are some of those out-lying rebelly rascals on the mountains."

"Dan," said Grady in a low tone, "you'll go through the world successfully. That I can easily foresee."

Let the historian detail the horrors of '98; we shrink from the task. The insurrection lasted eight months, and was characterized by a brutality scarcely paralleled in the annals of atrocity. The suspension of the Habeas Corpus Act jeopardized both life and property in Ireland, whilst the soldiery employed to suppress this unfortunate uprising were guilty of the most inhuman excesses. The gallant Sir John Moore, alluding to their outrages, exclaimed, "If I were an Irishman, I would be a rebel." With a free commission to kill and destroy, this motley army — made up of English militia, Scotch fencibles, and Irish yeomanry — perpetrated on the people of Ireland acts of wanton cruelty worthy of the savages of our western wilds. Lord Cornwallis, in a letter to the Duke of Portland, thus describes them: "The Irish militia are totally without discipline, *contemptible before the enemy*, when any serious resistance is made to them, but ferocious and cruel in the extreme when any poor wretches, either with or without arms, come within their power; in short, *murder* appears to be their favorite pastime." Martial law, in its worst sense, created a reign of terror, paralyzing the administration of justice and the commerce of the country. It is now an established fact that England encouraged this struggle to carry the Union — a measure which put a period to the existence of Ireland as a nation, and degraded her to the level of a province. The object of the Union was to consolidate England and Ireland under a common Parliament. The constitutional charter of 1782 restored Ireland to the rank and dignity of a free nation; the morning of January 1st, 1801, beheld the "Union Jack" floating over the tower of London, and the castles of Dublin and Edinburgh. This Union, so fatal to the liberties of Ireland, and so obnoxious to her people, was carried by force and fraud. When this measure was first introduced into the Irish Parliament, it was negatived by a majority of one. Finding their first effort unsuccessful, the Unionists changed their tactics, and, when brought forward a second time, the measure for the Union was carried by a considerable majority. The policy pursued in bringing about this fatal change was as unscrupulous as it was successful.

In the Irish Parliament, Grattan and Plunket, seconded by other noble patriots, stoutly protested against the Union; but opposed to them was a firm majority, in whom the love of country was overruled by ambition and the lust for gold. The voice of pub-

3

lic opinion was silenced, the press subsidized—every interest was carefully weighed and conciliated. New titles were created and freely dispensed, landed proprietors were richly indemnified, the tradesmen of the North were cajoled with promises of an enlarged commerce, whilst the Catholics, to whom any change was a relief, were flattered with the hope of speedy emancipation. To effect this deplorable measure cost England £1,500,000; but even this vast sum appears small when we consider that it was the price of Irish liberty.

Dublin boldly protested against the unpopular measure of the Union; and it was during this exciting period that O'Connell made his first speech. The occasion was offered at an anti-Union meeting, held at the Royal Exchange. The chair was filled by Mr. Ambrose Moore, and the resolutions denouncing the measure were drawn up by the renowned Philpot Curran. The meeting had not fairly begun before the notorious Major Sirr entered, with the intention of dispersing it. He demanded to see the resolutions; but finding nothing objectionable in them he turned on his heel, much disappointed, and left the hall.

Counsellor O'Connell rose, and, in a short speech, prefaced the resolutions. He said "that the question of Union was confessedly one of the first importance and magnitude. Sunk, indeed, in more than criminal apathy, must that Irishman be, who could feel indifference on the subject. It was a measure to the consideration of which we were called by every illumination of the understanding, and every feeling of the heart. There was, therefore, no necessity to apologize for introducing the discussion of the question amongst Irishmen. But before he brought forward any resolution, he craved permission to make a few observations on the causes which produced the necessity of meeting as Catholics — as a separate and distinct body. In doing so, he thought he would clearly show that they were justifiable in at length deviating from a resolution which they had heretofore formed. The enlightened mind of the Catholics had taught them the impolicy, the illiberality, and the injustice, of separating themselves on any occasion from the rest of the people of Ireland. The Catholics, had, therefore, resolved, and they had wisely resolved, never more to appear before the public as a distinct and separate body ; but they did not — they could not — then foresee the unfortunately existing circumstances of this moment. They could not then foresee that they would be reduced to the necessity, either of submitting to the disgraceful imputation of approving of a measure as detestable to them as it was ruinous to their country, or once again, and he trusted for the last time, of coming forward as a distinct body.

"There was no man present but was acquainted with the industry with which it was circulated, that the Catholics were favorable to the Union. In vain did multitudes of that body, in different capacities, express their disapprobation of the measure; in vain did they concur with others of their fellow-subjects in expressing their abhorrence of it — as freemen or freeholders, electors of counties or inhabitants of cities — still the calumny was repeated; it was printed in journal after journal; it was published in pamphlet after pamphlet; it was circulated with activity in private companies; it was boldly and loudly proclaimed in public assemblies. How this clamor was raised, and how it was supported, was manifest; the motives of it were apparent.

"In vain had the Catholics (individually) endeavored to resist the torrent. Their future efforts, as individuals, would be equally vain and fruitless; they must, then, oppose it collectively.

"There was another reason why they should come forward as a distinct class — a reason which, he confessed, had made the greatest impression upon his feelings. Not content with falsely asserting that the Catholics favored the extinction of Ireland, this, their supposed inclination, was attributed to the foulest motives — motives which were most repugnant to their judgments, and most abhorrent to their hearts; it was said that the Catholics were ready to sell their country for a price, or, what was still more depraved, to abandon it on account of the unfortunate animosities which the wretched temper of the times had produced. Can they remain silent under so horrible a calumny? This calumny was flung on the whole body; it was incumbent on the whole body to come forward and contradict it. Yes, they will show every friend of Ireland that the Catholics are incapable of selling their country; they will loudly declare that if their emancipation was offered for their consent to the measure, even were emancipation after the Union a benefit, they would reject it with prompt indignation. (*This sentiment met with approbation.*) Let us," said he, "show to Ireland that we have nothing in view but her good, nothing in our hearts but the desire of mutual forgiveness, mutual toleration, and mutual affection; in fine, let every man who feels with me proclaim, that if the alternative were offered him of Union or the re-enactment of the Penal Code in all its pristine horrors, that he would prefer without hesitation the latter, as the lesser and more sufferable evil; that he would rather confide in the justice of his brethren the Protestants of Ireland, who have already liberated him, than lay his country at the feet of foreigners. (*This sentiment met with much and marked approbation.*) With regard to the Union, so much had been said, so much had been written, on the subject that it was impossible that any man should not before now have formed an opinion on it. He would not trespass on their attention in repeating arguments which they had already heard, and topics which they had already considered. But if there was any man present who could be so far mentally degraded as to consent to the extinction of the liberty, the constitution, and even the name, of Ireland, he would call on him not to leave the direction and management of his commerce and property to strangers, over whom he could have no control."

His appearance on this occasion was dignified and prepossessing; his frame muscular, strongly knit, and active; and his face extremely comely, the features being softly mellowed, yet determined and manly. His fine countenance, which beamed with intelligence,

3*

had an expression of open frankness and inviting confidence, and showed nothing of that wily malignity imputed to him in after times by the tories. The hateful imputation was at once repelled by his bright and amiable blue eyes, the most kindly and honest-looking that can be conceived.

O'Connell's action at this meeting seems to have displeased his uncle Maurice, who, though adverse to the Union himself, was opposed to his young nephew compromising his prospects by entering the dangerous arena of politics.

In the year 1799, O'Connell, then residing in Dublin, became a member of the Society of Free and Accepted Masons. On learning there was an ecclesiastical censure attached to members of that order, he withdrew; not, however, before he had become master of his lodge.

Returning home one evening, in the winter of 1801, after a convivial party at Freemason's Tavern, he suddenly came upon a lumber yard in flames. At the same time he heard the cry of "Water!" and hastened to the aid of some laborers, who were endeavoring to clear a way to the water pipes. Excited by the claret, which he had too freely indulged in at supper, he seized a pick-axe, and speedily reached the plug. Not satisfied with his success, he continued to dig away, and refused to desist, though frequently ordered to do so by Sheriff Macready, who was present with a file of English militia. Finding he was not to be moved by entreaty, a soldier charged him with his bayonet, which was fortunately intercepted by his hunting watch. "If I had not had the watch," said O'Connell, when relating this adventure, "there was an end of the agitator."

For a few years subsequent to the exchange meeting, the young barrister appears to have renounced politics. In the interim, he applied himself diligently to the duties of his profession, and was rewarded with a success he could have hardly expected. Catholics, although admitted to the bar, could not wear the silk gown, and he rarely got an opportunity of addressing a jury. Although obliged to confine himself to cross-examination, O'Connell had so precise a knowledge of the habits and character of the people, he rarely failed in whatever he undertook.

On one occasion he was engaged in a will case. It was the allegation of the plaintiffs that the will was a forgery. The subscribing witnesses swore that the will had been signed by the deceased while "life was in him" — a mode of expression derived from the Irish language, and which peasants who have ceased to speak Irish still retain. The evidence was altogether in favor of the will, and the defendants had every reason to calculate on success, when O'Connell undertook to cross-examine one of the witnesses. He was struck by the persistency of this man, who, in reply to his questions, never deviated from the formula, "the life was in him."

"On the virtue of your oath, was he alive?"

"By the virtue of my oath, the life was in him," repeated the witness.

"Now I call on you in the presence of your Maker, who will one day pass sentence upon you for this evidence; I solemnly ask — and answer me at your peril—was there not a live fly in the dead man's mouth when his hand was placed on the will."

The witness was obliged to confess that the counsellor was right, for a fly had been actually inserted into the mouth of the deceased, to enable the witnesses to swear that life was in him.

Numerous anecdotes are told of our young barrister in his earlier legal experience. Many a hardened criminal escaped the ravenous jaws of the law; for O'Connell's success was soon recognized by these wrong doers who were most anxious to secure his services. On the other hand, many an honest unfortunate owed both life and property to his skill in puzzling witnesses, perplexing the judge, or bewildering the jury. An illustration of this is recorded by O'Connell himself:

"I recollect I once had a client, an unlucky fellow, against whom a verdict had been given for a balance of £1,100. We were trying to set aside that verdict. I was young at the bar at that time; my senior counsel contented themselves with abusing the adverse witnesses, detecting flaws in their evidence, and making sparkling points; in short, they made very flourishing, eloquent, but rather ineffective speeches. While they flourished away I got our client's books, and, taking my place immediately under the judge's bench, I opened the accounts and went through them all, from beginning to end. I got the whole drawn out by double entry, and got numbers for every voucher. The result plainly was, that so far from there being a just balance of £1,100 against our poor devil, there actually was a balance of £700 in his favor, although the poor slovenly blockhead did not know it himself. When my turn came, I made the facts as clear as possible to judge and jury; and the jury inquired if they could not find a verdict of £700 in his favor. 'I just tell you the circumstance," continued O'Connell, "to show you that I kept an eye on that important branch of my profession."

A farmer was captured in the act of killing game on the grounds of a landed proprietor, three of whose servants had secured the poacher, and were willing to swear they caught him in the act. O'Connell was asked by the attorney for the defence to cross-examine the witnessess. This request was reluctantly acceded to by O'Connell, who considered the case utterly hopeless. He had observed that each witness was anxious to claim for himself the sole credit of the arrest, and was willing to make any sacrifice rather than his companions should enjoy that privilege. O'Connell's keen perception soon took in the situation, and determined him to take advantage of it. Each witness, as he came upon the stand, undervalued the part played by his companions in arresting the prisoner. The third witness, mortified at the attempt of the others to belittle his services, determined to rebut their evidence. It was at this stage of the trial the young barrister came forward.

"Now, will you answer me one question?" said O'Connell to the last witness, "and then, perhaps, I'll have done with you."

"If you promise to ask me no more questions, I'll answer you any way you like."

"Very well! Remember you said so. Now, by

the virtue of your oath, is not the prisoner innocent?"

"By the virtue of my oath," said the witness, determined to deprive his colleagues of the merit of the
the capture, as he himself could not monopolize it all,
"by the virtue of my oath, he is innocent."

The poacher was acquitted.

An anonymous writer has graphically described
O'Connell's appearance at this period, as he jour-
neyed through the country, whilst attending circuit.

The writer was sitting at the window of a tavern
in a small village, as O'Connell came galloping up in
his "chariot and four," and thus faithfully records his
impressions:

"The inmate of the carriage was about five feet
eleven and a half inches high, and wore a portly,
stout, hale, and agreeable appearance. His shoulders were broad, and his legs stoutly built; and,
as he at that moment stood, one arm in his side
pocket, the other thrust into a waistcoat, which
was almost completely unbottoned from the heat of
the day, he would have made a good figure for the
rapid but fine-finishing touch of Harlowe. His head
was covered with a light fur cap, which, partly
thrown back, displayed that breadth of forehead
which I have never yet seen absent from real talent.
His eyes appeared to me at that instant to be between a light blue and a gray color. His face was
pale and sallow, as if the turmoil of business, the
shade of care, or the study of midnight, had chased
away the glow of health and youth. Around his
mouth played a cast of sarcasm, which, to a quick

eye, at once betrayed satire, and it appeared as if
the lips could be easily resolved into *risus sardonicus.*
His head was somewhat larger than that which a
modern doctrine denominates the 'medium size;"
and it was well supported by a stout and well-founda-
tioned pedestal, which was based on a breast full,
round, prominent, aud capacious. The eye was
shaded by a brow which I thought would be more
congenial to sunshine than storm, and the nose
was neither Grecian nor Roman, but was large
enough to readily admit him into the chosen band of
that 'immortal rebel' [1] who chose his body-guard with
capacious lungs and noses, as affording greater capa-
bility of undergoing toil and hardship. Altogether
he appeared to possess strong physical powers.

"He was dressed in an olive-brown surtout, black
trowsers, and black waistcoat. His cravat was care-
lessly tied — the knot almost undone from the heat
of the day; and as he stood with his hand across his
bosom, and his eyes bent on the ground, he was the
very picture of a public character hurrying away on
some important matter which required all of personal
exertion and mental energy. Often as I have seen
him since, I have never beheld him in so striking or
pictorial an attitude."

The judges with whom O'Connell had to contend differed from him in politics, and were always
ready to manifest their hostility to him. He proved
himself more than a match for the best of them —
"if they were haughty, he was proud; if they were
malevolent, he was cuttingly sarcastic."

[1] Cromwell.

Happening to be one day present in the courts in Dublin, where a discussion arose on a motion for a new trial, a young attorney was called upon by the opposing counsel either to admit a statement as evidence, or hand in some document he could legally detain. O'Connèll stood up and told the attorney to make no admission. "Have you a brief in this case, Mr. O'Connell?" asked Baron M'Cleland, with very peculiar emphasis.

"I have not, my lord; but I shall have one when the case goes down to the assizes."

"When *I* was at the bar it was not *my* habit to anticipate briefs."

"When *you* were at the bar I never chose *you* for a model, and now that you are on the bench, I shall not submit to your dictation."

Leaving the judge to digest this retort, he walked out of court, accompanied by the young attorney.

O'Connell was not always successful, however, for a cow-thief whom he had repeatedly defended, was finally transported. Many years after, this unfortunate man, who had served out his sentence in New South Wales, enlightened the Liberator on his *mode* of stealing cattle.

"When your honor goes for to shteal a cow, mind, it's no use your goin' of a fine night; but go to shteal her always of a black night, when it's rainin' torrents and blowin' whirlwinds; for nobody else will be out barrin' yourself on a bad night like that. The wilder the night, the easier you'll shteal the cow. And when your honor goes into the field where you're going to shteal her, don't be for takin' the cow that's crudlin' near the ditch, becase she's surely a lean cow; but shteal the cow that stands out in the rain. She's worth shtealin'. She's fat, and does not want shelther. That's the cow for your honor to shteal." O'Connell thanked his informant, and promised, with every appearance of sincerity, to follow his directions to the letter whenever he should abandon the painful drudgery of the law for the exciting and adventurous profession of a cow-stealer.

4

CHAPTER IV.

O'CONNELL's reputation at the bar was now fully
established. His first years earnings netted him £58,
the second, £150, the third, £200, and the fourth,
£300. Later in his career his income reached the
princely sum of £9,000.

O'Connell was thoroughly devoted to his profession. His success had been rapidly earned; it was
flattering in the highest degree; and yet in his heart
there was a void, which the companionship of a wife
could alone supply. His choice had been early made.
In his younger days he had pledged his love to his
cousin, Miss Mary O'Connell, of Tralee, and only
waited until his profession should enable him to
maintain a family.

"I never," said O'Connell, "proposed marriage to
any woman but one — my Mary. I said, to her 'Are
you engaged, Miss O'Connell?' She answered, 'I am

not.' 'Then,' said I, 'Will you engage yourself to me?' 'I will,' was her reply. And I said I would devote my life to make her happy."

The happy pair were united by Father Finn, parish priest of Irishtown, June 23d, 1802, in Dame St., Dublin, at the lodgings of James O'Connell, the brother of the bride. The ceremony was conducted with the utmost privacy. Mrs. O'Connell is described as an extremely amiable lady, possessed of excellent judgment, and during the course of her married life rendered great service to her husband by her discretion and prudence. Maurice O'Connell, on learning of his nephew's marriage, was greatly displeased. The real cause of his displeasure originated in the poverty of the young bride, who came dowerless to her husband. O'Connell thought his uncle's displeasure would end in cutting him off. It gave him no concern, however, for the partner of his choice was a far greater prize to him than the broad acres of Derrynane.

Marriage has been the turning point in many a great man's career. With O'Connell's marriage began the serious duties of his life. The careless habits of his youth were at once abandoned, and he marched forth, girt as a soldier for the battle of life, and was fully conscious of his power. The path which O'Connell chose for himself promised him little repose. He had learned that the real cause of Catholic apathy was a want of organization. Most of all, a leader was necessary, — a courageous, indefatiguable patriot, wise, patient, and determined. O'Connell felt himself urged onward by a resistless impulse to become that leader; and henceforth the regeneration of his country was the sole ambition of his life. Emancipation, which Pitt had promised the Catholics of Ireland in return for their submission to the Union, was as far away as ever. Pretext and evasion were sought in superfluous arguments and measures of expediency, showing the Catholics how sadly they had been duped. O'Connell's theory for emancipation was not based upon force. He had seen how ineffectual had been the insurrection of '98, and resolved upon agitation as the only means of bringing it about.

On the 23d of July, just one month after his marriage, the ill-starred insurrection of Emmet, to which he was greatly opposed, broke out. "I ask you," said he, "whether a madder scheme was ever devised by a Bedlamite? Here was Mr. Emmet, having got together about £1,200 in money, and seventy-four men; whereupon he makes war upon George III. with one hundred and fifty thousand of the best troops in Europe, and the wealth of the kingdom at his command! Why, my dear sir, poor Emmet's scheme was as wild as anything in romance." Emmet, however, had better reason to hope for success than would appear from O'Connell's view of it. First of all, he had been promised the support of Napoleon. Moreover, he expected a general uprising of the people; and had it not been for an accident, which precipitated his movement, a bold stand might have been made for Irish independence.

In the year 1803, O'Connell was still a member of the Lawyers' Corps, and constantly on duty. He himself tells us: "After I had stood sentry for three successive nights, Nicholas Purcell O'Gorman's turn came. He had recently been ill, and told me the exposure to the night air would probably kill him. 'I shall be in a sad predicament,' said he, 'unless you take my turn of duty for me. If I refuse, they'll accuse me of cowardice or croppyism; if I mount guard, it will be the death of me!' So I took his place, and thus stood guard for six consecutive nights."

Despairing of any voluntary concession from the government, the Catholics at length determined to make an effort in their own behalf. During 1803 and 1804, the suspension of the Habeas Corpus Act was continued in force, and they were obliged to hold their meetings at the houses of private individuals. These meetings were called for the purpose of organizing a line of action. At one of these conclaves, in 1805, a committee was appointed to wait upon Mr. Pitt, the English premier, and request him to lay their grievances before Parliament.

Pitt, acting under the advice of the king, who bitterly hated everything Catholic, gave them no encouragement, and the delegates were obliged to look elsewhere for an advocate. After some delay, Lord Grenville was prevailed upon to lay their petition before the House of Lords, whilst Mr. Fox pleaded their cause in the Commons. The Lords laid the matter on the table, while the Commons, regardless of the eloquent advocacy of Grattan, and the forcible pleadings of Fox, negatived the petition by a majority of 212. "At all events" writes John Mitchell, "the time was not yet come, nor the man; and in special one bold, blue-eyed young man, who was then carrying his bag in the hall of the Four Courts of Dublin, destined one day to hold the great leading brief in the mighty cause of six millions of his countrymen."

In the year 1807, we find O'Connell a member of a Catholic Committee, which was appointed on the 7th of February, and he appears to have done much to raise the spirits of his co-religionists. The young Agitator, conscious of his power, gave fresh hope and courage to all with whom he came in contact. Boldly and fearlessly he proclaimed the justice of his cause; and, like the drooping foliage after a refreshing rain, the Catholics of Ireland lifted their desponding hearts and lived again in the bright promise of their future Liberator.

On the 17th of February, a meeting was held at the Rotunda, again to petition Parliament. Lord Fingal acted as chairman. It soon appeared that the chairman, together with Lord Ffrench and others of the Catholic aristocracy present, were actually opposed to the real object of the meeting. These gentlemen talked of postponement and expediency; in fact re-echoed the very sentiments of Pitt and the Castle. O'Connell, who seemed to have had an intuitive perception of men's motives, could brook no such delay.

His words were: "Away, then, with all the objections to presenting a petition; there should be no delay. The man does not merit freedom who would hug his chains for a day. The present ad-

ministration has emancipated the negroes; they
would be entitled to praise as having done their duty,
if, instead of enabling his majesty to select admirals
and generals from our body, they introduced a clause
into their Slave Bill to raise Catholics to the rank of
freemen."

Signatures were obtained from the Catholics of
every county of Ireland, and, in 1808, the petition
was brought by Lord Fingal to London. This
year appeared to the Catholics one in every way favorable to their cause. Napoleon had triumphed
over Austria, Prussia had been crushed on the field
of Jena, and England was left singly opposed to the
"man of destiny." Their calculations, however, were
not correct. The noble petition-bearer received a
cold shoulder from the Duke of Portland; and, when
brought into the House of Commons, the lynx-eyed
Canning objected to the petition as it did not contain
original signatures, many persons' names appearing
who could not write, and Lord Fingal accordingly
returned to Ireland. In May of the same year, the
petition, this time bearing *genuine* signatures, was
again presented to the consideration of Parliament.
Bigotry and prejudice were immovable; in vain Grattan urged that concession to Catholics was not only
just but expedient and necessary; Catholic emancipation was as distant as ever. The petition was rejected by a negative majority of 152 votes. In the
course of Mr. Grattan's speech, he urged that the
Catholics were willing to concede the veto in order
to obtain emancipation. In this assertion he had
acted under the advice of Lord Fingal, from which

it was plainly evident this gentleman was willing to renounce his Papal allegiance. The object of the veto was to place the power of nominating Catholic bishops in the hands of the king, a wily invention of England that Ireland should sever her spiritual connection with Rome.

The Catholic hierarchy were deeply incensed at this false representation of their opinions. On the 14th of September following, a national synod of Catholic prelates assembled in Dublin, and offered resolutions denouncing the veto, which were signed by no less than twenty-three bishops, to the joy of every Catholic in Ireland. This bold vindication of Catholic rights did not escape the government. Unable to retaliate openly, the malignity of the tory cabinet manifested itself in renewed encouragement to the Orange party. On the 11th of September, the day following the synod, an Orange meeting was convened at Dawson St., Dublin, at which all the lodges of that body in Ireland and England were represented. At this assemblage it was not only resolved to exterminate the Catholics, but to oblige every member, under pain of expulsion, to exert his personal influence in seeing this ruthless measure enforced.

"From the most respectable authorities I have it," said O'Connell, at a Catholic meeting which took place subsequently, "that Orange lodges are increasing in different parts of the country, with the knowledge of those whose duty it is to suppress them. I have been assured that the associations in the north are re-organized, and that a committee of these delegates in Belfast have printed and distributed 500 copies of their new constitution. This I have heard from excellent authority; and I should not be surprised if the attorney-general knew it. Yet there has been no attempt to disturb these conspirators— no attempt to visit them with magisterial authority —no attempt to rout this infamous banditti. Perhaps my information is false; if so, I give the government an opportunity to rebut the charge."

During a flying visit which O'Connell paid his native county, about this time, he attended a meeting on the tithe question. At the meeting in question he succeeded in turning into complete and painful ridicule the well-prepared address of one of the previous speakers. It was the first exhibition of his powers as an orator which he had made in his native county. The upholders of the tithe system at this meeting,

> "Safe from the bar, the pulpit, and the throne,
> Were touched and shamed by ridicule alone."

The statements and arguments of "parsons much bemused with beer," which were paraded by their friends, were answered and overturned by O'Connell, who produced a decided impression on the assembly. He laughed to scorn the greedy avarice of the clergy of the Establishment, who insisted on taking a full tithe of the farmer's potatoes. He argued that if they took his staff of life out of his hands, they should carry the peasant on their shoulders. O'Connell carried triumphantly the anti-tithe resolutions.

The outrages perpetrated upon Catholics by the Orange Society at this period would not seem credible, if we were not familiar with the bloody acts of this body within the last decade of years.

About this time, there stood a fountain in Kevin St., Dublin, which some careless lads had decorated with green boughs and garlands. This was followed in the evening by a bonfire, around which young persons of both sexes had clustered, watching the bright flames ascend, and enjoying the excitement it produced. Suddenly, five cowardly Orangemen, with loaded muskets in their hands and deadly venom in their hearts, approached this scene of gayety. Having come within accurate range, they levelled their pieces, and, taking deliberate aim, discharged their contents into the unsuspecting crowd. One of the group fell dead upon the spot, whilst others were fatally wounded. A similar occurrence disgraced the neighborhood of Newry. Eighteen miscreants there fired upon a company of merry makers, killing and wounding many.

The fate of "Jack of the Roads," as related by O'Connell himself, may shed a light on the condition of Catholic Ireland in 1808. "Jack of the Roads," we may premise, was an idiot, who, covered with tatters, and apparently half-starved, was accustomed to keep pace with the Limerick mail-coaches. "He once made a bet of fourpence and a pot of porter," said O'Connell, "that he would run from Dublin to Limerick, keeping pace with the mail. He did so; and when he was passing through Mountrath, on his return, on the 12th of July, 1808, flourished a green bough at a party of Orangemen who were holding their orgies. One of them fired at his face; his eyes were destroyed; he lingered, and died; and there was an end to 'Jack of the Roads!'"

These outrages went unpunished, and were winked at by unworthy magistrates, who had sworn to maintain the peace and administer justice. Shame on ungrateful England, who permitted Catholic blood to be shed at home, whilst Catholic soldiers were gaining victories for her abroad!

O'Connell's influence was already felt amongst his co-religionists. His continuous cry was, "Agitate! agitate!" and these magic words fired the drooping courage of the Catholics, who had so long accustomed themselves to suffer in silence. Scarcely had they come together when discord began to poison their councils. This grieved O'Connell beyond measure. Disunion he felt had always been the curse of Ireland, and it was time that the sad lesson of the past should be heeded. O'Connell had reason to believe the aristocratic members of the Catholic Association had been tampered with by the government. Acting upon this conviction he resolved to bring the members of the Catholic Association to a sense of their duty, addressing them as follows :—

"The old curse of the Catholics is, I fear, about to be renewed; division, that made us what we are and keeps us so, is again to rear its standard amongst us ; but it was thus always with the Irish Catholics. I recollect that in reading the life of the great Duke of Ormond, as he is called, I was forcibly struck with a despatch of his, transmitted about the year 1661, when he was Lord-Lieutenant of Ireland. It was written to vindicate himself from a charge of having favored the Papists, and having given them permission to hold a public meeting in Dublin. His answer is remarkable. He rejects with disdain the foul calumny of being a favorer of Papists, though he admits he gave them leave to meet : 'because,' said he, 'I know by experience, that the Irish Papists never meet without dividing and degrading themselves.' I quote the words of the official despatch ; I can lay my finger on the very spot in 'Carte's Life of Ormond.'

"One hundred and fifty years have since elapsed, and we are still in thraldom, because no experience can, I fear, cure us of this wretched disposition to divide. He entreated of the respectable gentlemen who that day attended the Committee, to consider that their mistakes, if they had made any, ought not to be visited with so grievous a calamity as that of creating dissension amongst them."

O'Connell did not confine himself to the emancipation movement entirely. He was preëminently a nationalist, and was present at every occasion where Ireland's rights were brought forward for consideration. In fact, the great ascendancy the Liberator subsequently wielded over the minds and hearts of his countrymen was owing to their belief that behind this great movement of agitation there was an ultimate design of Irish Independence.

On Tuesday, September 18th, 1810, a meeting of citizens took place at the Royal Exchange, in Dublin to consider the subject of a Repeal of the Act of Union. Mr. O'Connell's speech on this occasion was a brilliant and exhaustive review of the manner in which the Union had been brought about. We give a brief extract.

"Alas! England, that ought to have been to us as a sister and a friend; England, whom we had loved, and fought and bled for; England, whom we have protected, and whom we do protect; England, at a period when out of 100,000 of the seamen in her service, 70,000 were Irish — England stole upon us like a thief in the night, and robbed us of the precious gem of our Liberty; she stole from us 'that which nought enriched her, but made us poor indeed.' Reflect, then, my friends, on the means employed to accomplish this disastrous measure. I do not speak of the meaner instruments of bribery and corruption. We all know that everything was put to sale — nothing, profane or sacred, was omitted in the Union mart — offices in the revenue, commands in the army and navy, the sacred ermine of justice, and the holy altars of God, were all profaned and polluted as the rewards of Union services. By a vote in favor of the Union, ignorance, incapacity, and profligacy obtained certain promotion; and our ill-fated but beloved country was degraded to her utmost limits, before she was transfixed in slavery."

Agitation lost none of its strength in this year. Another emancipation petition was framed and presented to Parliament; but, like its predecessors, was ignored and thrown aside. The frequent meetings and decided action of the Catholic party in Ireland had now become a source of apprehension to the government. Finding that O'Connell, undaunted by frequent defeat, was resolved upon uniting the Catholics of Ireland in concerted action, they determined to enforce the Convention Act. This act, which was passed in 1792, denied Catholics the right of petition, and of holding public meetings for such purposes.

"The truth is," writes a cotemporary, "that so long as the management of the Catholic affairs was confided exclusively to titled noodles, the thunders of the Convention Act were allowed to slumber; but the moment the sincerity of the young Agitator was likely to take the place of the treachery or folly of aristocratic imbecility, the government determined to act."

The government scheme for crushing Catholic agitation was well concerted. The first step was to carry the Militia Act, by which the Irish militia were to be transferred to England, and their place supplied by English soldiers. The former were made up almost exclusively of Catholics, and it was feared that, in case of trouble, they could not be depended upon. The Convention Act, already alluded to, would then be stringently enforced, and the Catholic Committee, it was thought, thus deprived of its meetings, would soon lose its influence. Should the Catholics then appeal to force, they were to have "sweltered in their own blood." This scheme was foiled in a most unexpected manner by O'Connell, whose resources seemed to enlarge as difficulties multiplied around him.

Despite the threats of the government, Lord Fingal, with other members of the Catholic Committee, assembled, and were arrested and brought to trial. The question of their right to meet was tested before a packed jury, in Dublin, in the person of Dr. Sheridan and Mr. Kirwan. At the trial, the whole question turned upon the meaning of the words in the Convention Act, "under *pretence* of petitioning." It was asserted by the crown counsel and chief justice that *pretence* meant *purpose*. They would fain revolutionize the English dictionary to prevent an improvement in the condition of the Irish nation. The Catholics really met, as every one knew, for the *bona fide* purpose of petitioning. The crown counsel endeavored to show that such a *purpose* was condemned by the Convention Act; that the meeting of delegates for the *purpose* of petitioning Parliament was an illegal meeting. The counsel for the traverser maintained that if delegates assembled really and truly to petition Parliament, and not for a different purpose under the pretext of petitioning, then the meeting was legal. Common sense and an intelligent jury declared for the latter interpretation. The traverser was acquitted. As O'Connell was not a leading counsel in the case, he confined himself merely to the cross-examination of the witnesses; but it was well known that the whole plan of the defence was arranged by him, and to his masterly management was it in a great degree attributable that the accused were acquitted. Roman Catholics acquitted by Protestants! Such an event was new and unexpected in Ireland, and created vast astonishment.

CHAPTER V.

THE joy of the Catholics on finding themselves victorious over the Attorney-General knew no bounds. They immediately determined to hold a meeting, that they might again petition for a redress of their grievances. The government, however, were not to be put off so easily; and the attempt to break up this meeting is thus described by the *Freeman's Journal* of that period:

"A few minutes before twelve o'clock yesterday, Counsellor Hare, a police magistrate, entered the Theatre, Fishamble Street, where the Catholic Committee were assembled, and took his station beside the chair, which was prepared for the reception of Lord Fingal.

"At two minutes after twelve his lordship arrived; and, upon the motion of Counsellor Hussey, seconded by Counsellor O'Connell, he was called to the chair.

"Mr. Hare was about to address Lord Fingal, when Lord Netterville stood up, and moved that the

Catholic petition be now read, which was seconded by Counsellor O'Gorman.

"Mr. Hare now addressed himself to Lord Fingal, evidently with a determination *to prevent the reading of the petition*, and persevered until he had accomplished this object.

"Mr. Hare. — My Lord Fingal, I beg to state what my object is in coming to this meeting. As chairman of this meeting, I have to inform you, that I come here, as a magistrate of the city of Dublin, *by directions of the Lord-Lieutenant*, his Excellency having been informed that this is a meeting of the Catholic Committee, composed of the peers, prelates, country gentlemen, and the persons chosen in the different parishes of Dublin. I beg to ask you, as chairman of this meeting, if that be the case, and what is your object?

"Lord Fingal. — Sir, we have met here for a legal and constitutional purpose.

"Mr. Hare. — Allow me to observe, that that is not an answer to my question; perhaps you did not distinctly hear me. I ask, is it a meeting of the Catholic Committee, composed of the peers, prelates, country gentlemen, and others in the city of Dublin?

"Lord Fingal. — I certainly do not feel myself bound to give you any other answer. We are met for the sole legal and constitutional purpose of petitioning.

"Mr. Hare. — My Lord, I ask you, as chairman of this meeting, in what capacity are you met?

"Lord Fingal. — We are met for the purpose of petitioning Parliament.

"Mr. Hare. — My Lord, that is not an answer to my question. I speak deliberately and distinctly, in order that every person may hear and understand me. (Here some little confusion occurred, owing to several persons speaking together.) Mr. Hare. — I hope I have leave to speak. ('Hear the magistrate,' from several persons.) I beg leave to ask your lordship again, is it a meeting of the Catholic Committee, constituted by the Catholic peers, prelates, country gentlemen, and the persons appointed in the different parishes of Dublin?

. "Lord Fingal. — I am not aware that I can give you any other answer than that which I have already given.

"Mr. Hare. — Then, my Lord, your answer is, that you are a meeting of Catholics, assembled for a legal and constitutional purpose? (From several voices — No, no; there was no answer given in such terms.)

"Counsellor O'Connell. — It is a most unusual thing for any magistrate to come into a public meeting to catechise, ask questions, and put his own construction upon the answers.

"Mr. Hare. — My Lord, am I to understand that you decline answering me fully what meeting you are, and the purpose of your meeting?

"Lord Fingal. — We are met for a legal and constitutional purpose.

Mr. Hare. — I wish to be distinctly understood: I have addressed your lordship explicitly two or three times. Am I to understand that you will give no other answer to my question? Do you give no other answer? (Here some confusion arose, in consequence of several persons speaking together — some crying out to have the petition read, others calling on Mr. Hay, and others requiring silence for the purpose of hearing Counsellor Hare.)

"Mr. Hare. — My Lord Fingal, I addressed myself to you so distinctly, that I thought my question could not be mistaken. I consider your declining to give me a direct answer, as an admission that this is the Committee of the Catholics of Ireland.

"Counsellor O'Connell. — I beg leave to say, that as what passes here may be given in evidence, the magistrate has received a distinct answer to his question; and it is not for him to distort any answer he has received into a meaning of his own. He is to take words in their literal signification.

"Mr. Hare. — My Lord, I consider your refusing to give any other answer as an admission of the fact of this being a Catholic Committee.

"Counsellor O'Connell. — Sir, if you please to tell gentlemen such is your belief, it is of no consequence to us; we are not to be bound by your opinion.

"Mr. Hare. — This is an admission of the fact that this is the Catholic Committee; and I consider your lordship's refusal —

"(Here the meeting was interrupted by the confusion incidental to a number of persons speaking together.)

"Mr. Hare. — Does your lordship deny that this is the Catholic Committee?

"Counsellor Finn.—No, no; my Lord Fingal has not given you either admission or denial.

"Counsellor O'Connell.—We do not want the gentleman's assistance to make out meanings for us. Let him not imagine that the character of this meeting can be affected, or that he can bind this meeting by any assertion he thinks proper to make.

"Mr. Hare.—Then I repeat that your lordship's refusal to give me a direct answer is an admission that this meeting is the Catholic Committee, and, as such, it is an unlawful assembly.

"Counsellor O'Connell.—Mr. Hare is now speaking in his magisterial capacity, therefore, whatever he says, give it attention.

"Mr. Hare.—My Lord, I say that this is an unlawful assembly, and, as such, I require it to disperse. I beg leave to say, that it is my wish to discharge my duty in as mild a manner as possible. I hope that no resistance will be offered, and that I need not have recourse to those means with which I am entrusted for the purpose of causing the meeting to disperse.

"Lord Fingal.—It is not our intention to do anything improper, or to act in resistance to the laws of the land; but it is my determination not to leave the chair until I am obliged by some person to do so, in order that I may bring my legal action against the person who shall remove me.

"Mr. Hare.—My Lord, I shall remove you out of the chair; and in doing so, it will be an actual arrest.

"Here, as might be naturally expected, some confusion arose, in consequence of a noise in the gallery, which, we. are informed, was occasioned by police constables.

"Mr. Hare.—My Lord if you'll have the goodness to leave the chair, that is a legal arrest.

"He then took Lord Fingal by the arm and gently pushed him from the chair.

"On the motion of Counsellor O'Gorman, seconded by Dr. Luby, Lord Netterville was immediately called to the chair, from which he was removed by Counsellor Hare, in the same way that he had put Lord Fingal out of it.

"There was then a universal cry for Lord Ffrench . to take the chair. His lordship, who was in a bad state of health, either had not arrived, or was not within hearing of those who called him to the chair.

"The Hon. Mr. Barnwall was then called to the chair; but before he had taken it, Lord Ffrench had arrived, and was proceeding to his post, when, at the recommendation of Sir Edward Bellew, and at half-past twelve o'clock, the meeting dispersed.

"After the Catholic meeting had been dispersed in Fishamble Street, a number of gentlemen repaired to Mr. D'Arcy's, the Crown and Anchor Tavern, Earl Street, for the purpose of signing a requisition to call an aggregate meeting of the Catholics of Ireland. While the requisition was preparing, Counsellor Hare, accompanied by Alderman Darley, went into the room where they were assembled, and asked whether that meeting was a meeting of individual gentlemen. Being answered in the affirmative, and being about to make a speech, Lord Ffrench told him they did not want to hear any *of his speeches*, nor would they listen to them; if he came there for the purpose of *acting*, he must proceed without delay.

"Mr. Hare said that he merely wished to say, that as they had acknowledged themselves to be a meeting of individual gentlemen, he would not molest them.

"A Catholic requisition for an aggregate meeting, to be held on Thursday next, at the Theatre, Fishamble Street, has been drawn up *and signed by upwards of three hundred persons.*

"We have just learned that Lord Fingal interrogated the police magistrates, after the dispersion of of the committee, if he was to procure bail to their arrest, *and that they deny having arrested him!*"

Again, in May, 1811, the petition was presented for the consideration of the Commons, and was rejected by a majority of 104. Grattan's speech on this occasion teemed with illustrations of Catholic wrongs, and must have made a deep impression upon the minds of British legislators. If England disregarded the Catholic remonstrance, it was no longer in her power to say she was ignorant of the abuses to which five millions of British subjects were subjected. No one more appreciated Mr. Grattan's noble effort than O'Connell, who seems to have had a high estimate of that gentleman's ability.

On one occasion Mr. O'Neil Daunt asked O'Connell who, in his opinion, was the greatest Irishman.

"*Next to myself,*" he answered, "I think old Henry Grattan was."

Mr. O'Connell's mode of carrying on his agitation is thus fully described by himself. "There are many men," said he, "who shrink from repeating themselves, and who actually feel a repugnance to deliver a good sentiment or a good argument, just because they have delivered that sentiment or that argument before. This is very foolish. It is not by advancing a political truth once, twice, or even ten times, that the public take it up and finally adopt it. No; incessant repetition is required to impress political truths upon the public mind. That which is but once or twice advanced may possibly strike for a moment, but will then pass away from the public recollection. You must repeat the same lesson over and over again, if you hope to make a permanent impression; if, in fact, you hope to impress it on your pupil's memory. Such has always been my practice. My object was to familiarize the whole people of Ireland with important political truths, and I could never have done this if I had not incessantly repeated those truths. I have done so pretty successfully. Men, by always hearing the same things, insensibly associate them with received truisms. They find the facts at last quietly reposing in a corner of their minds, and no more think of doubting them than if they formed part of their religious belief. I have often been amused when, at public meetings, men have got up and delivered my old political lessons in my presence as if they were new discoveries, worked out by their own ingenuity and research. But this was the triumph of my labor. I had made the facts and sentiments so universally familiar, that men took them up and gave them to the public as their own."

"You have seen O'Connell," says an American writer. "Is he not a chieftain? Did you ever see a creature of such power of the tongue? I never saw anyone that could converse with an audience like him. Speeches may be as well made by other men, but I never heard such *public talk* from anybody. The creature's mind plays before ten thousand, and his voice flows as clearly and as leisurely as in a circle round a fireside; and he has the advantage of the excitement it affords to arouse his powers."

Strange to say, Orangemen frequently retained O'Connell's legal services. The following anecdote offers an explanation: "Hedges Eyre, of Orange notoriety, invariably engaged O'Connell as his counsel. On one accasion a brother Orangeman severely censured Hedges Eyre for employing the Catholic leader: 'You've got seven counsel without him,' quoth this sage adviser; 'and why should you give your money to that Papist rascal!' Hedges did not make an immediate reply; but they both remained in court watching the progress of the trial. The counsel on the opposite side pressed for a non-suit, and carried the judge (Johnson) along with them. O'Connell remonstrated against the non-suit, protesting against so great an injustice. The judge seemed obdurate. 'Well *hear* me at all events!' said O'Connell. 'No, I won't,' replied the judge; 'I've already heard the leading counsel.' 'But *I* am conducting counsel, my lord,' rejoined O'Connell, 'and more intimately aware of the details of the case than my brethren. I entreat, therefore, that you will hear me.' The judge ungraciously consented; and in five minutes O'Connell had argued him out of the non-suit. '*Now*,' said Hedges Eyre, in triumph, to his Orange confrere, '*Now* you see why I gave my money to that Papist rascal.'"

After the arrest and prosecution of the Catholic Committee, and their subsequent acquittal, that body gradually dwindled away; but the zeal which had animated its deliberations, though suffered to languish, was not extinct. From the effete Catholic Committee sprang the young and vigorous Catholic Board. This new organization carefully avoided everything that could be construed into a *representative* character. The Catholic Board of 1812 was the school of the emancipation of 1829. The greatest evil the new organization had to contend with was the Catholic aristocracy, who formed its representative head. O'Connell, ever on the alert, soon discovered the conspiracy which threatened not only to alienate the members of the Board from its great purpose of unrestricted emancipation, but, worse than all, from Rome herself. The Veto, so strongly advocated by the English Catholics, was strongly supported, as we have seen, by Lord Fingal and the aristocratic coterie under his lead. O'Connell, backed by the Catholic hierarchy and people of Ireland, openly condemned the movement.

At a meeting of the Board he offered the following resolution, viz. :

"That the respectful thanks of the Catholic Board be given to the Most Reverend and Right Reverend the Catholic Prelates, for their *communication* to this Board, and for their ever vigilant and zealous attention to the interests of the Catholic Church in Ireland."

Imagine the result of the English ministry controling the appointment of Catholic bishops!—Ireland cut off from the spiritual jurisdiction of Rome. Every careful student of history has witnessed the result in Germany and England; it is to be hoped that Ireland will never suffer the curse of *Reformation*.

CHAPTER VI.

THE Catholic aristocracy at length grew jealous of O'Connell. The increasing force of his eloquence, his immense popularity with the people, his success at the bar, and, most of all, his fearless denunciation of the Veto, gave them reason to believe the leadership of the Catholic party would speedily pass beyond their control. This fear gave rise to a spirit of bitter antagonism in the deliberations of the Board, which called forth the best efforts of the Agitator. O'Connell, who seemed omnipresent, gave himself up unsparingly to the interests of the people. It seems surprising that, in the midst of a large professional practice, he still found time to give to National or Catholic interests. But so untiring was his industry, that no meeting held at the Royal Exchange, or in the Theatre in Fishamble Street, found him absent.

With surprising fertility of resources, his speeches followed one another in rapid succession, each developing fresh power and projective enterprise. Our space in this brief compilation does not permit us to follow him through his eloquent denunciations of English trickery and aristocratic turpitude. Alive to the necessity of united action, he endeavored on all occasions to heal the divisions which threatened to retard the progress of emancipation. In short, had it not been for O'Connell, Catholic emancipation might have been put back a century.

O'Connell by his assiduous labors — first, in the Catholic Committee; secondly, in the Catholic Board — was laying the foundation, and, indeed, building the superstructure, of that world-wide renown which he subsequently enjoyed. "I have been sometimes amused at the whimsical mode in which the popular devotion to him manifested itself," says his secretary. "He lived in the hearts of old and young. Ascending the mountain road between Dublin and Glencullen, in company with an English friend, O'Connell was met by a funeral. The mourners soon recognized him, and immediately broke into a vociferous hurrah for their political favorite, much to the astonishment of the Sassanach, who, accustomed to the solemn and lugubrious decorum of English funerals, was not prepared for an outburst of Celtic enthusiasm on such an occasion. A remark being made on the oddity of a political hurrah at a funeral, it was replied, that the corpse would have cheered lustily too — if he could!"

O'Connell possessed a buoyancy of spirits which

the turmoil of his public life, and the anxieties of his
profession, were unable to crush. His mind was
stored with a rich fund of droll and humorous anecdotes and personal reminiscences which rendered his
domestic circle the delight of every one fortunate
enough.to come within its influence. He was master
of the art of story-telling, for which his fluency, his
great memory, his intricate knowledge of human nature, and, above all, his great control over his features, eminently qualified him.

Passing by a gravel-pit, one day, O'Connell remarked to a companion, "There is the very spot
where Brennan the robber was killed. Jerry Connor
was going from Dublin to Kerry, and was attacked
by Brennan at that spot. Brennan presented his
pistol, crying, 'Stand!' 'Hold!' cried Jerry Connor. 'Don't fire—here's my purse.' The robber,
thrown off his guard by these words, lowered his
weapon, and Jerry, instead of a purse, drew a pistol
from his pocket, and shot Brennan in the chest.
Brennan's back was supported at the time against
the ditch, so he did not fall. He took deliberate aim
at Jerry, but feeling himself mortally wounded,
dropped his pistol, crawled over the ditch, and slowly
walked along, keeping parallel with the road. He
then crept over another ditch, under which he was
found dead the next morning."

We are reminded by the above incident, of an adventure of his own, whilst travelling near Nenagh.
He thus describes it:

"Some years ago, when this neighborhood was
much infested with robbers, I was travelling on cir-

cuit. My horses were not very good, and just at this spot I saw a man whose movements excited my suspicions. He slowly crossed the road, about twenty yards in advance of my carriage, and awaited my approach with his back against the wall, and his hand in the breast of his coat, as if ready to draw a pistol. I felt certain I should be attacked, so I held my pistol ready to fire, its barrel resting on the carriage door. The man did not stir, and so escaped. Had he but raised his hand, I should have fired. Good God! what a miserable guilty wretch I should have been! How sincerely I thank God for my escape from such guilt!"

O'Neil Daunt, the author of "Personal Reminiscences of O'Connell," has recorded the following:

"At a part of the road between Kildare and Rathcoole, O'Connell pointed out the place where Leonard McNally, son to the barrister of the same name, alleged he had been robbed of a large sum. To indemnify himself for his alleged loss, he tried to levy the money off the county. 'A pair of greater rogues than father and son never lived,' said O'Connell; 'and the father was busily endeavoring to impress upon every person he knew, a belief that his son had been really robbed. Among others, he accosted Parsons, then M. P. for the King's county, in the hall of the Four Courts. "Parsons! Parsons, my dear fellow!" said old Leonard, "did you hear of my son's robbery?" "No," answered Parsons quietly, "I did not. Whom did he rob?"

O'Neill Daunt having mentioned a conservative barrister named Collins, who, in 1800, had written an anti-Union pamphlet, predicting the ruin of the country from that measure, and who lived long enough to see his predictions verified:

"Ah! I knew Collins, too," said O'Connell; "he was a clever fellow. He had talent enough to have made a figure at the bar, if it had not been for the indolence induced by his comfortable prosperity. His wife was a Miss Rashleigh, an uncommonly beautiful woman. He and I went circuit together. Going down to the Munster circuit by the Tullamore boat, we amused ourselves on deck, firing pistols at the elms along the canal. There was a small party of soldiers on board, and one of them authoritatively desired us to stop firing. 'Ah! corporal, don't be so cruel,' said Collins, still firing away. 'Are you a corporal?' asked I. He surlily replied in the affirmative. 'You must have got yourself reduced to the ranks by misconduct, for I don't see the V's on your sleeve.' This raised a laugh at his expense, and he slunk off to the stern, quite chopfallen."

In August, of 1813, O'Connell visited Limerick. During this visit an altercation arose between a certain Councillor Magrath and O'Connell, in the county courthouse, where they were both professionally engaged. Cards were exchanged, and the combatants met in the regular duelling-ground of the neighborhood. Nicholas P. O'Gorman acted as second for O'Connell, whilst a Mr. Bennett did that friendly service for Magrath. The contestants, pistol in hand, having taken position, awaited the signal to fire. At this critical moment mutual friends arrived, and insisted upon a compromise. Finally Magrath declared aloud he was sorry for what had happened, and O'Connell, ever ready to forgive, declared he entertained no feelings of enmity to his rival; and the would-be combatants shook hands, and rode back to the town side by side, conversing cheerfully.

To give our readers some idea of the duelling mania of that period, we shall briefly notice some incidents in the life of one of the most notorious of Irish duellists. This was no other than Mr. Bagenal, of Dunleckny, County Carlow, whose high lineage, princely income, and boundless hospitality, had earned for him the title of King. This jolly gentleman gathered around his table the wild youth of the county, whom he took much delight in initiating into the mysteries of the cup and the etiquette of the *code*. At these entertainments, two pistols were placed on either side of his plate. With one he tapped his wine, the other he held in reserve for that one of his guests who refused to do it justice.

King Bagenal had fought many duels during his adventurous lifetime, but perhaps the most remarkable occurred in his seventy-ninth year. His highness was informed that some of his neighbor's pigs had strayed into his enclosure, and rooted up some flowers. King Bagenal caused the ears and tails of the intruders to be chopped off, and sent them to their owner, with a message regretting that he (the owner) did not possess a tail to be cut off also. This message brought about a challenge. Bagenal, as the challenged party, selected pistols, and stipulated that, owing to his advanced age, he should fight sitting in his arm chair. At three o'clock on the following afternoon the combatants met. Twelve paces were measured off, and at the word fire, the redoubtable old duellist winged his antagonist, whilst the arm of the chair in which he sat was shattered to pieces. The evening terminated in a glorious carouse, at which the claret was tapped as usual, and the long life of King Bagenal was freely drank.

O'Connell had little time, however, for quarrels. In the autumnal assizes of 1813, twenty-six cases were tried in the Limerick Record Court, and in each one of these O'Connell held a brief. One can fancy the great Agitator at this period making his way through the crowds which surrounded the court-house, and the friendly greetings that met his ear as he passed. His reputation at the bar had now become so well established, that, in addition to the briefs above mentioned, he was likewise retained in every criminal case tried in the same circuit. The splendid talents of O'Connell were not alone employed in cases where fame or emolument were to be gained. Often he came to the relief of the poor and oppressed, as in the following case :

"On Tuesday, 25th May, 1813, O'Connell, in the Court of Common Pleas, moved for a conditional order against the Rev. Wm. Hamilton, for illegal and oppressive conduct as a magistrate of the county of Tipperary; and, in addressing the presiding judge, said: 'The facts of the case are really curious, and would be merely ludicrous but for the sufferings inflicted on my client. The affidavits stated that a peasant girl named Hennesy had a hen which laid — not golden eggs — but eggs strangely marked with red lines and figures. She, on the 21st of April, 1813, brought her hen and eggs to the town of Roscrea, near which she lived, and of which the defendand was the Protestant curate. It appeared by the result that she brought her eggs to a bad market, though at first she had some reason to think differently; for the curiosity excited by those eggs attracted some attention to the owner; and as she was the child of parents who were miserably poor, her wardrobe was in such a state that she might almost literally be said to be clothed in nakedness. My lord, a small subscription to buy her a petticoat was suggested by the person who makes the present affidavit, himself a working weaver of the town, James Murphy, and the sum of fifteen shillings was speedily collected. It was a little fortune to the poor creature. She kissed her hen, thanked her benefactors, and, with a light heart, started on her return home. But — *diis aliter visum* — at the moment, two constables arrived with a warrant signed by the Rev. William Hamilton. This warrant charged her with the strange offence of a *foul* imposition. It would appear as if it were issued in some wretched jest, arising from the sound not the sense. But it proved no joke to the girl, for she was arrested. Her hen, her eggs, and her fifteen shillings were taken into custody and carried before his worship. He was not at leisure to try the case that day. The girl was committed to Bridewell, where she lay a close prisoner for twenty-four hours, when his Rev. Worship was pleased to dispose of the matter. Without the mockery of any trial, he proceeded at once to sentence. He sentenced the girl to perpetual banishment from Roscrea. He sent her out of the town guarded by three constables, and with positive injunctions never to set foot in it again. He decapitated her hen with his own sacred hands. He broke the eggs and confiscated the fifteen shillings. When the girl returned to her home — the fowl dead, the eggs broken, and the fifteen shillings in his reverence's pocket — one would suppose justice quite satisfied. But no! his Worship discovered that Murphy had collected the offending money; he was therefore to be punished. He was, indeed, first tried; but under what law, think you? Why, literally, my lords, under the statute of good manners. Yes, under that act, wherever it is to be found, was Murphy tried, convicted, and sentenced. He was committed to Bridewell, where he lay for three days. The committal states "that he was charged on oath with having assisted in a foul imposition on public credulity, contrary to good manners." These are the words of the committal; and he was ordered to be detained until he should give security "for his good behavior." Such is the ridiculous warrant on which an humble man has been deprived of his liberty for three days. Such are the details given of the vexatious proceedings of the reverend magistrate. It was to be hoped that those details would turn out to be imaginary; but they are sworn to — positively sworn to — and require investigation, the more especially as motives of a highly culpable nature were attributed — he (O'Connell) hoped unduly attributed — to the gentleman. He was charged, on oath, with having been actuated by malice towards this wretched girl because she was a Catholic. It was sworn that his ob-object was to establish some charge of superstition against her, upon no better ground than this, — that one of those eggs had a mark on it nearly resembling a cross.' The rule was granted; but Mr. Hamilton compromised the case, in consequence of the public exposure of his conduct."

Everywhere O'Connell went during this circuit the people received him with marked expressions of their devotion to him. A vote of thanks was tendered him on August 7th, 1813, at Louth. Subsequently, like honors were shown him at Kilkenny, Galway, Tralee, and Wexford. At Cork, the enthusiastic populace carried him in a chair, lifted above their heads, through the principal thoroughfares.

In this year, another bill for Catholic emancipation was brought before Parliament without success.

The Orange element, encouraged by this defeat, gave vent to their usual passion for outrage and blood. In the market place of Armagh, there stood, for more than 700 years, an Irish cross, beautifully ornamented with Catholic symbols, at once the veneration of the Catholic and the admiration of the antiquarian. On the 12th of July, the Orangemen destroyed this venerable relic. In their bigoted malice they hurled it to the ground, blasted the pedestal with gunpowder, and converted the base into a trough for swine. In Belfast the streets ran crimson with blood. A party of Orangemen, whilst celebrating their annual orgies in a tavern of that town, were startled by the crash of broken glass in the front of the house. Seizing their muskets, they rushed into the street, and, without a word of warning, discharged their pieces at the passers by. Three unfortunate men were slaughtered, and numbers wounded. It was folly to expect the law to reach such offenders. A trial followed. The jury was Orange, and the judge Orange. The Orange sign passed from the assassins to the jury, and their acquittal immediately followed. One outrage followed another, the object being to *frenzy* the Catholics into open hostilities. O'Connell, ever the guardian of the people, could not be ensnared even by so cruel a test of human forbearance, and he took occasion to warn the people of their danger. He thus counsels them:

"Alas! for poor Ireland!" said O'Connell. "Her liberties depend upon the prudence of a people of the most inflammable passions, goaded almost to madness, on the one hand, by Orange insults, and exposed at the same time to the secret seductions of the agents and emissaries of those very Orange oppressors. Do you wish to gratify the Orangemen? If you do, the way is before you. You have only to enter into some illegal or traitorous association— you have only to break out into turbulence or violence, and the Orangemen will be delighted, because it will afford them the wished-for opportunity of revelling in your blood."

7

CHAPTER VII.

O'CONNELL never tired of relating his adventures while going circuit, and often spoke of the inns at which he put up, and the roads over which he travelled.

"In 1780," said O'Connell, "the two members for the county Kerry, when preparing to visit Dublin, sent to the metropolis for a noddy. The noddy took eight days to get to Kerry, and they, when seated in it, took seventeen days to get to Dublin! Each night the two members, owing to the absence of inns, quartered themselves at the house of some friend; on the seventeenth day they reached Dublin, just in time for the commencement of the session."

Speaking of a favorite inn at Millstreet, he said:

"The improved roads have injured that inn. I well remember when it was the regular end of the first day's journey from Tralee. It was a comfortable thing for a social pair of fellow-travellers to get out of their chaise at night-fall, and to find at the inn (it was then kept by a cousin of mine, a Mrs. Cotter) a roaring fire in a clean, well-furnished parlor, the whitest table-linen, the best beef, the sweetest and tenderest mutton, the fattest fowl, the most excellent wines (claret and madeira were the high wines there — they knew nothing about champagne), and the most comfortable beds. In my early days it was by far the best inn in Munster. But the new roads enable travellers to get far beyond Millstreet in a day; and the inn, being therefore less frequented than of old, is of course not so well looked after by its present proprietor."

"There was the Coach and Horses Inn, at Assolas, in the county Clare, close to the bridge," said O'Connell. 'What delicious claret they had there! It is levelled with the ground these many years. Then there was that inn at Maryborough; how often have I seen the old trooper who kept it smoking his pipe on the stone bench at the door, and his fat old wife sitting opposite him. They kept a right good house. She inherited the inn from her father and mother, and was early trained up to the business. She was an only child, and had displeased her parents by a runaway match with a private dragoon. However, they soon relented, and received her and her husband into favor. The worthy trooper took charge of the stable department, for which his habits well adapted him; and the in-door business was admirably managed by his wife. Then, there was that inn at Naas, most comfortably kept — and excellent wine. I remember stopping to dine there one day, posting up from the Limerick assizes. There were three of us in the chaise, and one was tipsy; his eyes were bloodshot and his features swollen from hard drinking on the previous night, besides which he had tippled a little in the morning. As he got out of the chaise, I called him 'Parson!' to the evident delight of a Methodist preacher, who was haranguing a crowd in the street, and who deemed his own merits enhanced by the contrast with a sottish minister of the establishment."

O'Connell tells the following interesting incident in relation to the antiquary Grose:

"Grose," said he, "came to Ireland full of strong prejudices against the people, but they gave way beneath the influences of Irish drollery. He was very much teased, when walking through the streets of the Irish capital, by the Dublin butchers besetting him for his custom. At last he got angry, and told them to go about their business, when a sly, waggish butcher, deliberately surveying Grose's fat, ruddy face and corpulent person, said to him, 'Well, plaise your honor, I won't ask you to buy, since it puts your honor in a passion. But I'll tell you how you'll sarve me?' 'How?' inquired Grose, in a gruff growl. 'Just tell all your friends that it's Larry Heffernan that supplies your honor with *mate;* and never fear but I'll have custom enough.'"

This market scene naturally recalls to memory the celebrated encounter of O'Connell with Mrs. Biddy Moriarty. There was in Dublin at that time a noted character named Biddy Moriarty, who kept a huckster's stall on one of the quays, nearly opposite the Four Courts Biddy's reputation as a termagant was well known throughout the Irish capital, and as the virulence of her tongue was ably seconded by the great dexterity of her fist, few dared to confront her. She was the very embodiment of slang; and it occurred to a waggish friend of O'Connell's, whose power of invective was likewise well known, to pit him against the redoubtable vender of small wares. The matter was accordingly broached to O'Connell, who expressed himself delighted to enter into this war of words. Bets were freely offered and accepted, and the Agitator, accompanied by a few friends, proceeded to the huckster's stall, where O'Connell commenced the attack:

"What's the price of this walking-stick, Mrs. What's-your-name?"

"Moriarty, sir, is my name, and a good one it is; and what have you to say agen it? and one-and-sixpence 's the price of the stick. Troth, it's chape as dirt; so it is."

"One-and-sixpence for a walking-stick! Whew! why, you are no better than an imposter, to ask eighteen pence for what cost you twopence."

"Twopence, your grandmother!" replied Mrs. Biddy. "Do you mane to say that it's chating the people I am? Impostor, indeed!"

"Ay, impostor; and it's that I call you to your teeth," rejoined O'Connell.

"Come, cut your stick, you cantankerous jackanapes."

"Keep a civil tongue in your head, you old *diagonal*," cried O'Connell, calmly.

"Stop your jaw, you pug-nosed badger, or by this and that," cried Mrs. Moriarty, "I'll make you go quicker nor you came."

"Don't be in a passion, my old *radius*. Anger will only wrinkle your beauty."

"By the hokey! if you say another word of impudence, I'll tan your dirty hide, you bastely common scrub; and sorry I'd be to soil my fists upon your carcass."

"Whew! boys, what a passion óld Biddy is in! I protest, as I am a gentlemen —"

"Jintleman! jintleman! the likes of you a jintleman! Wisha, by gor, that bangs Banagher. Why, you potato-faced pippin-sneezer, when did a Madagascar monkey like you pick enough of common Christian dacency to hide your Kerry brogue?"

"Easy, now — easy, now," cried O'Connell, with imperturbable good humor. "Don't choke yourself with fine language, you old whiskey-drinking *parallelogram.*"

"What's that you call me, you murderin' villin?" roared Mrs. Moriarty, stung to fury.

"I call you," answered O'Connell, "a parallelogram; and a Dublin judge and jury will say that it's no libel to call you so."

"O tare-an-ouns! O holy Biddy! that an honest woman like me should be called a parrybellygrum to her face. I'm none of your parrybellygrums, you rascally gallows-bird; you cowardly, sneaking, plate-lickin' blaggard!"

"O, not you, indeed!" retorted O'Connell. "Why, I suppose you'll deny that you keep a *hypothenuse* in your house."

"It's a lie for you, you bloody robber. I never had such a thing in my house, you swindlin' thief."

"Why, sure your neighbors all know very well that you keep not only a hypothenuse, but that you have two *diameters* locked up in your garret, and that you go out to walk with them every Sunday, you heartless old *heptagon.*"

"O, hear that, ye saints in glory! O, there's bad language from a fellow that wants to pass for a jintleman! May the devil fly away with you, you micher from Munster, and make celery-sauce of your rotten limbs, you mealy-mouthed tub of guts."

"Ah! you can't deny the charge, you miserable *submultiple* of a *duplicate ratio.*"

"Go, rinse your mouth in the Liffey, you nasty tickle pitcher. After all the bad words you speak, it ought to be filthier than your face, you dirty chicken of Beelzebub.

"Rinse your own mouth, you wicked-minded old *polygon.* To the deuce I pitch you, you blustering intersection of a st—ng superfices!"

"You saucy tinker's apprentice, if you don't cease your jaw, I'll—" But here she gasped for breath, unable to hawk up any more words; for the last volley of O'Connell had nearly knocked the wind out of her.

"While I have a tongue I'll abuse you, you most inimitable *periphery.* Look at her, boys! there she stands,—a convicted *perpendicular* in petticoats. There's contamination in her *circumference,* and she trembles with guilt down to the extremities of her *corollaries.* Ah! you're found out, you *rectilinear antecedent,* and *equiangular* old hag! 'Tis with you the devil will fly away, you porter-swiping *similitude* of the *bisection of a vortex!*"

Overwhelmed with this torrent of language, Mrs.

Moriarty was silenced. Catching up a saucepan, she was aiming at O'Connell's head, when he very prudently made a timely retreat.

"You have won the wager, O'Connell; here's your bet!" cried the gentleman who proposed the contest.

O'Connell, whilst in Limerick, in 1812, during the Assizes, was asked by Standish O'Grady to go with him to the play. O'Connell declined, observing that the Limerick grand-jurors were not the pleasantest folk in the world after dinner. O'Grady went, but soon returned. "Dan," said he "you were quite right. I had not been but five minutes in the box when ten or a dozen noisy gentlemen came into it. It was small and crowded; and, as I observed that one of the party had his head quite close to a peg on which I had hung my hat, I said very politely, ' I hope, sir, my hat does not incommode you; if it does, pray allow me to remove it.' 'Faith,' said he, 'you may be sure it does not incommode me; for if it did, d—n me but I'd have kicked it out of the box, and yourself after it!' So, lest the worthy juror should change his mind as to the necessity of such a vigorous measure, I quietly put my hat on, and took myself off."

O'Connell used to relate an amusing case in which he was engaged against a parson for a breach of promise of marriage. The lady was a Miss Fitzgerald; the gentleman, Parson Hawkesworth.

"Hawkesworth," said he, "had certainly engaged the lady's affections very much. He had acquired fame enough to engage her ambition. He was a crack preacher; had been selected to preach before the Lord-Lieutenant; his name occasionally got into the papers, which then was not often the case with private persons; and, no doubt, this notoriety had its weight in the lady's calculations. The correspondence read upon the trial was comical enough. The lady, it appeared, had at one period doubted his fidelity; whereupon the parson writes to reassure her in these words: 'Don't believe any one who says I'll jilt you! They lie, who say so; and I pray that all such liars may be condemned to an eternity of itching without the benefit of scratching!' £3,000 damages were given against him. He was unable to pay, and decamped to America upon a preaching speculation, which proved unsuccessful. He came back to Ireland, and *married the prosecutrix!*"

Another of O'Connell's stories was about a physician who was detained for many days at the Limerick assizes, to which he had been subpœnaed as a witness. He pressed the judge to order him his expenses. "On what plea do you claim your expenses?" demanded the judge. "On the plea of my heavy personal loss and inconvenience, my lord," replied the simple applicant. "I have been kept away from my patients these five days, and, if I am kept here much longer, *how do I know but they'll get well?*"

CHAPTER VIII.

THE trial of John Magee, which took place in July, 1813, was the occasion of O'Connell's greatest forensic effort. Had O'Connell bequeathed to Ireland no other illustration of his genius than the masterly and patriotic defence of his client on this trial, it alone would have earned for him the lasting gratitude of his countrymen.

Mr. Magee, the defendant, was proprietor of the *Dublin Evening Post*, a patriotic journal widely circulated among Catholics. In that journal, Mr. Scully (the author of an able work on the Penal Laws), on the retirement of the Duke of Richmond, reviewed the various viceroys who had preceded him in that office. As this article was anonymous, the proprietor of the *Post* was held responsible, and arraigned for libel. A trial in which the government took so prominent a part did not fail to create an immense sensation throughout Ireland. There was a full bar on either side. The Attorney and

Solicitor Generals conducted the prosecution, assisted by Sergeants Moore, Ball, and McMahon, whilst the counsel for the defence consisted of O'Connell, Wallace, Hamilton, Finlay, and Phillips.

"In his defence of Magee, O'Connell surpassed himself. In the law of the case he was invincible; in the construction of the libel he was triumphant; and in the politics involved in the question victorious. The Attorney-General said that Magee was indicted as proprietor of a newspaper. O'Connell in his speech denied the fact, and appealed to the indictment itself. The Attorney-General said Magee was indicted as printer. O'Connell denied the fact, and again appealed to the indictment. The Attorney-General said that Magee was indicted for calling the duke 'a murderer!' O'Connell denied the fact, and once more appealed to the indictment. The indictment contained no such statements. In short, O'Connell's speech, which occupied four hours in the delivery, remains to his country and his descendants a monument of industry, acuteness, political courage, and of the mental powers of the admirable advocate. In the Solicitor-General's reply there was passion, rhetoric, and legal knowledge; but the attributes which he usually exhibited in his more felicitous efforts — richness of illustration, polished zeal, glowing imagery, and philosophic views — were utterly absent."

We wish that space was allowed us to give this speech in full. No admirer of the great Agitator should fail to peruse it. Departing from "the rigid rule of his professional conduct," he felt himself "compelled" to be political, and availed himself of the opportunity of giving a condensed history of Ireland, demonstrating the ends of British misrule. He felt assured, moreover, his speech would be read both in England and on the Continent, and O'Connell never neglected a chance of vindicating the integrity, or of making public the wrongs, of his country.

O'Connell thus concluded his speech: "There are amongst you men of great religious zeal, of much public piety. Are you sincere? Do you believe what you profess? With all this zeal, with all this piety, *is* there any conscience amongst you? *Is* there any terror of violating your oaths? Be ye hypocrites, or does genuine religion inspire ye? If you be sincere, if you have conscience, if your oaths can control your interests, then Mr. Magee confidently expects an acquittal. If amongst you there be cherished one ray of pure religion, if amongst you there glow a single spark of liberty, if I have alarmed religion, or roused the spirit of freedom in one breast amongst you, Mr. Magee is safe, and his country is served; but if there be none — if you be slaves and hypocrites — he will await your verdict, and despise it." The verdict, of course, was for the Crown.

The interest centred in this trial was so general, that ten thousand copies were sold on the day of its publication. It was translated into French and Spanish, and thus the cause of Ireland was laid open for the consideration of all Europe.

O'Connell's life was one of perpetual excitement

and unceasing vigilance. In the courts he was confronted by the prejudice of both judge and jury, and in the Catholic Board by the envy and jealousy of the aristocracy. Fortunately, there were periods of repose. After · the business labors of the day were ended, he crossed the threshold of his home, where all was peace and happiness.

O'Connell's lucrative practice and social position had called for a change of residence, and, in 1811, he moved into a mansion in the fashionable atmosphere of Merrion Square. The Agitator's life in this happy home was extremely enviable — it was the home of the Christian gentleman. Sheil, in his "Sketches of the Irish Bar," has given us a description of its interior, and the following extract will be found worthy the brilliant pen of the author of "The Apostate:"

"If any of you, my English readers, being a stranger in Dublin, should chance — on your return on a winter's morning from one of the small and early parties of that raking metropolis, that is to say, between the hours of five and six o'clock — to pass along the south side of Merrion Square, you will not fail to observe that, among those splendid mansions, there is one evidently tenanted by a person whose habits differ materially from those of his fashionable neighbors. The half-opened parlor shutter, and the light within, announce that some one dwells there whose time is too precious to permit him to regulate his rising with the sun's. Should your curiosity tempt you to ascend the steps, and, under cover of the dark, to reconnoitre the interior, you will see a tall, able-bodied man standing at a desk, and immersed in solitary occupation. Upon the wall in front of him there hangs a crucifix. From this, and from the calm attitude of the person within, and from a certain monastic rotundity about his neck and shoulders, your first impression will be that he must be some pious dignitary of the Church of Rome absorbed in his matin devotions. But this conjecture will be rejected almost as soon as formed. No sooner can the eye take in the other furniture of the apartment — the bookcases, clogged with tomes in plain calf-skin binding, and blue-covered octavos that lie about on the tables and on the floor, the reams of manuscript, in oblong folds and begirt with crimson tape — than it becomes evident that the party meditating amidst such objects must be thinking far more of the Law than of the Prophets."

At home, surrounded by his family and friends, O'Connell gave himself up to unrestrained enjoyment. His conversation was replete with anecdote; and the most interesting of all his narrations, were those in which he figured personally. We have added a few of his stories, sparkling with national wit, and dressed in the livery of his easy, graceful style. His memory was wonderful; his imagination vivid; and nothing escaped his quick eye that flavored of the odd or ridiculous. He tells this laughable incident of an ingenius Kerry lad, who had been "taken in" by a newsboy.

"One day during the war, James Connor and I dined at Mr. Mahony's, in Dublin, and after dinner we heard the newsvenders, as usual, calling out,

'*The Post! The Dublin Evening Post!* Three packets in to-night's *Post!*' The arrival of the packets was at that time irregular, and eagerly looked for. We all were impatient for the paper, and Mahony gave a fivepenny piece to his servant, a Kerry lad, and told him to go down and buy the *Post.* The boy returned in a minute with a *Dublin Evening Post* a fortnight old. The roguish newsvender had palmed off an old newspaper on the unsuspecting Kerry tiger. Mr. Mahony stormed, Connor and I laughed; and Connor said, 'I wonder, gossoon, how you let the fellow cheat you! Has not your master a hundred times told you that the dry papers are always old and good for nothing, and that new papers are always wet from the printing-office? Here's another fivepenny. Be off now, and take care to bring us in a *wet Post.*' 'Oh, never you mind the fi-penny, sir,' said the boy, 'I'll get the paper without it;' and he darted out of the room, while Mahony cried out, 'Hang that young blockhead! he'll blunder the business again.' But in less than five minutes the lad re-entered with a fresh, wet paper. We were all surprised, and asked him how he managed to get it without money. 'Oh, the aisiest way in life, your honor,' said the urchin; 'I just took the dry ould *Post,* and cried it down the street a bit — *Dublin Evening Post! Dublin Evening Post!* and a fool of a gentleman meets me at the corner, and buys my ould dry paper. So I whips across to a newsman I sees over the way and buys this fine, fresh, new *Post* for your honor with the money I got for the ould one.'"

"Lord Clare's enmity to Ireland," said O'Connell, "was once nearly ended by an assassin. In 1794, he was carrying a bill through Parliament for compelling the accountant of the Court of Exchequer to return his accounts whenever called upon by the Court.

"Baron Power then filled the office of accountant. This man had used the public funds to gratify his extravagant habits, and felt that discovery would ruin him. He had many times endeavored to dissuade Lord Clare from pressing this bill, but that nobleman was inexorable. Driven to desperation, the baron armed himself with a brace of pistols, and ordered his coachman to drive him to Ely Place, where he asked to see Lord Clare. Not finding him at home, Baron Power then resolved on suicide, and ordered his coachman to drive him along the North Wall. When he had got to a considerable distance out of town, he quitted the carriage, desired the coachman to await his return, and walked on alone to the Pigeon House. He tied his hands together, in order to deprive himself of the power of swimming, and jumped into the sea, from the pier. It was afterwards remarked as a curious fact that he walked off to drown himself, using an umbrella to protect him from the rain. One would think the sprinkling of a shower could not much incommode a fellow who was resolved on a watery grave. Such is the result of habit."

O'Connell, in his personal recollections, frequently alluded to a member of the Munster Bar, familiarly known as "Jerry Keller." Jerry was a member of the celebrated Convivial Society, known as the

"Monks of the Screw," and, we have no doubt, added much to the enjoyment of that jovial circle.

"Jerry," said O'Connell, "was an instance of great waste of talent. He was the son of a poor farmer, near Kanturk, named *Keleher*, which Jerry anglicized into *Keller*, when he went to the bar. He was an excellent classical scholar, and had very considerable natural capacity; but although he had a good deal of business at the bar, his success was far. from being what he might have attained, had he given his whole soul to his profession. His readiness of retort was great. Baron Smith once tried to annoy him on his change of name, at a bar dinner. They were talking of the Irish language. 'Your Irish name, Mr. Keller,' said the baron, 'is *Diarmuid Ua Cealleachair*.' 'It is,' answered Jerry, nothing daunted; 'and yours is *Laimh Gabha*.'[1] There was a great laugh at the baron's expense — a sort of thing that nobody likes.

"Another time," said O'Connell, "when the bar were dining together on a Friday, a blustering young barrister named Norcott, of great pretension, with but slender materials to support it, observed that Jerry was eating fish instead of meat, and by way of jeering Jerry (who had been originally a Catholic), said to him: 'So you won't eat meat! Why, I did not think, Jerry, you had so much of the *Pope* in your belly.' 'For all the meat in the market,' said Jerry, 'I would not have as much of the *Pretender* in my head as you have.'"

Another of O'Connell's odd stories was about a Miss Hussey, to whom her father bequeathed £150

---

[1] William Smith.

per annum, in consideration of her having a red nose. "He had made a will," said O'Connell, "disposing of the bulk of his fortune to public charities. When he was upon his death-bed, his housekeeper asked him how much he had left Miss Mary. He replied that he had left her £1,000, which would do for her very well, if she made out any sort of a good husband. 'Heaven bless your honor,' cried the housekeeper, 'and what decent man would ever take her and the red nose that's on her?' 'Why, really, that is very true,' replied the dying father; 'I never thought of her nose!' and he lost no time in adding a codicil that gave Miss Mary an addition of £150 a-year, as a set-off against her ugliness!"

We have already cited the honors which the principal cities of Ireland had bestowed upon the great Agitator, and their open expressions of respect, admiration, and gratitude. The capital was not to be outdone in showing its appreciation of a patriot, who, during a period of ten years, had labored so earnestly in behalf of its liberties. At a meeting composed of the first Catholics of Dublin, it was *Resolved:* — "That a service of plate, of the value of 1,000 guineas, be presented to Daniel O'Connell, Esq., on the part of the Catholic people of Ireland, as a small tribute of their gratitude for the unshaken intrepidity, matchless ability, and unwearied perseverance with which, in despite of power and intolerance, he has uniformly asserted the rights and vindicated the calumniated character of his Catholic countrymen."

Owing to the disaffection of Lord Fingal and his

aristocratic associates, O'Connell and his supporters convened a meeting in Capel Street, Dublin, in January, 1815, to establish a more liberal organization. The result of this meeting was the formation of THE CATHOLIC ASSOCIATION, which afterwards achieved such noble results. At one of these meetings O'Connell made use of the following language, which was followed by most tragic consequences:

"I am convinced that the Catholic cause has suffered by neglect of discussion. Had the petition been last year the subject of debate, we should not now see the *beggarly Corporation of Dublin* anticipating our efforts by a petition of an opposite tendency. The Duke of Sussex in the Lords, and Mr. Whitbred in the Commons, appear to me persons worthy to be intrusted with our petition."

Finding the Catholic leaders unshaken by the blow struck in dissolving the Catholic Board, their enemies conceived the idea of doing away with O'Connell. They felt assured that with him would end all effort at agitation. Duelling was frequently an apology for murder, at this period, and many a rival candidate on the hustings fell a victim to the superior marksmanship of his opponent.

Duelling, in fact, was so common an occurrence, that all disputes were settled at fifteen paces. It was, therefore, quite natural that the enemies of O'Connell should have chosen an "affair of honor" as the surest and most convenient way of ridding themselves of the object of their fear and hatred. They found in Mr. D'Esterre, a member of the Dublin corporation, the proper person to effect the desired end. This man, who possessed abundant animal courage, and was, at the same time, an unerring shot, already enjoyed considerable reputation as a duellist. The following incident conveys some idea of this adventurer's reckless daring: D'Esterre was serving as a marine in the British navy when the famous "Mutiny of the Nore" broke out. Refusing to join the mutineers, he was tried by them, and sentenced to be hanged. The rope was already about his neck, when a leader of the revolt made a final effort to induce him to renounce his allegiance. "Hang away, and be d—d!" was the savage reply of the reckless desperado. His intrepidity saved him.

D'Esterre, who was hopelessly involved in debt, had been promised a liberal reward in case O'Connell should meet death at his hands. Having accepted the offer, he had no difficulty in provoking a quarrel. O'Connell had called the corporation "beggarly." As a member of that body, he considered himself insulted. Urged on by his friends, he paraded the streets of Dublin, armed with a pistol and cowhide, in search of O'Connell. The latter had been warned of the trap laid for him, and, ever anxious to preserve the peace, had prudently avoided an issue. Not finding the object of his search on the street, D'Esterre addressed a note to O'Connell on Thursday, the 26th of January. This note called attention to the fact that the term "beggarly" had been applied to the Corporation, of which he was a member, and he desired to know if he (O'Connell) had used such language. O'Connell, in his reply, neither admitted nor denied the charge; but, "from the calumnious manner in which the religion and character of the Catholics of Ireland had been treated in that body, no terms attributed to him could exceed the contemptuous feelings he entertained for that body in its corporate capacity." He concluded by desiring that "this reply should close all *correspondence* on the subject." D'Esterre's reply was returned unopened, accompanied by a note from Mr. James O'Connell, in which he assured the gentleman "his brother (Daniel) was surprised that his communication had been made *in writing.*"

From Friday, the date of O'Connell's reply, until Wednesday of the following week, Dublin was the scene of the wildest excitement. The sympathies of the people were thoroughly aroused. Wherever O'Connell appeared, the people received him with more than ordinary enthusiasm. On one occasion he was obliged to seek refuge in a house on Exchequer Street, to avoid the concourse of friends who followed him through the street. On Wednesday morning, at nine o'clock, Sir Edward Stanley waited on O'Connell for an explanation regarding " the D'Esterre affair." O'Connell, however, refused to discuss the matter, and referred him to his friend Major MacNamara, "who would transact any business the subject called for." At twelve o'clock of the same day, these gentlemen met at the major's house. A brief conference followed, which ended in Sir Edward delivering the challenge of his principal. MacNamara coolly accepted the message on behalf of O'Connell, and fixed at once the time and place,—viz., three o'clock of the same day, at Bishop's Court, Co. Kildare. This speedy conclusion · rather startled the civic knight, who wished to postpone the meeting until the next day. The major was inexorable, and presumed, he said, that one pistol fire would satisfy both gentlemen. "No, sir; that will not do," said Sir Edward; "not if they fired five-and-twenty shots each. Mr. D'Esterre will never leave the ground until Mr. O'Connell makes an apology." "Well, then, if blood be your object, blood you shall have, by G—!" replied Major MacNamara.

The meeting was finally arranged for half-past three, at Lord Ponsonby's demesne, thirteen miles from Dublin. O'Connell was promptly on hand, looking calm and collected as if he were entering the Four Courts. D'Esterre did not arrive until half an hour later. Those who had urged him into this unfortunate encounter cruelly deserted him at the last moment. Both combatants displayed the utmost courage: O'Connell coolly surveyed the spot, which was then white with snow, whilst the seconds made the necessary arrangements. D'Esterre had come attended only by his second and surgeon, whereas a number of the most respectable gentlemen of Dublin had followed O'Connell. They now awaited with profound anxiety the issue of the contest. As the . Liberator's keen eye surveyed this friendly group, he caught sight of the diminutive form of Jerry McCarthy, his tailor: "Well, Jerry," he humorously exclaimed, "I never missed you at an aggregate meeting." The *Evening Post* thus describes the concluding scene :

"The friends of both parties retired, and the combatants, having a pistol in each hand, with directions to discharge them at their discretion, prepared to fire. They levelled, and before the lapse of a second both shots were heard. Mr. D'Esterre was first, and missed. His bullet struck the ground. The moment D'Esterre discharged his pistol, he bent his right knee, and wheeled away a little, as if he sought to avoid the sight of O'Connell, or wished to present his back to his antagonist; but why he did so — whether from contempt, levity, or apprehension — it is impossible to say. Mr. O'Connell's shot followed instantaneously, and took effect in the groin of his antagonist, about an inch below the hip. Mr. D'Esterre, of course, fell, and both the surgeons hastened to him. They found that the ball had traversed the hip, passed through the bladder, and possibly touched the spine. It could not be found. There was an immense effusion of blood. All parties prepared to move towards home, and arrived in town before eight o'clock. We were extremely glad to perceive that Major MacNamara and many respectable gentlemen assisted in procuring the best accommodation for the wounded man. They sympathized in his sufferings, and expressed themselves to Sir Edward Stanley as extremely well pleased that a transaction which they considered most uncalled for had not terminated in the death of D'Esterre. We need not describe the emotions which burst forth along the road and through the town when it was ascertained that Mr. O'Connell was safe."

"Nothing," says another authority, "could be

more correct or honorable than the conduct of the parties upon the ground. Mr. O'Connell displayed all the gentleness of heart so peculiarly belonging to his character, and his particular request to his medical friend, before taking his ground, was this: 'Should any fatality happen to my opponent, I entreat you to consider him as your patient — treat him with all the care you would devote to me.'"

D'Esterre died of his wound a few days after the duel, shamefully abandoned by those who had led him on to destruction. If ever a duel was justifiable, surely such was the one just recorded. Yet O'Connell never forgave himself for having participated in it. He afterwards pensioned the widow of his antagonist, and never passed her house without lifting his hat, and breathing a prayer for the repose of the soul of her brave but ill-starred husband.

Great was the joy of the people throughout Ireland on learning that O'Connell was safe. No less than seven hundred gentlemen left their cards at his house the day following the duel. "God be praised! Ireland is safe!" exclaimed Dr. Murray, Archbishop of Dublin, on learning that the great defender of the faith had survived the encounter. Ireland scarcely knew how much she loved her cherished son until his life had been threatened; then, with a heart overflowing with generous confidence, she freely consigned to his leadership the destinies of her people.

CHAPTER IX.

IN 1815, a Catholic petition was introduced into the House of Commons by Sir Henry Parnell. During the debate which followed, O'Connell was made the especial target of the ministerial opponents of the bill. None, however, surpassed Sir Robert Peel in his abuse — his attack upon the Agitator was most virulent and insulting. Reviewing the conduct of this statesman, O'Connell publicly defied his traducer to repeat in his presence the language which he had used under the shelter of parliamentary privilege. This open challenge was not long in finding its way to the ear of Mr. Peel, who lost no time in accepting it. The *friends* of both gentlemen met, and, with chivalrous despatch, made the necessary arrangements. Mrs. O'Connell, however, had got wind of the "affair," and privately informed the sheriff. O'Connell was accordingly arrested, and bound over to keep the peace under the penalty of £10,000. For a while the matter seemed to have blown over; but the truth was, O'Connell had been mortally offended, and only awaited an opportunity of obtaining satisfaction. At length O'Connell learned that Mr. Peel was in London, and he immediately started in search of him. On his arrival in London the challenge was renewed, and arrangements made to fight at Ostend. O'Connell's earnestness now became a source of anxiety to Mr. Peel. A duel with the best shot in Ireland was not a very desirable thing at best. Mr. Peel's father shared the uneasiness of his son, and offered a reward of fifty guineas for the arrest of the disturber of his peace. This tempting offer at once aroused the vigilance of the metropolitan police, and O'Connell was arrested at four o'clock in the morning, just as he was preparing to leave for Dover. Again he was bound over to keep the peace, and returned to Ireland thoroughly disgusted.

From 1816 to 1819, an interval of three years, nothing seems to have transpired worthy of comment. A lethargy seized upon the Catholics of Ireland that appeared to affect O'Connell himself.

Henry Grattan died in 1820. In that year his son offered himself as a candidate for the parliamentary representation of Dublin. O'Connell eagerly espoused the cause of young Grattan, and, on the hustings, took occasion to eulogize the memory of Ireland's departed patriot and statesman.

"We are met on this melancholy occasion," said O'Connell," "to celebrate the obsequies of the greatest man Ireland ever knew. The widowed land of his birth, in mourning over his remains, feels it is a nation's sorrow, and turns with the anxiety of a parent to alleviate the grief of the orphan he has left. The virtues of that great patriot shone brilliant, pure, unsullied, ardent, glowing. Oh! I should exhaust the dictionary three times told, ere I could enumerate the virtues of Grattan. In 1778, when Ireland was shackled, he reared the standard of independence; and in 1782 he stood forward as the champion of his country, achieving, gloriously, her independence. Earnestly, unremittingly, did he labor for her, bitterly did he deplore her wrongs; and if man could have prevented her ruin — if man could have saved her — Grattan would have done it! After the disastrous act of Union, which met his most resolute and most determined opposition, he did not suffer despair to creep over his heart, and induce him to abandon her, as was the case with too many others. No; he remained firm to his duty in the darkest adversity; he continued his unwearying advocacy of his country's rights. Of him it may be truly said, in his own words: 'He watched by the cradle of his country's freedom — he followed her hearse!' His life, to the very period of his latest breath, has been spent in her service, and he died, I may even say, a martyr in her cause. Who shall *now* prate to me of religious animosity? To any such, I will answer by pointing to the honored tomb of Grattan, and I will say, 'There sleeps a man, a member of the Protestant community, who died in the cause of his Catholic fellow countrymen!'"

No one was more grateful than O'Connell for the

support given by Protestants to the cause of Catholic emancipation.

George IV. ascended the throne of England in this year, and the aristocracy in Ireland were desirous of manifesting their loyalty, in an address to his majesty. They accordingly assembled for this purpose at the Court-house of Kilmainham. When Lord Howth, with other members of the meeting, arrived, they were surprised to find the court-house and its approaches filled by the people. Finding it impossible to penetrate the crowd before the door, the new comers were obliged to enter the building through one of its windows. This ludicrous proceeding so amused the audience, that when the chairman arose to open the meeting, he could not be heard in consequence of the shouts and laughter that greeted him. It is necessary to state that the action of the king towards his unhappy queen, had rendered the course about to be pursued by the aristocracy exceedingly unpopular with the people. O'Connell stood in the centre of the hall, surrounded by his friends. Lord Frankfort was proposed as chairman. O'Connell objected to the appointment; whereupon the sheriff demanded to know "if he was a freeholder of the county?" O'Connell's reply was most emphatic, and must have surprised his officious interrogator:

"I *am* a freeholder of this county. I have a hereditary property which, probably, may stand a comparison with the person's who interrogates me; and I have a profession which gives me an annual income, greater than any of the personages who sur-

round the chair are able to wring from the taxes."
A dispute followed, and the sheriff, finding himself unable to preserve order, called in the military, who drove out the people at the point of the bayonet.

O'Connell and his friends having succeeded in breaking up one meeting, now determined to hold another of their own. Open-air meetings were forbidden at that time, but a chair was placed in the doorway of a tavern near at hand, and thus they managed to evade the law. It had been the intention of the dissenters to propose a counter address to the king, denouncing his treatment of the queen. This address was now called for, but was nowhere to be found. O'Connell had fortunately prepared one himself, which was adopted, and duly forwarded to his majesty. The meeting concluded by drawing up a memorial to the Lord-Lieutenant, deprecating the outrageous conduct of the sheriff; which, of course, was never heeded by that dignitary.

. In January, 1821, O'Connell addressed one of his famous letters "to the people of Ireland," which created a profound sensation through Ireland, and even in England. It was written with a view of arousing the people to a sense of their condition, and to prepare them for those great demonstrations which preceded emancipation. In this year, Mr. Plunket, who, since the retirement and death of Grattan, had advocated the Catholic cause in the Commons, introduced his Relief Bill. Mr. Plunket labored under the same mistaken idea of what the Catholics required as Mr. Grattan did. The first sections of the Act were truly admirable, but the remaining provisions were favorable to the Veto. The Commons received the bill favorably, and passed it by a majority· of nineteen. It was then carried to the House of Lords, where, fortunately, it was defeated. O'Connell rejoiced at the rejection of this bill, which, had it passed, would have transferred the censorship of Rome to the British capital. He condemned it in the most emphatic terms. Letter after letter emanated from his busy pen, warning the people of the dangerous tendency of Plunket's measure, and characterizing it as "abominable." These letters were written whilst he was on circuit, in the intervals of his laborious professional practice, and exhibit the vigilance with which at all times he watched over the interests of his religion and country.

O'Connell, subsequently, recommended that the Irish Catholics should throw their numerical strength into the ranks of the English Radicals, and carry reform in the first place, and emancipation afterwards. No sooner had the news of this intended combination reached the ears of the English cabinet than they took measures to anticipate the result. Indeed this masterly suggestion filled the English cabinet with consternation. The Radicals were already a rapidly-increasing power at home; but what would they not effect if joined to the Irish Reformers? Something must be done to ward off the threatened danger, and interpose a barrier between the coalescing factions. It was the result of this fear that induced George IV. to visit Ireland, in 1821. The Irish journals were soon apprised of the intended visit, and the nation

placed on the tip-toe of expectation. On the 12th
of August of that year, salutes of artillery roaring
in the Park and at the Pigeon House, and the jan-
gling joy-bells of the city, announced the arrival of
the royal visitor. His majesty set out from England
in regal state, employing his leisure in discussing
goose-pie, and washing it down with prodigious quan-
tities of whiskey. Landing at Howth, he entered a
carriage, and was driven rapidly by the North-Circu-
lar Road to the Viceregal Lodge. Meanwhile, his
ill-treated consort, whom he had left in the throes of
death, ended her unhappy career. To save appearances, the king remained for three days buried in
seclusion, as if lamenting her death. In the meantime, Dublin, alive with excitement, made extensive
preparations for his triumphat entry into the city.

On the morning of the 17th, the streets of the
Irish capital were swarming with an expectant multitude, assembled to do honor to their royal guest.
In due time, the king, habited in the uniform of a
field marshal, and wearing in his chapeau a bunch
of shamrocks, issued forth from the Park. On
either side of the carriage in which he sat, rode a
brilliant escort, and as his majesty came in sight of
the people, a shout of welcome met his ear, such as
none but the warm-hearted Celt can give. The royal
equipage now took its place in the procession, which
was of imposing length, and made up of the nobility, gentry, the professions, corporations, and trades.
Arriving at the head of Sackville Street, a barrier of
evergreens, representing the gates of the city, intercepted the royal *cortége*. His majesty must obtain

the freedom of the city from the Lord Mayor before
he dare enter. The ceremony of opening the gates
was carried out with the utmost-punctilio, and the
gorgeous cavalcade moved on, amidst the wildest
demonstrations of popular joy. The king, rising in
his carriage, returned the salute of the people, and
slowly moved on to the castle, where he alighted and
entered.

Ireland's reception of George IV. was in every
respect a triumph. The national heart throbbed
with unrestrained satisfaction; its sincerity was un-
mistakable; and the Irish people trusted that the
presence of their sovereign was an earnest of his
clemency and good-will. O'Connell himself shared
the kindly spirit of the people, and had impressed
them with the necessity of welcoming their royal vis-
visitor. He felt it would further the interests of the
Catholic cause, by creating a favorable influence in
England.

"This," said O'Connell, speaking of the king's
visit long afterwards, "this was the most critical
period of my political life, and that in which I had
the good fortune to be most successful. If I have
any merit for the success of the Catholic cause, it
is principally to be found in the mode in which I
neutralized the most untoward events, and converted
the most sinister appearances and circumstances into
the utmost extent of practical usefulness to the
cause of which I was the manager. Abuse of George
IV. would have been then so bad policy, that the
enemies of religious liberty would gladly avail themselves of any such abuse to render the king more

desperate in his opposition. George IV. came to
Ireland with the most ample prospects of national
benefit. He came, he assured us, as the father of
all his people — to reconcile *all* his people to each
other — to establish the liberty and prosperity of *all*
the Irish. Nor did his actions, whilst in Ireland, be-
lie his declarations. For the first time for two centuries were the Catholics received by the Executive
on terms of perfect equality with the Protestants.
The Catholic prelates were received by the king in
their ecclesiastical costume, with their golden crosses
and chains. It was the first official recognition of
their dignity as prelates. To the Earl of Fingal, as
head of the Catholic laity, the ribbon of the order of
St. Patrick was given, at an installation at which the
king himself presided. The rest of the Catholic
laity were received and cherished precisely as the
Protestants were; and, to crown all, the celebrated
Sidmouth letter was issued, full of present kindness
and gratitude to the Catholics, and of future hope
and expectation of conciliation — a conciliation which
everybody knew could never be effected without
legal and perfect equalization of political rights.
How little can any person removed from the scene
appreciate the difficulties I had to encounter, and
the management which was necessary to prevent the
Catholics from marring, or being accused of marring, these bright prospects. How much of just
resentment was it necessary to suppress! How
much of — but I promised you to be as brief as possible. I will therefore abstain from following up
this topic; yet I am entitled to this fact — that no

part of my political life obtained—I will say deservedly—so much of the gratitude and confidence of my countrymen, as the mode in which I was enabled to convert the king's visit to Ireland from being a source of weakness and discomfiture to the Catholics, into a future claim for practical relief and political equalization."

"O'Connell," said a London newspaper, vilipending the Agitator, "escorted his majesty to Kingstown; followed him (literally) into the sea, in order to present him with a laurel crown, and knelt in the water when offering him the wreath."

O'Connell answered this attack by quoting the words of his assailant, and then refuting them. "*He escorted his majesty to Kingstown*—quite untrue. I did not escort his majesty at all that day. He was, in the morning, in the county Wicklow. I rode with some gentlemen to Kingstown, and there remained until the king's arrival. I did not see him that day until his arrival at Kingstown. *He followed him (literally) into the sea, in order to present him with a laurel crown.* This is so circumstantially false, that it must be called literally a lie. I did not follow the king at all; nor did I go nearer the water when presenting the laurel crown than about twenty paces. *He knelt in the water*—totally untrue. I presented the crown to the king in a tent, the nearest part of which to the water was at least twenty feet from the water's edge. I presented it at the end of the tent farthest from the water, in as dry a place as ever king stood upon. I, of course, knelt one knee in presenting the crown; but so far is it from being true that I was guilty of any unbe-coming servility, that I did not even kiss the hand which the king held out to me for that purpose."

The king entered his royal yacht, and sailed away for England. It is said he was charmed by the en-chanting scenery of the Irish coast, and lingered on the stern of his vessel, looking through a spy-glass at the long and beautiful outline of the Wicklow hills, until they faded from his view. If George IV. had entertained a generous impulse for Ireland, the sight of the English shores speedily put it to flight. Meanwhile, the aristocracy of both countries were enjoying the success of their plan, and laugh-ing at the people who had been so easily duped. The dread alliance with the English Radicals had been frustrated. The Irish people never afterwards had cause to bless his memory.

The following is an interesting anecdote of O'Con-nell whilst on circuit, in 1822. Illicit trade then was alarmingly on the increase at the town of Dingle, and the government resolved to suppress it speedily. Accordingly, one John Flood, formerly employed as a lamp-lighter in the Crow-Street Theatre, Dublin, through moneyed influence, was appointed to a posi-tion in the revenue, and sent down to look after government interests.

Flood, on his arrival, however, instead of manning a cutter, set up a theatre. He became the centre of attraction in the "out of the way" town, and gave himself up to social amusements of all kinds. He subsequently proved more hostile to the neighboring farm-yards than to the smugglers, and was on more than one occasion before the "justices." Flood grew anxious for his position, as evil reports of his conduct had already reached Dublin. He now felt the necessity of mending his ways, and resolved to take the first opportunity of re-establishing himself in the good graces of his superiors. Fortunately, a person by the name of O'Connor, a shop-keeper of Dingle, was caught in the act of smuggling tobacco. Flood, of course, lost no time in bringing the offender into court. O'Connor secured the services of O'Connell.

Flood, who was half intoxicated at the trial, had given his evidence, and was about to leave the witness-box when he was held by O'Connell for cross-examination.

"Come back, Alonzo!" cried O'Connell. It would appear O'Connell knew the former career of the witness, and was prepared to take advantage of his shortcomings. Flood, turning around, exclaimed, "Alonzo the brave and the fair Imogene." O'Connell at once opened on him, by asking "who was your Imogene in Dingle?" Flood was obliged to confess how many Imogenes he had, how many parties he had given, how many hen-roosts he had pillaged. At length the witness grew exasperated under the sharp lash of O'Connell's tongue, and, losing control of himself, leaped towards his persecutor. Reaching the space between the witness-box and the bench, he lost his balance and fell forward on the floor amidst the laughter of the entire court. As Flood had frequently contradicted himself during the cross-examination, his evidence was not accepted, and O'Connor was acquitted.

A distinguished member of the Irish bar narrates the following humorous anecdote:

"When Lord Manners retired from the Chancellorship, a great part of the public looked to Plunket, the Attorney-General, then in the zenith of his fame as an orator and a statesman, as the successor to the high place. The newspapers announced it, the people received it as a fact, and the known object of his ambition seemed already in the possession of the preëminent laborer. English policy, however, or it may be the inability to spare such an ally from the House of Commons, stopped his promotion for the time, and Sir Anthony Hart, of the English bar, sat as Lord Chancellor of Ireland. A brilliant gathering of the 'Long Robe' received the stranger on his first sitting, with the customary obeisance. The disappointed, if not insulted, Attorney-General was there, and Saurin, and Goold, and Bushe, and Wallace, and Joy, and, amongst the juniors, Blackburn and Sheil; but, greatest amongst the great, 'the observed of all observers,' the future Liberator. 'How does Plunket look this morning, Dan?' cries Sheil in a shrill whisper. 'Very sore at *Hart*,' responded Dan, rolling his large gray eye towards the bench; and the timely hit soon ran round the gay circle and the buzzing and crowded hall, adding to the long roll of the great Dan's hard yet pleasant sayings."

CHAPTER X.

THREE names were assumed, and successively abandoned, by the governing body of the Irish Catholics
during the life-time of O'Connell. The Committee
became the Board, and the Board was succeeded by
the first Association. The government abolished
the Committee and Board, whilst the first Association died a natural death.

To re-unite the broken thread of Catholic interest,
a letter, the joint effort of O'Connell and Sheil, was
addressed to those members who had been prominent in the late organizations. The result proved a
success. In a house on Sackville Street, long known
as Tyrrell's Library — which was then occupied as a
tavern, and owned by a man named Dempsey, who
enjoyed a great reputation for dressing beefsteak —
a few Catholics met on the 28th of April, 1823.

This meeting was convened by O'Connell. Some one present moved that Lord Killeen (son of Lord Fingal) be made chairman, which was followed by that gentleman presiding. O'Connell then arose to explain why the meeting had been called.

"Some persons," said he, "must take upon themselves the trouble of managing the affairs of the Catholics. They need not assume a representative character, and every Catholic gentleman will be eligible to act by subscribing one guinea to a fund which shall be formed, to meet contingent expenses. Such a body will be useful in repelling calumny abroad, and in procuring redress for victims of rancor who are not well able to avenge their own wrongs."

Two vital measures were adopted at this meeting. The people at large were to be enrolled in this great enterprise, with an annual assessment of one shilling each; the clergy were to be interested in the undertaking, first, to keep alive the spirit of the organization, and secondly, to collect and forward assessments to the treasurer of the association, as they became due.

On Monday, the 12th of May, in accordance with the resolutions passed at an aggregate meeting held two days before, O'Connell and his fellow-chiefs formally established the Catholic Association. The Catholic Association, when first founded, was eminently successful. At one of the meetings, fifty individuals demonstrated their sincerity by each paying a pound to its funds. The aristocracy seemed to hail it with hope, and crowd round it with satisfaction. But when it had, in their eyes, served its purpose, and O'Connell no longer thought of his threatened junction with the English radicals, "the respectable classes" began to grow cold, and O'Connell could not, on many occasions, muster as many votaries of freedom as would constitute a meeting of ten. According to the rules, without ten a meeting could not be held. That O'Connell labored hard to render the Association worthy of its great mission, may be inferred from the following incident of one of the meetings: At twenty-three minutes past three on that afternoon, there were but seven persons present, including Mr. O'Connell himself and the *inexorable* Purcell; the latter, as usual, watch in hand, not in the least moved by the anxiety so plainly depicted in Mr. O'Connell's face. Another minute, and Mr. O'Connell could remain in the room no longer. He ran towards Coyne's shop, down-stairs, in the faint hope of finding somebody. On the stairs the *eighth* man passed him going up. In the shop itself were fortunately two young Maynooth priests, making some purchases. The rules of the Association admitting all clergymen as honorary members without special motion, he eagerly addressed and implored them to come up but for one moment, and help to make the required quorum. At first they refused, there being a good deal of hesitation generally on the part of the clergy to put themselves at all forward in politics, and these young men in particular having all the timidity of their secluded education about them. But there was no withstanding him; partly by still more earnest solicitations, and partly by actual *pushing*, he got them towards the staircase, and upon it, and finally into the meeting-room, exactly a second or two before the half-hour, and so stopped Mr. O'Gorman's mouth; and the required number being thus made up, the chair was taken.

At a meeting held February 29, 1824, O'Connell brought forward his great project of the "Rent." We have already alluded to the shilling assessment which had been proposed on a former occasion. At this meeting, O'Connell, whose master-mind had not only conceived the intellectual, but even the financial arrangements of this plan, placed the matter so forcibly before the minds of his hearers that it was unanimously adopted. O'Connell calculated that by his penny-a-month subscription, £50,000 could be easily realized. This fund was to be applied in the following manner: £5,000 were to be used in carrying measures in Parliament, and keeping at London an agent who would carefully watch the movements of the enemy; for the press, £15,000; for law proceedings, in preserving legal privileges of the Catholics and prosecuting Orange aggressors, £15,000; for the use of Catholic schools and the purchase of books, £5,000; for educating Catholic priests for the service of America, £5,000. The remaining sum, £5,000, was to be retained as a sinking fund, as well as a balance to meet the current expenses of the Association.

"Every peasant," says Thomas Wyse, "every Catholic inhabitant, from the child of seven to the grandfather of seventy, was invited to contribute; and thus arose in a few weeks 'the Catholic Rent.' Between £700 and £900 were received during each week of the first year of this society's organization. Thus the 'Rent' became a success from the start. It was the lever which opened the long closed gates of Parliament to Catholic emancipation."

In December of this year, O'Connell made a speech that came near giving him serious annoyance. In this speech the following objectionable language was used: "He hoped that Ireland would never be driven to the system pursued by the Greeks. He trusted in God they would never be so driven. He hoped Ireland would be restored to her rights; but if that day should arrive — if she were driven mad by persecution, he wished that a new Bolivar might arise — that the spirit of the Greeks and of the South Americans might animate the people of Ireland!" For this O'Connell was indicted, but the grand jury threw out the bill. To the credit of the reporters present when the speech was delivered, it may be said they refused to give evidence against the accused. The only exception was a reporter of *Saunders' News-Letter*, and this gentleman was afterwards obliged to admit he was asleep during most of the meeting.

During this year O'Connell paid a visit to Paris, accompanied by his son Morgan, who, in 1821, returned from South America. In Paris he had the pleasure of visiting his distinguished kinsman, General Count O'Connell, whose history has been glanced at on pages 6 and 7 of this work. At this time the general was eighty, and though seamed by innumerable wounds, received in his long and illustrious military career, still enjoyed good health. Forty years before, at the siege of Gibraltar, a shell from the English batteries bursting at his feet, left him streaming in blood, inflicting nine wounds on his person; and a bullet, whizzing by his head, swept away a considerable portion of his ear.

In Paris, O'Connell parted with his son Morgan, who proceeded to Austria, where he obtained a cornetcy in a regiment of light dragoons. The remainder of the Agitator's family were, at this time, at Tours, owing to the declining health of Mrs. O'Connell, who was seeking relief in the genial climate of Southern France.

O'Connell's uncle, "Old Hunting-Cap," died in 1824, at the ripe age of ninety-six. In his will he bequeathed his entire landed property, worth £4,000 per annum, to his nephew, Daniel O'Connell. The Agitator was keenly affected by the old man's death; which affliction was shared by the poor, who had lost at once a sincere friend and generous advocate.

At the opening of Parliament in 1825, the king's speech was singularly unfriendly to Ireland, although he began by saying that Ireland was prosperous. Still he felt the Catholic Association was breeding sedition, and should at once be suppressed. Accordingly, on the 10th of February, a bill was brought before the national Legislature for the "suppression of unlawful associations." O'Connell and Sheil were sent over by the Catholic Association to demand a hearing at the bar of the House of Commons. O'Connell was present during the entire debate on this bill, awaiting an opportunity of being heard. Lord Brougham, who fought hard to defeat the measure, moved that the Irish delegation should be allowed to plead their cause. This was not granted, however, and that part of their mission ended.

O'Connell was warmly welcomed, and courteously entertained, during his visit, by many leading Whigs, and had a favorable opportunity of laying the Catholic question before them in its very best light.

The attention shown O'Connell during his stay in London was not inspired by sincerity. The aristocracy were anxious to learn how far the Catholics of Ireland sympathized with the Radicals of England. O'Connell's cheerful manner and habitual courtesy soon convinced them there was little to fear on that score; and finding the bill could be carried without endangering their interests, they lost no time in securing its acceptance. O'Connell returned to Ireland on the 1st of June, 1825, no doubt heartily glad to be freed from the restraints of English society, where he could scarcely move or speak without the utmost caution, so closely was he watched on all sides. Mrs. O'Connell and his daughters met him at Howth, which was then the landing-place for English packets, and he was escorted to his house in Merrion Square by the enthusiastic populace, who removed the horses, and drew along the carriage themselves. On his arrival at the house, he was obliged to address the people from the balcony before they could be induced to disperse. In sunshine and storm, in summer and winter, by day, and even at night, O'Connell stood on that balcony from time to time, and, to the no small annoyance of his Protes-

tant neighbors, responded to the calls of a grateful and faithful people.

Before the deputation left London there was an Emancipation bill pending, which afterwards passed the Commons, but was fortunately lost in the upper house. Tacked to this bill were two conditions, called "wings." The Catholic clergy were to be paid by the government, but the forty-shilling freeholders were to be disfranchised. The first condition was intended as a conciliatory measure towards the priesthood, but would have had the effect of rendering them "stipendiaries of the crown." It was a wily scheme to sever the tie which joined the priest and people. The second condition would have destroyed the political power of the vast majority of the Irish people, and placed the nation under the control of the landed proprietors, who had no sympathy with the real progress of Ireland. O'Connell, during his stay in England, was led to believe this bill, even with its "wings," would have been of advantage to the Catholics. "There can be no question," says Fagan, "that O'Connell was treated with great perfidy in the course of these negotiations. He was led to believe that emancipation was certain, provided it were accompanied with the 'wings.' Every one at the time, in London, who was mixed in the matter, believed it. Blake, the chief remembrancer, who was then in London, and on terms of political intercourse with the leading political men of the day, has since often stated his conviction that the matter was settled. Plunket was himself deceived, and was thus the means of deceiving O'Connell and the rest of the deputation. The system of deceit was carried so far as to induce O'Connell to attend the levee of the Duke of York."

O'Connell's opinion on the forty-shilling freehold question was made the ground of a dastardly attack upon his character. Alas! it has been too frequently the lot of Irish patriots to find reproaches where they should have received unqualified support. The men who criticised the Liberator on this occasion were unable to appreciate the labors and sacrifices he underwent for the cause of emancipation. O'Connell was not to be intimidated or disheartened by these curs, whose bark was the limit of their power of offence. He boldly entered a meeting held to denounce him, and defended his policy with great vigor and success. He was resolved at any cost, no matter who was opposed to him, to stand up for Ireland. He finally concluded by calling upon those present to be united.

"I now," he said, "call upon and conjure you, gentlemen, to bury animosity and captious irascibility, and to join with me in fighting the common enemy. I can only say that if the entire country were to turn against me, I would not, like Scipio, go to lay my bones in foreign earth, but I would go to the aggregate meeting on Wednesday to reproach them by exerting myself to serve them, if possible, twenty times more. (Laughter and applause.) I am happy to be able to tell you that I have the report already prepared; it will probably pass in the committee to-day, and will be presented at the aggregate meeting on Wednesday; where we shall all

meet, I hope, with no other object than the success
of our common cause — no other view than the interests of the people."

O'Connell's popularity was not lessened; the country at large only awaited an opportunity of showing
their renewed confidence in him. This opportunity
was afforded shortly afterwards whilst he was on circuit. In Galway, the horses were taken from his
carriage, and he was drawn through the principal
streets in the midst of a shouting and admiring multitude, greeted with cheers, blessings, and acclama-
tions. In Cork, an eloquent address was presented
to him, with the view of proving to his detractors
that "his purity of intention and devotion to Irish
interests continued unimpeached in the public esti-
mation." In Mallow, he was obliged to entreat the
people, for the sake of Mrs. O'Connell, who accompanied him, and whose health was delicate, to allow
his carriage to pass on without taking off the horses.
"It is not possible," says a popular writer, "to convey in language an idea of his popularity at this period. He was absolutely adored by the Irish people." At Wexford, the Agitator was met at "the
pass" by a fleet of boats and obliged to enter a triumphal barge, superbly decorated. The rowers were
dressed in green and gold, and, from the gala appearance of boats and people, it resembled a Venetian
carnival. He was finally landed at the bridge, in
Wexford, amid ringing plaudits from the crowded
banks, and, in the evening, was entertained at a public dinner.

At the close of this year (1825), O'Connell re-

ceived a challenge from a Kerry barrister, named
Leyne. This gentleman took offence at some language said to have been used by the Agitator, and
even went so far as to call O'Connell a liar and
coward. The sad result of duelling had made a profound impression on O'Connell's religious mind, and,
instead of fighting, he had Mr. Leyne bound over to
keep the peace. Finding his father unwilling to re-
sent the insult offered, Maurice O'Connell forth-
with challenged Mr. Leyne, who refused to accept.
O'Connell, on finding his son still bent upon bringing the "affair" to a climax, had them both arrested,
and bound over to keep the peace.

One of the fourteen-day meetings held at this
time was rendered memorable by a controversy which
took place between O'Connell and the newspapers.
O'Connell complained that the reports were inaccu-
rate. The press was not slow to reply. "He asserts," said the *Morning Register*, "that the reports
did not contain all that he delivered. We admit
that they did not in length go much beyond seventy
columns; but seventy columns could not have done
him great injustice. They certainly did not include
all that the learned gentleman had spoken; for to do
that would require Mr. Thwaites' broad sheet. Any
one who measures by a stop-watch will find that Mr.
O'Connell pours out about 200 words in one minute.
These 200 words will make 22 lines of small print.
These 22 lines are about one-eighth of an ordinary
column, so that it will give Mr. O'Connell only seven
or eight minutes' trouble to fill a column of small
print, if he must be followed exactly through epi-

sodes, parentheses, and all. What are eight minutes'
speaking to Mr. O'Connell? What are forty?
What one hundred and fifty? In a five hours' sitting he will contrive sometimes to be three hours on
his legs; and in three hours he will positively pour
out twenty-two columns and a quarter of oratory;
to catch all of which, with a view to speedy publication, would require more space than is furnished by
the London 'broadsheet' itself. We must, therefore, acknowledge that we had not published all that
Mr. O'Connell delivered; but he had, as we calculate, his seventy columns." The *Freeman's Journal*
was much severer in its strictures on O'Connell, in
rebutting his attack upon the press.

11

CHAPTER XI.

THE new Catholic Association was next to be formed. At an aggregate meeting, the Catholics agreed to leave the somewhat dangerous task of re-organizing in the hands of a committee of twenty-one gentlemen. This committee sat fifteen days in secretly deliberating upon the best means of evading the recent act of supression. From this body originated the "fourteen days' meetings," which, whilst they outwitted the law, were productive of the most marked results.

The old Association had imitated the House of Commons; its sessions spread over months; its discussions embraced every possible variety of political subject. The object of the suppression bill was to destroy this resemblance. To effect this, the meetings of the Catholics for the purpose of petitioning were limited, by the suppression bill, to fourteen days. The object was to restrict: it enlarged!

It brought together what had not been assembled by all the former weekly meetings in the metropolis. A large concourse of gentlemen and clergy flocked in from the country, and thus superadded a new assembly in the character of a convention to the ordinary meetings of the Association. Under the masked battery of education and charity, every complaint was uttered, every shaft was levelled which could have been permitted in the open field of the old Association. The limitation of. their meetings to fourteen days was instantly seized for the purpose of additional agitation. It was made good ground for the convening of a new species of assembly, — the provincial meetings. Each province of Ireland was summoned by requisition ; the Catholics invited their Protestant friends; both met on an appointed day, in a town, chosen in rotation, in one or other of the counties of the province. They generally remained sitting for two days, and usually dined together on the third. The result was most important; it was not only another convention like that of the fourteen days — it was a convention of Protestants and Catholics. It familiarized both sects with each other.

The re-organized Catholic Association soon exhibited a vigor that amazed its enemies throughout the length and breadth of Ireland. Its funds were used in securing first-class lawyers to protect the people in extreme cases of oppression, such as the wrecking of a Catholic chapel, or bringing to justice Orange rioters and assassins.

In the Northern Courts, a Catholic heretofore had

little or no chance of obtaining justice. It must have surprised those rascally magistrates to find themselves suddenly confronted by Dublin attorneys, vastly superior to themselves in the knowledge of the law, prepared to question their decisions and expose their injustice.

There was another channel in which the funds of the Association were employed with surprising effect; viz., in the election of members for Parliament. The first notable success was in Wexford. The Beresford family had long represented that county, and the idea of successfully opposing so powerful an interest never entered into the mind of any one. It must be remembered that all Catholics possessing forty shillings were entitled to vote, although no Catholic was legally entitled to sit in Parliament. The landlords, who carried in their pockets the destinies of the tenants, had been in the habit of driving them to the hustings like so many sheep. A refusal to vote according to the proprietor's direction was equivalent to an ejection. Hence the great security of the Beresfords, who were large landed proprietors, and controlled a vast number of votes. In 1826, Lord George Beresford was opposed by Mr. Stuart, who was favorably disposed to the Catholic cause. O'Connell went down from Dublin, as counsel to Stuart, at a fee of 600 guineas. At this crisis, a steamboat was sent up the Blackwater, by Beresford, to bring down to Waterford the Duke of Devonshire's tenants, who had been weaned over to vote in his favor. No sooner had O'Connell heard of this scheme, than he set off rapidly for Lismore, and arrived in advance of the steamer. Having assembled the people of the town, he delivered a long harangue on the dangers of embarking on a "tin kittle," referring, of course, to the steamboat, and so wrought on the fears of their wives and daughters that they would not suffer their relations to go on board. The steamer was obliged to return to Waterford without a single voter on board, to the no small mortification of the Beresfords and their Orange adherents. At the hustings, an aged patriot in the crowd cried out, "I propose Daniel O'Connell as a fit person to represent the county of Waterford in Parliament." This gave O'Connell an opportunity of delivering his opinion on the hustings, which he turned to good effect. His speech was one of the most eloquent of his life, lasting over two hours, and at its close he withdrew his claim, which, of course, he had no intention of prosecuting. Beresford withdrew, and Mr. Stuart was triumphantly elected.

Sheil used to tell an anecdote of this election, of which he vouched for the accuracy. Lord Waterford was dying at the time, but the ruling passion was strong in death. He heard that his own huntsman, Manton, was going to "vote against him." He sent for the old and faithful follower; but, though the poor man's heart was sore, both from affection for his old master, and the knowledge of the consequence of exercising his right, he refused to vote "against his country and his religion." The dying peer had his revenge. Manton was dismissed, deprived of his farm, and driven out on the world a beggar.

This success gave an impetus to the cause of freedom. The people began to feel their power and assert their independence. O'Connell returned to Dublin, and, after the municipal election, set out with his entire family to Derrynane, which had now become the property of the Agitator, the princely bequest of his uncle, "Old Hunting-Cap." The journey thither was a continuous ovation. The people lined the roads, and welcomed him as he passed. He was met at Cahirciveen by peasants furnished with ropes, who detached the horses from his carriage, and drew the Liberator and his family in triumph to their home. O'Connell's life at Derrynane was a source of joy and edification to his friends and tenantry. He maintained a domestic chaplain, and the Holy Sacrifice of the Mass was each day offered beneath that hospitable roof. His friends gathered about him in numbers, listening to his interesting anecdotes and stories, and enjoying the sunshine of a presence that sent a thrill of delight over all who came under its genial rays. Children, guests, and domestics seemed animated by a common spirit of affection and respect towards him.

During his stay at Derrynane, O'Connell frequently engaged in field-sports. His followers were surprised on these occasions at the agility and endurance he exhibited, outstripping in activity his wild Kerry scouts, who had both youth and practice to back them.

A rough northern lawyer, who was his guest at Derrynane, was greatly surprised one day at his faculty of bestowing attention on different subjects at once. The lawyer consulted him about an Act of Parliament, and was reading aloud the disputable sections of the Act, when he suddenly stopped short, exclaiming "Oh, Mr. O'Connell, I see you are reading something else! I'll wait till you have done." "Go on! go on, man!" said O'Connell, without raising his eyes from the document with which he was engaged; "I hear you quite distinctly. If you had as much to do as I have, you would long ago have been trained into the knack of devoting the one moment to two occupations." The other obeyed, and when he concluded his queries, O'Connell put aside the second object of his thoughts, and delivered a detailed reply to all the questions of his visitor.

In his irregularly-built house, he resembled an old king in an Irish story, as he sat at his breakfast-table, arrayed in a reddish, well-quilted dressing-gown, with a tasselled cap upon his head, reading his letters and newspapers, which the postman early each morning brought over the hills from Cahirciveen. Speaking of the sofas in his breakfast-room to a visitor, he said, "These were once present at high Orange orgies. I bought them at the auction of that petticoat-Robespierre, Lord Clare, who never named Catholics without some epithet of hatred and contempt."

O'Connell, in 1828, had attained so exalted a position in the hearts of the people, and exerted so commanding an influence over the destinies of Ireland, that the popular impulse of the nation was bent on seating him in Parliament. It was yet a matter of conjecture how this could be brought about, as the law still denied a Catholic that privilege, when a most fortunate circumstance, from an unexpected source, solved the difficulty and brought the question to an issue.

There was at this time in Dublin a gentleman named Sir David Rosse, who, though a Tory in politics, was, from motives of gratitude, a sincere well-wisher of O'Connell's. One morning, in June of 1828, Sir David met Vincent Fitzpatrick, son of a noted bookseller of Dublin, and suggested that as Vesey Fitzgerald had vacated his seat for Clare, O'Connell should himself stand for that county. Fitzpatrick seized the idea with avidity, and thanking the gentleman for his suggestion, flew off immediately to acquaint the Agitator. O'Connell received the proposition very coolly. Fitzgerald, he said, had always been a friend to the Catholic cause, and, moreover, the law rendered it impossible for him to sit in Parliament, even if elected. Fitzpatrick, however, was obstinate, and would not be refused. He urged the matter so persistently that O'Connell was obliged to yield, and they both marched off to the office of the *Evening Post*, where he wrote his memorable letter to the electors of Clare. This famous letter, which we give in full, is as follows:

"TO THE ELECTORS OF THE COUNTY OF CLARE."

"DUBLIN, June, 1828.

"FELLOW-COUNTRYMEN,—Your county wants a representative. I respectfully solicit your suffrages to raise me to that station.

"Of my qualifications to fill that station. I leave you to judge. The habits of public speaking, and many, many years of public business, render me, perhaps, equally suited with most men to attend to the interests of Ireland in Parliament.

"You will be told I am not qualified to be elected. The assertion, my friends, is untrue. I am qualified to be elected, and to be your representative. It is true that, as a Catholic, I cannot, and of course never will, take the oaths at present prescribed to members of Parliament; but the authority which created these oaths (the Parliament) can abrogate them; and I entertain a confident hope that, if you elect me, the most bigoted of our enemies will see the necessity of removing from the chosen representative of the people an obstacle which would prevent him from doing his duty to his king and to his country.

"The oath at present required by law is, 'that the Sacrifice of the Mass, and the invocation of the Blessed Virgin Mary, and other sàints, as now practised in the Church of Rome, are impious and idolatrous.' Of course I will never stain my soul with such an oath. I leave that to my honorable opponent, Mr. Vesey Fitzgerald. He has often taken that horrible oath. He is ready to take it again, and asks your votes to enable him to swear. I would rather be torn limb from limb than take it. Electors of the county of Clare! choose between me, who abominate that oath, and Mr. Vesey Fitzgerald, who has sworn it full twenty times! Return me to Parliament, and it is probable that such a blasphemous oath will be abolished forever. As your representative, I will try the question with the friends in Parliament of Mr. Vesey Fitzgerald. They may send me to prison. I am ready to go there to promote the cause of the Catholics, and of universal liberty. The discussion which the attempt to exclude your representative from the House of Commons must excite, will create a sensation all over Europe, and produce such a burst of contemptuous indignation against British bigotry in every enlightened country in the world, that the voice of all the great and good in England, Scotland, and Ireland, being joined to the universal shout of the nations of the earth, will overpower every opposition, and render it impossible for Peel and Wellington any longer to close the doors of the constitution against the Catholics of Ireland.

"Electors of the county of Clare, Mr. Vesey Fitzgerald claims, as his only merit, that he is a friend to the Catholics. Why, I am a Catholic myself; and if he be sincerely our friend, let him vote for me, and raise before the British Empire the Catholic question in my humble person, in the way most propitious to my final success. But no, fellow-countrymen, no; he will make no sacrifice to that cause; he will call himself your friend, and act the part of your worst and most unrelenting enemy.

"I do not like to give the epitome of his political life; yet, when the present occasion so loudly calls for it, I cannot refrain. He took office under Perceval, — under that Perceval who obtained power by raising the base, bloody, and unchristian cry of 'No Popery' in England.

"He had the nomination of a member to serve for the borough of Ennis. He nominated Mr. Spencer Perceval, then a decided opponent of the Catholics.

"He voted on the East Retford measure — for a measure that would put two virulent enemies of the Catholics into Parliament.

"In the case of the Protestant Dissenters in England, he voted for their exclusion — that is, against the principle of the freedom of conscience; that sacred principle which the Catholics of Ireland have ever cultivated and cherished, on which we framed our rights to emancipation.

"Finally, he voted for the suppression of the Catholic Association of Ireland!

"And, after this, sacred Heaven! he calls himself a friend to the Catholics.

"He is the ally and colleague of the Duke of Wellington and Mr. Peel. He is their partner in power; they are, you know, the most bitter, persevering, and unmitigated enemies of the Catholics; and, after all this, he, the partner of our bitterest and unrelenting enemies, calls himself the friend of the Catholics of Ireland.

"Having thus traced a few of the demerits of my right honorable opponent, what shall I say for myself?

"I appeal to my past life for my unremitting and disinterested attachment to the religion and liberties of Catholic Ireland.

"If you return me to Parliament, I pledge myself

to vote for every measure favorable to Radical RE-FORM in the representative system, so that the House of Commons may truly, as our Catholic ancestors intended it should do, represent all the people.

"To vote for the repeal of the Vestry Bill, the Subletting Act, and the Grand Jury Laws.

"To vote for the diminution and more equal distribution of the overgrown wealth of the Established Church in Ireland, so that the surplus may be restored to the sustenation of the poor, the aged, and the infirm.

"To vote for every measure of retrenchment and reduction of the national expenditure, so as to relieve the people from the burdens of taxation, and to bring the question of the REPEAL OF THE UNION, at the earliest possible period, before the consideration of the Legislature.

"Electors of the county of Clare! choose between me and Mr. Vesey Fitzgerald; choose between him who so long cultivated his own interest, and one who seeks only to advance yours; choose between the sworn libeller of the Catholic faith, and one who has devoted his early life to your cause, who has consumed his manhood in a struggle for your liberties, and who has ever lived, and is ready to die, for the integrity, the honor, the purity, of the Catholic faith, and the promotion of Irish freedom and happiness.

"Your faithful servant,

DANIEL O'CONNELL."

This address electrified the nation, and was regarded by the people as a bold and open challenge to the government.   In England it spread consternation among the aristocracy, for this great moral revolt could not be put down by force of arms.

To prosecute this undertaking, the friends of O'Connell found it would be necessary to collect a large fund to meet the expenses of the election. They accordingly went earnestly to work, and in a short time were in possession of over £14,000.   The contest on the hustings was at hand.   O'Connell left Dublin in an open carriage, accompanied by N. P. O'Gorman, and two other gentlemen.   As they moved away from the Court of Exchequer, the barristers, in wig and gown, swarmed about the carriage, and it was with difficulty the crowd were induced to open a passage for the Liberator and his companions. O'Connell stood up and bowed to the throng, who returned his salute with deafening cheers, and was soon rattling along on his way to Clare.   Arriving at the hustings, the practical work began at once. Some idea may be formed of the temper of the opposition from the fact that five noblemen gave £4,000 each to defray the expenses of Fitzgerald's election. The partisans of this gentleman resorted to the most extreme shifts to further their interests.   One Hickman, a Tory barrister, paraded the town with two pistols in his belt.   Swelling with anger, he suddenly encountered O'Connell.   "Hallo! O'Connell," exclaimed Hickman, with the tone of a bully, "mark my words, if you canvass one of my tenants, I'll shoot you."   O'Connell calmly replied, as he turned away, "I'll canvass every one of them;" and so he did.

At the hustings a very singular incident occurred. Just as proceedings were about to commence, a tall man seated himself on the railings of the gallery, with his feet dangling over the heads of those below. The High Sheriff, Mr. Molony, who was strongly attached to the cause of the aristocracy, was greatly annoyed at this proceeding. What worried the sheriff still more was that the individual wore on his breast the medal of the "Order of Liberators," and a large green sash across his shoulders. "Who are you?" demanded the sheriff. "My name is O'Gorman Mahon," replied that individual, in a loud tone. "I tell that gentleman," said Mr. Molony, "to take off that badge." O'Gorman paused a moment, and then replied with amusing courtesy. "This gentleman (laying his hand on his breast) tells that gentleman (pointing with the other to the Sheriff) that if that gentleman presumes to touch this gentleman, this gentleman will defend himself against that gentleman, or any other gentleman, while he has got the arm of a gentleman to protect him." The sheriff sat down.

The political contest meanwhile waxed hot. Every species of intimidation was made use of by the landlords to force their tenants into voting for Mr. Fitzgerald. It is said that one of those gentleman rode into Ennis, seated in his carriage in the guise of a footman, to watch his tenantry, who, three hundred strong, followed after him under military escort. As they passed O'Connell's hotel, he came on a stand, and addressed the voters, who halted to listen to him. His eloquence soon prevailed over the threats of their landlord. Meanwhile, the crowd dexterously separated the jealous owner of the soil from his tenants, who were left to vote as they pleased. The most marked feature at the hustings was the order and sobriety of the people. Not even a blackthorn was exhibited, and only one man was found intoxicated, who proved to be, singularly enough, the coachman of O'Connell, a Protestant Englishman. The candidates were about equal at the close of the first day. On the second O'Connell was considerably ahead. At length, the unwilling High Sheriff was obliged to announce that the Agitator had triumphed.

At the close of the election, O'Connell was chaired through Ennis. Thousands had poured in from every quarter of the county, each bearing a green bough in his hand. Every house and cabin was waving with laurels and verdure. It was a most extraordinary scene. Sixty thousand men surrounded O'Connell — a moving mass of waving foliage! Similar honors awaited him in Limerick. In one town, four thousand, in another, fifteen thousand horsemen formed his escort. All along the way from Clare to Dublin, his progress was one vast triumphal procession.

O'Connell did not take his seat in Parliament at once. He went to London to defend his election, in case it might be petitioned against; but as there was a promise of immediate emancipation, he was unwilling to endanger its prospects by urging his own claims.

CHAPTER XII.

THE bill of Catholic Emancipation, so long and patiently waited for, at length passed both houses, and, on the 13th of April, 1829, the royal signature made it a law. The king, a most bitter enemy of Catholicity, protested against the measure to the last, and only sanctioned it under the pressure of circumstances, and after a puerile display of resistance, which lasted for twenty-four hours. After signing the act, he is said to have petulantly exclaimed, "The Duke of Wellington is King of England, O'Connell is King of Ireland, and I suppose I am only Dean of Windsor."

After the Emancipation Act had passed, O'Connell presented himself at a *levée* in London. He approached the royal presence with the usual ceremonies; but as he saw "the royal lips moving," he advanced, believing that he was addressed. Whatever the king had said was inaudible, so O'Connell kissed hands and passed on. In a few days some curious reports appeared in the papers. It was said the king had used some strong language, which was not unusual; it was said also that he had cursed some one at the *levée*, which *was* unusual; and more, that the individual favored by the royal anathema was Irish. O'Connell met the Duke of Norfolk soon after, and asked if he could explain the newspaper reports. "Yes," he replied, "you are the person alluded to. The day you were at the *levée*, his majesty said, as you were approaching, 'There is O'Connell. G— d— the scoundrel!'"

For thirty years, O'Connell had devoted himself unremittingly to the cause of Catholic Ireland. He had laid at the feet of his country not only his brain and heart, but, with a generosity equal to his patriotism, had sacrificed his private fortune to further the interests of Emancipation. Of all nations the Irish may be regarded as the most generous. No sooner were his financial embarrassments made public, than the purse-strings of the nation were unloosed. A subscription-list was at once opened, which was appropriately called "The O'Connell Tribute." From every section of country contributions came pouring in, until at length this spontaneous offering reached the princely sum of £50,000.

To exclude O'Connell from Parliament, a clause had been added to the Emancipation Act which rendered it necessary that Catholics should be elected "after the commencement of the Act," in order to be entitled to a seat in the House. O'Connell, therefore, found himself contronted by a fresh obstacle. To obviate this difficulty, he approached Sir Edward Denney with an· offer of £3,000 for one of his boroughs, but that gentleman met him with a flat refusal. He therefore determined to demand his seat, which he accordingly did, on the 15th of May. The following extract from the London *Times* of that date thus describes his appearance in the House:

"The attempt was made by Mr. O'Connell last night to take his seat in the House of Commons, and the narrative of the proceeding will be read with interest in our parliamentary report. Yet that can convey but an imperfect idea of the silent, the almost breathless attention with which he was received in the House, advancing to and retiring from the table. The benches were filled in an unusual degree with members, and there is no recollection of so large a number of peers brought by curiosity into the House of Commons. The honorable gentleman was introduced by·Lords Dungannon and Ebrington; a perfect stillness ensued. By his action he evidently declined the first oath which was tendered to him — that of supremacy and allegiance — and required the oath prescribed by the late Act. The explanation by the Speaker to the House of what had taken place was clear, his expression of countenance and manner towards the honorable gentleman, on whom he fixed his regards, extremely courteous, and his declaration that 'he must withdraw,' firm and authoritative. Mr, O'Connell for a moment looked round, as one who had reason to expect support, and this failing, he bowed most respectfully and withdrew. After his departure, Mr. Brougham spoke, but in a somewhat subdued tone ; some discussion followed, but the debate on the subject is fixed for Monday next."

May 18th, 1829, was a memorable day in the history of O'Connell's eventful life. Mr. Peel, in the House of Commons, moved, in the midst of the most intense excitement, that O'Connell should be heard at the bar of the House, which was granted

The Liberator advanced to the bar, attended by his solicitor, Mr. Pierce Mahony, the whole House regarding him the while with mingled feelings of curiosity and interest. O'Connell, in the speceh which followed, clearly demonstrated his right; but neither his eloquence nor the explanation of his able solicitor was able to move the preconcerted verdict of the House, and O'Connell's claim was not accepted.

On the following day, O'Connell appeared at the bar for the third time, and was told by the Speaker that he could not take his seat unless he took the oath of supremacy.

"Are you willing to take the oath of supremacy?" asked the Speaker.

"Allow me to look at it," replied O'Connell.

The oath was handed to him, and he looked at it in silence for a few seconds; then raising his head, he said, "In this oath I see one assertion, as to a matter of fact, which I *know* to be untrue. I see a second assertion as to a matter of opinion, which I *believe* to be untrue. I therefore refuse to take this oath."

A writ was immediately issued for a new election. One of the chief causes of alarm to the aristocracy in England, and indeed in Ireland, was the great admiration of the soldiers for O'Connell. In fact, this was one of the principal reasons which induced the ministry to concede emancipation. A majority of the army were Catholic, and many of the regiments in Ireland, originally Protestant, had been gradually recruited with Catholics. In the event of a rebellion, which the Agitator could have excited by a single word, these brave fellows could not be relied on to slaughter the people. "There are two ways of firing," said a soldier at that time, "*at* a man and *over* a man; and if we were called out against O'Connell and our country, I think we should know the difference."

"There he is — look at him. That's the man for the people, and for the soldiers too," said a young soldier, as he uncovered his head, and reverently approached O'Connell, whose bland and genial manner encouraged him to speak.

His first words were uttered in a low voice: "Are you O'Connell, sir?" O'Connell's reply was kindly made, and the young soldier became more confident and collected. "I am going to leave my country, sir, and perhaps I may never see it again; but my sorrow is lighter now that I see *you* before I go. Many a time I have prayed for you at my mother's knee and in the house of God; and now my heart is proud that I can pray to God, in your own presence, to bless you and prosper your cause." The patriot soldier knelt as he spoke, and cast a glance to heaven and on the beloved object of his prayers. O'Connell seemed greatly moved; and as he stretched forth his hand to raise the gallant youth at his feet, his eye glistened with honest pride and feeling. He made an effort to speak, but his heart was too full. The soldier snatched his hand and pressed it eagerly to his lips and heart. "Remember," said he, "remember that though I wear *this* badge, I would die for *you !*" His head sank, sobbing, for an instant of intense feeling, upon the hand of O'Connell; but ere expression could come on either side, he started to his feet and hurried away.

O'Connell himself related the following incident: "After the Clare election," said he, "I met a remarkably fine young man named Ryan, as handsome a fellow as ever I saw, who had been made a sergeant, though not more than a year in the army. In one of our popular processions, we encountered a marching detachment; and, as my carriage passed, this young sergeant walked away from his men, and asked me to shake hands with him. 'In acting as I now do,' said he, 'I am infringing military discipline. Perhaps I may be flogged for it; but I don't care; let them punish me in any way they please; let them send me back to the ranks; I have had the satisfaction of shaking the hand of the father of my country.' There were unequivocal indications of a similar spirit in the army; and doubtless such a spirit in the troops was not without its weight on the duke. As to my enthusiastic young friend the sergeant, I afterwards understood that his little escapade was overlooked ; and right glad I was to find that his devotion to me entailed no punishment on him."

On the night O'Connell refused to take the oath, he returned to his hotel, and wrote his second address to the electors of Clare. In that address he said :

"The House of Commons have deprived me of the right conferred on me by the people of Clare. They have, in my opinion, unjustly and illegally deprived me of that right; but from their decision there is no appeal save to the people. I appeal to you. In my person the county of Clare has been insulted. The brand of degradation has been raised to mark me, because the people of Clare fairly selected·me. Will the people of Clare endure this insult, now that they can firmly but constitutionally efface it forever? Electors of the county of Clare, to you is due the glory of converting Peel and conquering Wellington. The last election for Clare is admitted to have been the immediate and irresistible cause of producing the 'Catholic Relief Bill.' You have achieved the religious liberty of Ireland. Another such victory in Clare, and we shall attain the political freedom of our beloved island." That victory, he told them, was necessary to prevent Catholic rights and liberties from being "sapped and undermined by the insidious policy of those men who, false to their own party, can never be true to us, and who have yielded — not to reason, but to necessity, in granting to us freedom of conscience. . . . A sober, a moral, and a religious people cannot continue slaves; they become too powerful for all oppressors; their moral strength exceeds all physical powers; and their progress towards prosperity is in vain opposed by the Peels and the Wellingtons of society. These poor strugglers for ancient abuses yield to a necessity which violates no law and commits no crime; and having once already succeeded by these means, our next success is equally certain if we adopt the same virtuous and irresistible means."

It is impossible to describe the enthusiasm shown by the people during O'Connell's journey down to Clare. Every town through which he passed — Naas, Kildare, Monasterevan, Maryborough, Mountrath, Roscrea — was waving with verdure, crowded with people, resounding with shouts, and filled with excitement. Nenagh lighted his way with a blaze of candles from every window of the town. He entered Limerick at eight in the morning, thoroughly worn out, and retired at once to rest. During his repose, a large tree, root and branch, was hauled up to the front of his hotel, and, from its thick foliage invisible musicians sent forth delightful strains of welcome. The Agitator awoke. He descended to the door of the house, and, on the spur of the moment, delivered one of those harangues which always went deep into the hearts and minds of the hearers. He then entered his carriage, and was escorted out of town by an enthusiastic procession of tradesmen flaunting their banners, and regaling his ears with shouts of commendation. At Ennis he was seated on a triumphal car, and, surrounded by the exulting multitude, received the homage of a king. To prepare our readers for the issue of that celebrated election, we shall briefly advert to the state of the elective franchise at this period.

The same Parliament which had granted emancipation, had likewise disfranchised the forty-shilling freeholders, who numbered 300,000 voters. This measure was carried with the object of weakening the strength of the Catholics, who formed the great bulk of the poorer classes, and, if possible, of defeating O'Connell. The forty-shilling freeholders were succeeded by the ten-pound freeholders, and O'Connell had no small work in prevailing on these men to register their freeholds, and qualify themselves for voting.

At length this work was accomplished, and O'Connell once more nominated as a candidate for the county of Clare. The Agitator's personal canvass of the freeholders encountered opposition from a quarter where it was least expected. William Smith O'Brien, who now appeared in politics for the first time, addressed a letter to the electors of Clare, in which he gave them to understand that O'Connell had retarded rather than advanced the Catholic cause. O'Brien certainly placed himself in a very troublesome predicament. O'Connell ridiculed him by tracing his ancestry to a tinker's apprentice, and Tom Steele was not satisfied until he had exchanged shots with him.

During the interval between his triumphant reception at Ennis and his re-election, O'Connell went up to Dublin. In the course of a speech made during his stay, he seems to have mortally offended a certain crazy attorney, named Toby Glascock. This limb of the law, who was most diminutive in stature, went about the town swearing vengeance against the Liberator. Not finding the object of his ire, he boasted he would have O'Connell flogged by his servant. At length he became so annoying, that O'Connell had him bound over to keep the peace.

Before the court, the irate attorney endeavored to show the absurdity of a Liliputian like himself attacking a Colossus like the plaintiff. As for his servant, he would soon convince the court of his harmlessness. Stooping down, with some difficulty, he hauled from beneath a table his attorney's bag, and out jumped a dwarfish darkey, grinning from ear to ear. For the first time in his life, O'Connell had the laugh against him, but for all that Sir Toby had to keep the peace.

On the 3d of July, 1829, O'Connell was a second time returned for Clare. It was, indeed, to use the words of O'Connell, "a great day for Ireland." He had twice knocked at the "Portals of Intolerance" as a suppliant, — they now opened to receive him as a conqueror.

The overpowering fatigues of the Clare hustings sorely taxed O'Connell's strength; he felt the need of repose much. In the autumn succeeding his election, therefore, he retired to the quiet of Derrynane, whose refreshing breezes were sure to restore his health and vigor. But even here rest was denied him.

One bright October morning, O'Connell, as he gazed from his windows of Derrynane, caught sight of a horseman rapidly approaching towards him. The jaded steed was soon pulled up before the hall door, and the rider, dismounting, was ushered into the presence of the Liberator. His message was soon delivered. .He had ridden ninety long miles to entreat the "friend of the people" to defend four poor Catholics of Doneraile, who were falsely accused, on the evidence of informers, of murdering their landlord.

"There is no time to be lost," suggested the horseman; "the trial comes on to-morrow morning; and unless you are in the court before the trial opens, every man of them will be hanged, though as innocent as the child unborn."

O'Connell could not refuse; he promised to undertake their defence. William Burke, of Ballyhea — for such was the name and address of the stranger — after a hurried repast, turned his horse's head from Derrynane, and sped quickly with the glad tidings to Cork.

Relays of fresh horses were stationed along the road, and, as O'Connell galloped down to Cork, his mad pace tested the temper of them all. Burke reached Cork at eight o'clock, O'Connell two hours later. The trial had already begun when O'Connell arrived. His face was soiled by the dust of the road, his dress was in disorder. These, however, gave him no concern; human lives were in the balance, and he rapidly elbowed his way through the throng who surrounded the courthouse, and entered. Solicitor-General Doherty's heart sank within him at the unexpected appearance of the Liberator, and he con-

tinued his speech, in which he had been surprised,
with many misgivings as to its effectiveness.

As the Solicitor-General proceeded, O'Connell, who
was coolly discussing his breakfast, kept his well-dis-
ciplined ear on the alert, and frequently interrupted
the speaker with "That is not law, sir!" The
judges, who knew that such an assertion was sure to
prove correct, were obliged to sustain it. The evidence for the prosecution was next produced, but
witness ofter witness broke down under the ordeal of
O'Connell's terrible cross-examinations. One of these
unfortunate victims, finding himself cornered and
confused, shrieked out, in his desperation, "It's little I thought I'd have to meet you here, Mr. O'Connell."

When once aroused, O'Connell was most unmerci-
ful in the use of his tongue, which cut like a two-
edged sword. He ridiculed the Solicitor-General in
the most open and scornful manner. "You may go
go down, sir," said Doherty, addressing a witness in
an accent which was offensively cockney. "Naw
daunt go dawn, sir," said O'Connell, mimicking and
ridiculing the affectation of the law-officer. And
when Doherty, on another occasion, said, "The allegation is made on false facts," O'Connell laughed
at the expression as an egregious blunder, exclaiming, "False facts! How can facts be false?"

O'Connell not only scouted the informers out of
court, but subdued and cowed the Solicitor-General,
and the trial resulted in the acquittal of the prisoners.

At the end of this year (1829), O'Connell was severely criticised by the *Times*, and other prominent

journals.   Whilst the Clare election was in progress, Pierce Mahony, who acted as solicitor for O'Connell before Parliament, desired to secure the latter's services in the Waterford election.   Lord George Beresford proposed standing for that county, and induced Mahony to engage O'Connell.   At first O'Connell consented, feeling it might bring about a friendly spirit between both creeds ; he, however, saw the imprudence of the step afterwards, and withdrew.   Hence the " Thunderer's " three hundred leading articles against the acknowledged champion of the people. In replying to the *Times*, O'Connell rebutted the charges laid at his door, and concluded by calling that journal " The venal lady of the Strand."   This will account for the manner in which Thomas Carlyle, in his " Life of John Sterling, makes Sterling, *Pater*, who supplied the *Times* with " thunder," speak of O'Connell.

CHAPTER XIII.

WHEN Parliament opened, O'Connell was early in his place. The very first evening of the session he arose to address the House. Here, before the assembled representatives of Great Britain, stood the man who had so long and earnestly clamored for the rights of the people, the terror of every minister for the preceding twenty years, the acknowledged champion of over five millions of oppressed Catholics. Every eye was fixed upon him as he rose to speak, and the ears of all were anxious to learn the power of his eloquence. His rich Kerry brogue filled the entire chamber, and evidently created a profound impression. For half an hour he reviewed the king's speech. He was frequently applauded during his address, and when he concluded, he sat down amidst the deafening cheers of the House.

O'Connell brought the illegal conduct of Mr. Doherty in the Doneraile trial before Parliament early

in the session.   The Attorney-General did not fear
the effect of this speech upon the House, and contented himself with criticising O'Connell's mode of
speaking.   He contrasted the defiant boldness of
the Agitator addressing a mob at home with his
courtesy when addressing the House of Commons,
and drew the unfavorable inference that O'Connell
was not what he appeared.   Lord Leveson Gower
defended Doherty, and thereupon brought forth from
the Liberator one of his oft-quoted nicknames.

"He has ventured to censure my conduct out of
this House; out of this House or in this House, I
hold his censure at nought — nor do I undervalue it.
He has taken upon himself, forsooth, to· arraign
my conduct.   I have a right to retaliate upon him
as a public man.   For his taste, for his judgment, I
have no regard; I rejoice that he disapproves of my
conduct — I should be sorry he approved of it.   He
is mighty in his own conceit — he is little in mine.
If he served my country, I would value him.   But
what has he done?   What one act of his official life
has been useful in Ireland?   Where shall I find his
services?   He has condescended to accept the sal-
ary of an officer amongst us.   I take it for granted
that he has received the emoluments of that office —
I do not know how he has earned them.   He has ornamented by his presence the apartments of Dublin
Castle.   But has he done any act of liberality? — has
he promoted any one friend of civil or religious liberty? — has he, in short, raised himself into importance or consideration by any one act of his administration?   I deny that he has.   He is an apprentice

in politics, and he dares to censure me, a veteran in
the warfare of my country. His office is a mere ap-
prenticeship. The present Premier was Secretary in
Ireland — the present Secretary of State was Secretary in Ireland — so was the present Chancellor of
the Exchequer. Their juvenile statesmanship was
inflicted upon my unhappy country. I have heard
that barbers train their apprentices by making them
shave beggars. My wretched country is the scene of
his political education — he is the shave-beggar of
the day for Ireland! I have now done with the noble Lord. I disregard his praise — I court his censure. I cannot express how strongly I repudiate his
pretensions to importance, and I defy him to point
out any one act of his administration to which my
countrymen could look with admiration or gratitude,
or with any other feelings than those of total disregard. His name will serve as a date in the margin
of the history of Dublin Castle — his memory will
sink into contemptuous oblivion."

O'Connell's success in Parliament was beyond
question, and in this his first campaign he established
quite a reputation as a debater.

"From the icy coldness with which that extraordinary man was received when he first entered the
House," says an anonymous writer, "he has risen
perhaps to be the most attractive debater the assembly possesses. Mr. O'Connell has great advantages
of person. He has all that appearance of power
which height and robust proportions invariably give
to the orator, without being the least corpulent or
fleshy — without coming under Cicero's anathema

against the 'vastus.'   He has great girth of chest—
stands firm as a rock — his gestures are free, bold,
and warm — his countenance plays with all he utters
—his mouth, in particular, indicates with great felicity the passion of the moment — frank in conciliation, bitter in scorn.   Indeed the shape of the lips is
rather a contradiction to the manlier traits of the
orator's fine athletic person — it is so pliable in character, so delicate in outline.   It indicates, according
to the science of physiognomy, a quick, and even
over-quick, susceptibility.   Eyes light, full, and clear
— the dark *Brutus* — the throat nervous and finely
shaped, always free in the loosened neckcloth — a
small nose, but with deep-set, regular nostrils — complete a very striking and characteristic *tout ensemble.*
Well, then, fancy the orator on his legs — and now
for the voice.   The Irish accent in its more polished
dialect does not detract from a voice by far the most
clear, flexible, and lucidly distinct you ever heard.
You can't escape into a corner of that ill-built house
to avoid it.   Shut your ears — it will creep into
them.   Yet he speaks in a much lower tone than
other speakers, and in a much mellower key.   As to
matter, he throws himself at once upon the strong
bearing of the subject — he seizes the question by
its common sense.   Unlike other lawyers, you
never find him prying into the little holes and corners — niggling his soul into the crannies of a question.   As was said of Chatham — it is the one broad
view which he takes and insists upon; and that that
view should allow him to be so popular in the House

of Commons, is a striking proof how democratic that assembly has become."

At length the death of that intolerant voluptuary, George IV., caused the dissolution of Parliament, and necessitated O'Connell's re-election. From an establishment in Stephen's Green, rented by himself, and which he called the "parliamentary office," he issued an order for a meeting of his friends. At this meeting he made known his intention of standing for Waterford instead of Clare.

The question then arose who should be his successor. Both Major McNamara and O'Gorman Mahon were put forward as candidates. O'Connell had previously promised his assistance to the major, but was subsequently freed from the obligation in a conversation with that gentleman. O'Connell finding himself free, declared in favor of O'Gorman Mahon. Through some misunderstanding, McNamara took umbrage at the preferment of his late rival, and gave O'Connell a great deal of annoyance, which at one time threatened serious consequences. The major's resentment was soon followed by the displeasure of Mahon, who, strange to say, in his turn, fell out with the Liberator. This culminated in a personal recontre. It happened thus: O'Connell was being drawn along one of the high roads of Clare in a triumphal car, surrounded by an enthusiastic gathering of the people, when Mahon, seated in a chair in the midst of a similar gathering, rapidly approached the Liberator. Both processions were moving in the same direction, but it soon became evident the new comers were bent upon taking the lead. The O'Connell demonstration held the van of the line by right, and were determined not to take the dust of the intruders. The aggressors, however, advanced with some difficulty, until the vehicle of Mahon was alongside of O'Connell's triumphal car. In the midst of the uproar and confusion, Mahon climbed to the platform of the car, as if with the intention of ousting O'Connell. With a single effort, O'Connell hurled back the intruder into the midst of the excited crowd. With great presence of mind, he speedily regained his self-possession, and called upon his followers to halt, and allow the opposite party to pass on, thus avoiding an encounter which would have proved serious and disgraceful. Leaving Clare, O'Connell passed on to Waterford, from which city he was triumphantly returned.

No sooner had emancipation been conceded than O'Connell directed his energies towards Repeal. On his return to Dublin, after the Waterford election, he plunged once more into the vortex of agitation. His presence was everywhere sought after; but wherever he appeared, either at "dinners," "meetings," or "entertainments," the burden of his speeches was Repeal. Finding one association in which he figured proscribed by law, he immediately established another. One of these was called "The Irish Volunteers for the Repeal of the Union." When public meetings were suppressed, he established "Reform breakfasts," humorously remarking that if these were forbidden him he would then resort to a political "lunch." The government at length proscribed even these table gatherings, on which occasion O'Connell nicknamed the late Lord Derby, "Egg-shell Stanley;" but the Liberator still determined to exercise a right to which he felt himself entitled under the laws, and accordingly continued to hold them. This course drew upon him the displeasure of the government, and, on the 19th of January, 1830, he was arrested in his house at Merrion Square, and brought to the head police office. The government, however, feared the effects of a vigorous course in regard to O'Connell, and he was permitted to give bail, which was set at £1,000, and two securities, of £500 each. The anxious collection of friends who were assembled outside the building were determined to make a demonstration, and O'Connell was obliged to return to the house of Mr. Fitzpatrick, on George's Street, to escape their enthusiasm. Finding. however, the people still congregated, and determined to be addressed by him, he approached the window, and delivered the following short but impressive harangue:

"Yesterday I was only half an agitator," cried O'Connell; "henceforth I am a whole one. Day and night will I now strive to fling off despotism — to redeem my country, to repeal the Union, and to establish on a permanent basis the happiness and legislative independence of my native land. Many an honest man who was yesterday opposed to the present agitation, will be, before the close of the day, a determined, unflinching friend of Repeal."

O'Connell had fixed the 3d of January for his departure to England. The road leading to Kingstown on that day was lined on either side by dense crowds of people. An immense concourse of tradesmen, six miles in length, escorted him on his way, with banners flying, and bands of music discoursing national airs. Each member of the procession wore a collar of blue ribbon, to which was attached a large-sized Repeal medal, bearing the likeness of the Liberator. He took good care, however, not to let these people know that he had received that morning, before setting out, a summons to appear before the court on the following day. Had O'Connell's devoted followers known this, there would have been bloodshed in Dublin before night. The trial which took place immediately after, was a renewal of the former charge of holding illegal meetings, and resulted in his acquittal, upon which he set out for Parliament in the most private manner possible.

In 1832, the tithe agitation attained its height, and Rathcormac was the scene of a most horrible massacre. At a place called Harvey, the people assembled in thousands to resist the payment of the tithes. Out of the twenty-three armed police who marched against them, only five escaped with their lives.

For this encounter, twenty-five men were arrested, and sent to Kilkenny for trial, and O'Connell was retained for the defence. The first prisoner placed at the bar was Michael Kennedy; and the principal witness against him was one of the escaped policemen. In his cross-examination this man preserved the utmost coolness, and O'Connell was about to give up in despair, when his attorney handed him a piece of paper, on which was written, "The witness's father was a sheep-stealer."

O'Connell went on with his cross-examination, much to the surprise of the attorney, without taking any notice of the circumstance. Just as the witness was about to escape, as he hoped, finally, O'Connell called him back.

"Are you fond of mutton?"

"I like a good piece well enough," replied the unsuspicious witness.

"Did you ever know any expert sheep-stealers?"

The witness colored crimson, but replied quietly, "I have met with a few in the discharge of my duty as a policeman."

"Just so; only in the discharge of your duty? Did you ever know a sheep-stealer before you entered the police?"

"Never," replied the witness.

O'Connell put the question again, mildly, and received the same reply, and then, in tones of thunder, charged at the unhappy man, and obliged him to admit the truth, and likewise admit himself a perjurer. An *alibi* was proved for the prisoner, and he was acquitted.

Returning to London, from which he had been called to attend the trial just alluded to, O'Connell threw himself zealously into the debate on the Reform Bill, which at that time was agitating the whole empire. The Whigs, it would appear, impressed O'Connell with the conviction that they were sincerely interested in the welfare of Ireland; it is even alleged they offered him the Attorney-Generalship of Ireland. But the Liberator would not accept, being already familiar with British policy, which, in the case of many prominent Irishmen before him, had advanced the leaders at the expense of the people. On his return to Dublin the trades turned out in great numbers, and presented him with an address. In his reply, through fear of weakening the Whig party, then in power, he made no allusion to Repeal, to the great disappointment of those who had assembled to hear him. For a time he seems to have abandoned that great question, which he had heretofore strongly advocated, and promulgated the idea that the first duty of the Catholics was to keep the Whig party in power.

During this year a quarrel arose between O'Connell and the Dublin reporters. The "Knights of the Quill," finding themselves aggrieved by a remark made by him, held a meeting, at which they agreed not to report any more of his speeches. At a meeting held in Corn Exchange, the reporters plied their pencils with great industry until O'Connell rose to speak, when they simultaneously threw them down, and sat perfectly motionless.

"What!" exclaimed O'Connell, alluding to the conduct of the reporters, "am I, who fluttered the ministers in the cabinet of England, to be nibbled at in Dublin by a parcel of mice?"

"Do you call me a mouse, sir?" croaked out Elrington, a quondam Catholic, very coolly looking up at the Liberator, opposite to whom he happened to sit.

"No, indeed I do not," exclaimed O'Connell, with great bitterness; "I could not be guilty of such a misnomer, for, as every one knows, you are a large rat!"

This pointed allusion to the recantation of Elrington was relished by every one present, save the chopfallen object of the sarcasm, who was filled with confusion by the roar of laughter which followed O'Connell's reply.

CHAPTER XIV.

The Coercion Bill — O'Connell's Opposition to it — His Philan-
thropy — His Ideas of Slavery — The Household Brigade — At
War with the London Reporters — O'Connell forced to introduce
the Repeal Question into Parliament — Its Defeat — Reflections
on Westminster Abbey — "Gully the Boxer" — O'Connell in
Canterbury Cathedral — The Anti-Tory Association — G. P. O. —
Curious Incident in a Lunatic Asylum — "O'Connell and his Rad-
ical Crew" — O'Connell's Reply to Col. Sibthorp — He calls
Lord Alvanley a "Bloated Buffoon" and receives a Challenge —
Morgan O'Connell accepts in Behalf of his Father — The Duel —
Disraeli's Ingratitudet o O'Connell — The Liberator reviews that
Gentleman's Ancestry — Disræli's Challenge, and what became
of it.

During the debates on the Coercion Bill, in 1833,
O'Connell fought long and desperately to stay the
passage of that measure, which had for its object the
dethronement of every right common to constitutional liberty. To secure its passage, the wily
Peel treated the House of Commons to anecdotes of
the barbarity of the Irish, and endeavored to prove
the necessity of "putting them down." O'Connell,
in his reply, admitted that there had been outrages,
but clearly demonstrated that the responsibility lay
at the door of those "who gave the peasants stones for
bread, and martial-law for justice." O'Connell certainly made a brilliant defence against the arguments
of such able speakers as Lord Grey, Stanley, Lord
Brougham, Peel, and Macauley. With the exception

of Sheil, O'Connell stood alone in this war of arguments; and, if the bill passed, he could yet console himself with the reflection that he had offered a protest before the nation.

Probably one of the most beautiful traits in the character of O'Connell was his broad philanthropy. To his mind all men were free and equal. When the negro emancipation question was introduced into Parliament, he was one of the few members who advocated its passage. His keen sense of justice was aroused, and, in many a telling speech, he held up the slave-owner to scorn, and pleaded the cause of the slave. His position carried so much influence with it, that the opponents of the bill approached him with an offer of their votes on any measure for Ireland, he might in the future bring forward, providing he would lend no further aid to the abolitionists. His reply was as sublime as it was generous:

"Gentlemen, God knows I speak for the saddest people the sun sees; but may my right hand forget its cunning, and my tongue cleave to the roof of my mouth, if to save Ireland — even Ireland — I forget the negro one single hour."

O'Connell was now seconded in his parliamentary struggles by what he called his "household brigade," consisting of his three sons and two sons-in-law, who held seats in the first reformed Parliament. His experience in the House of Commons had rendered him familiar with the tactics of the several parties which controlled it, and his speeches exhibited, if possible, a greater fire and energy than ever. His terrible sarcasms rung in the tingling ears of his opponents, and he hurled back with effective argument the slanders of his country's traducers. On one occasion, addressing the Whigs, of whose insincerity he was now fully convinced, he said: "You have brains of lead, hearts of stone, and fangs of iron."

It was during this year O'Connell's famous quarrel with the London reporters took place. We have already seen how their fellow-quillsmen fared in Dublin. The reporters of London were not more successful.

O'Connell complained that their reports were designedly false, and, at a public meeting in London, boldly defied "their utmost power and ingenuity."

This was followed by a letter in the *Times* from the reporters, in which they stated, until O'Connell withdrew his charge, they would not report him. O'Connell lost no time in bringing them to terms, which he did in the following summary manner: Reporters are simply tolerated in the House of Commons, as any member, by simply calling attention to the fact that "strangers" (non-members) are present, can have the galleries immediately cleared. O'Connell availed himself of this privilege, and the reporters were obliged to succumb, promising thereafter to report him correctly.

In April, of 1834, the first practical effort for Repeal was made. On the 23d of that month, O'Connell fiormally presented the question for the consideration of Parliament. The Repeal newspapers, urged on by the Hotspurs of the Catholic party, at last forced O'Connell to precipitate this question, even against his own good judgment, to the no small delight of the government, who were satisfied it would never pass. Moreover, Fergus O'Connor, member from Cork, had threatened to introduce the subject if O'Connell further delayed; and, rather than Repeal should manifest any signs of weakness, the Agitator was willing to hazard the onus of defeat. The entire sentiment of England was opposed to Repeal, and the imbecile sovereign, William IV., even looked upon the question as treasonable. As was expected, the motion for a Repeal committee was negatived in the House by an enormous majority, only forty members voting in its favor. O'Connell opened the debate in a speech that lasted five hours. He drew a vivid picture of Ireland's wrongs, rehearsed the crimes committed by England against her sister island from the earliest date of their connection, and concluded this brilliant summary by moving "for a select committee to inquire and report on the means by which the destruction of the Irish Parliament had been effected." Although his oratory made a forcible impression on the minds of his hearers, and ably sustained his motion, the conviction that he was leading a forlorn hope materially lessened that magnetic power which invariably accompanied his more successful efforts.

On the evening of the 23d, O'Connell walked leisurely down to the House of Commons, from his house in Langham Place, leaning on the arm of a friend. His mind, which was filled with the great subject of the evening, seemed suddenly controlled by some overpowering influence, as he came in view of Westminster Abbey. Taking off his hat, he blessed himself, and gazing with admiration on that venerable and majestic pile, exclaimed: "May the Lord have mercy on your soul, Henry VII., who left us so magnificent a monument of your piety! You provided at your death to have Masses said perpetually for your soul; but from the time that ever-execrable brute, Henry VIII., seized on the revenues of the Church, and confiscated your endowment along with the rest, perhaps no human being ever took thought to breathe the words, 'Lord have mercy on your soul!'" At this moment, a smart tap on the back compelled him to turn round, and Gully, the boxer, M. P., stood before him. With the frank heartiness of manner which characterized the ex-pugilist, he exclaimed, "There you are, Dan, going down quietly and coolly to your work." "And tell me, Gully, is not that the way to go to work?" asked O'Connell, squaring his fists at him in the manner of a boxer. After the exchange of a few additional words, the two senators shook hands and parted, and O'Connell resumed his walk to the House of Commons.

O'Connell frequently expressed a wish that he might be spared to see Mass one day offered up in Westminster Abbey. He was, moreover, a great student of mediæval architecture, and never neglected an opportunity of gratifying this fondness when in the vicinity of an old cathedral.

There was a slight incident connected with his visit to Canterbury Cathedral, which he took pleasure in frequently recording. "While walking through the noble old Catholic pile," said he, "I chanced to remark to my daughter, who accompanied me, that it was not a little singular that not one Protestant prelate had ever been interred within its walls. This remark was overheard by the female guide who shows the cathedral to visitors. She listened attentively, and, after some apparent hesitation, said, 'May I take the liberty, sir, of asking a question?' 'Certainly,' said I. 'Then may I make so bold as to ask, if all those Archbishops were Papists?' 'Every one of them, madam,' said I. 'Bless me!' cried the woman in astonishment, 'I never knew that before.' I then described the effect of the high altar lighted up for the celebration of Mass in Catholic times, when the great aisle, now boxed up into compartments by the organ loft, stretched its venerable and unbroken length from the altar to the portal, thronged with kneeling worshippers. The picture delighted the woman. 'Oh!' cried she, clapping her hands, 'I should like to see that!' 'God grant you may!' returned I." Then he would sometimes add, "And He may yet grant it. England is steadily and gradually returning to the Catholic faith."

Comparing the cathedrals of Catholic times with those erected since the Reformation, he observed, "Westminster Abbey and St. Paul's afford us good specimens of this sort of contrast; the very architecture of the former seems to breathe the aspiring sentiment of Christianity; but St. Paul's — it is a noble temple, to be sure; but as for any peculiarity of Christian character about it, it might just as well be a temple of Neptune!"

In 1834, O'Connell established the Anti-Tory Association, and the defeat of the Peel and Wellington administration was in a great measure owing to his powerful exertions. When the Whig party, of which Lord Melbourne was the head, came into power, every measure for the benefit of the Irish people was frustrated, and flung out by the House of Lords, and O'Connell found it necessary to visit the principal towns of Great Britain, and agitate against those titled "conservators of injustice." In Edinburgh, he made several eloquent speeches against the aristocracy, one of which he delivered to an immense gathering of over 50,000 Scotchmen.

In this year Lord Haddington was sent as Lord-Lieutenant to Ireland. This nobleman landed at Kingstown, and as he rode up to Dublin was puzzled by the letters G. P. O., which he saw on every milestone along the way. To satisfy his curiosity, he inquired of a gentleman the meaning of these *mystic* letters.

"Those letters are a convincing proof, my lord," said the Irish gentleman, whose name was Thomas Reynolds, "of the warm affection which the Irish people cherish for my illustrious friend and countryman, Daniel O'Connell. G. P. O., my lord, stands for 'God preserve O'Connell.'"

It is unnecessary to state that this evidence of O'Connell's popularity was by no means acceptable to the noble lord.

Sugden was sent to Ireland at the same time as Lord Chancellor. Of this man O'Connell told a curious anecdote.

"The present Lord Chancellor," he said, "is very

fond of inspecting the management of lunatic asylums. He made an agreement with the surgeon-general to visit, without any previous intimation, a lunatic asylum kept by Dr. Duncan in this city. Some person sent word to the asylum that a patient was to be sent there in a carriage that day, who was a smart little man that thought himself one of the judges, or some great person of that sort, and who was to be detained by them. Dr. Duncan was out when Sir Edward was admitted and received by the keeper. He appeared to be very talkative, but the attendants humored him and answered all his questions. He asked if the surgeon-general had yet arrived, and the keeper assured him that he was not yet come, but that he would be there immediately. 'Well,' said he, 'I shall inspect some of the rooms until he arrives.' 'Oh no, sir,' said the keeper, we could not permit that at all.' 'Then I shall walk for awhile in the garden,' said his lordship, 'while I am waiting for him.' 'We cannot let you go there either, sir,' said the keeper. 'What,' said he, 'don't you know that I am the Lord Chancellor!' 'Sir,' said the keeper, 'we have four other Lord Chancellors here already!' He got into a great fury, and they were beginning to think of a strait-waistcoat for him, when fortunately the surgeon-general arrived. 'Has the Lord Chancellor arrived yet?' said he. The man burst out laughing at him, and said: 'Yes, sir; we have him safe, but he is by far the most outrageous patient we have.'"

To divert O'Connell's attention from the Repeal agitation, by absorbing it in the party contests of the British nation, appears to have been the chief aim of the aristocracy during 1835; and to some extent they succeeded. The following may serve as an instance of this crafty strategy: Lord Melbourne became for the second time Prime Minister, and informed the House of Lords that he had formed a cabinet. Lord Alvanley rose and asked him whether he had or had not the powerful aid of O'Connell and his party? Acting apparently on the celebrated principle of statesmanship, that the use of words is not to express but to conceal ideas, Melbourne publicly declared that he had taken no means to secure O'Connell's assistance, and was not aware that he possessed it. On hearing this, Lord Londonderry rose, and congratulated Lord Melbourne: "He was glad to hear that he had repudiated O'Connell and his radical crew, as he was sure that any ministerial connection with him or his 'tail' would be the curse of the country."

A few nights subsequently, in the House of Commons, Colonel Sibthorp, who was remarkable for the hirsute appendages of his face, declared that he did not like the countenances of the gentlemen opposite. "He earnestly hoped that the House should have a safe and speedy riddance of the band." This afforded O'Connell an opportunity of rising to reply, which he did, to the cost of each of these gentlemen. He began by complimenting Sibthorp on his good humor; and, alluding to his face, he said, "I will not abate him a single *hair* in point of good humor." Alluding to Lord Alvanley, he stigmatized that gentleman as a "bloated buffoon." The indignant, but

cautious, Lord endeavored to have O'Connell expelled from the Brooks Club, and not succeeding,
sent him a challenge *two days after the Liberator
had left for Ireland.* O'Connell, in his reply, ridiculed the tardiness of the message, and declined to
accept it on conscientious scruples. Meantime, Morgan O'Connell felt it incumbent upon him to accept
the challenge offered his father, and a hostile meeting took place at Barnet Road, near Regent's Park.
After exchanging three shots each, without injury to
either of the contestants, Lord Alvanley left the
field, and the affair terminated.

The Tories having learned that Morgan O'Connell
was ready to accept all challenges sent to his father,
that gallant young gentleman was at once considered
by them as a species of target. Mr. Disraeli, the
present Premier of England (1875), was at that time
struggling for prominence in the arena of politics.
He began his career as a Reform Radical, and, in
canvassing the borough of Wickham, solicited the assistance of O'Connell, who gave him a letter of recommendation. This letter he caused to be placarded
everywhere throughout the borough, and appeared in
every way grateful for the kindness shown him.
Disraeli was not successful, however, as a Radical,
and at once determined to go over to the Tories.
To conciliate that party, he inaugurated his change
by attacking O'Connell in a speech at Taunton, in
England, in which he poured a torrent of abuse on
the Liberator. O'Connell was surprised by this unexpected attack from a source whence he had reason
to expect nothing but good-will and kindness, and of

all men he was the last to suffer such an insult to go unpunished. At a meeting of the Dublin Franchise Association, O'Connell alluded to Disraeli's abuse, and seems to have surpassed himself in withering sarcasms.

After reviewing the sudden political change of his traducer, and branding his life as "a living lie," he concluded by alluding to his Jewish origin. His name, he said, shows that he is by descent a Jew. His father became a convert. He is the better for that in this world, and I hope, of course, he will be the better for it in the next. There is a habit of underrating that great and oppressed nation — the Jews. They are cruelly persecuted by persons calling themselves Christians — but no person ever yet was a Christian who persecuted. The cruellest persecution they suffer is upon their character, by the foul names which their calumniators bestowed upon them before they carried their atrocities into effect. They feel the persecution of calumny severer upon them than the persecution of actual force and the tyranny of actual torture. I have the happiness to be acquainted with some Jewish families in London, and amongst them more accomplished ladies, or more humane, cordial, high-minded, or better educated gentlemen, I have never met. It will not be supposed, therefore, that when I speak of Disraeli as the descendant of a Jew, that I mean to tarnish him on that account. They were once the chosen people of God. There were miscreants amongst them, however, also; and it must have certainly been from one of those that Disraeli descended. He possesses just the qualities

of the impenitent thief who died upon the cross —
whose name, I verily believe, must have been Disraeli. For aught I know, the present Disraeli is descended from him, and with the impression that he
is, I now forgive the heir-at-law of the blasphemous
thief who died upon the cross!"

Disraeli immediately demanded satisfaction of
Morgan O'Connell. That gentleman denied Disraeli's right to challenge him, as he was not responsible for the language of his father. Disraeli published an abusive public letter, headed "to Daniel
O'Connell;" but it would have applied to the whole
human family as well. He then addressed Morgan
O'Connell a second time. "Now, sir, it is my hope
that I have insulted him; assuredly it was my intention to do so; and I fervently pray that you or some
one of his blood may attempt to avenge the inextinguishable hatred with which I shall pursue his existence." Morgan O'Connell, no doubt, acting under
the advice of his father, still refused to fight, and
Mr. Disraeli was obliged to nurse his wrath.

CHAPTER XV.

Banquets given O'Connell in Liverpool and Birmingham — Unsuccessful Effort to Unseat O'Connell in Parliament — O'Connell refuses to Apologize at the Bar of the House — Death of Mrs. O'Connell — O'Connell makes a Retreat at Mount Melleray Abbey — Description of the Abbey and its Inmates — He concludes his Retreat — How O'Connell spent his Time in London — Assassination of Lord Norbury — It is attributed to O'Connell's Agitation — His Defence before the House of Commons — The Coal-Porters of Dublin — Meeting at the Corn Exchange — The Repeal Association founded — O'Connell's Speech — He is accused of Bigotry by his Enemies — He defends his Position in a Letter to Archbishop MacHale — O'Connell's Liberality towards his Protestant Daughter-in-Law — Field Sports at Derrynane.

In January, of 1836, O'Connell was entertained at a public banquet in Liverpool, and sat down with a dinner-party numbering one thousand persons. His claim upon these hospitable people was his marked hostility to the aristocracy. He was also a guest at a similar entertainment, equally as well attended, in the "Town Hall" of Birmingham.

William IV., King of England, died in June, 1837, and Queen Victoria ascended the throne during the same month. A general election followed. The opening of her reign was little auspicious to the cause of Ireland.

O'Connell was at this time member for Dublin, but the malice of his enemies would not suffer him to retain that honor. Petitions poured into the House, a committee was appointed, and O'Connell was unseated. The member from Kilkenny, however, retired, and the Liberator was returned to Parliament a few days after, so that his absence was scarcely observed. Finding they could not get rid of O'Connell, his enemies attempted to undermine his popularity by writing him down. He was accused, in *Blackwood's Magazine*, of having taken a bribe of £1,000 for proposing to have the Factory Bill discussed in committee.

O'Connell clearly proved his innocence, and indignantly denied the false charge. Still, this fact proves how much his power was dreaded by the aristocracy, who lost no opportunity of attacking him.

A public dinner was given to O'Connell in February, of 1838, at the Crown and Anchor Tavern, London. Four hundred persons were present, and O'Connell was introduced by the chairman as "the object of the attention of the whole empire, and the admiration not only of England, but of the world."

The Liberator, in his response, accused the Tory committee, on the Irish Reform Bill, of perjury. A few nights after, Lord Maidstone asked O'Connell, in the House of Commons, if he had made such an assertion. O'Connell replied by reiterating the charge; whereupon he was reprimanded at the bar of the House. When the speaker had concluded his reprimand, O'Connell, to the amazement of the House, replied, "I express no regret; I retract nothing; I repent nothing. I do not desire unneces-

15*

sarily to use harsh or offensive language. I wish I could find terms less objectionable and equally significant; but I cannot. I am bound to reassert what I asserted." The Tories, who had assembled to enjoy a triumph, were confounded; but they dared not carry the matter further—they felt O'Connell had the right on his side. "I did expect," said O'Connell, speaking afterwards on this subject, "that I would have been sent to the Tower for the assertion of a principle; and if the Tories had the courage, they ought to have sent me there. I had made arrangements for such a contingency."

In this year O'Connell received from the government an offer to be appointed Lord Chief Baron, but declined it, feeling he could not accept it consistently with the interests of Ireland.

Mrs. O'Connell died at Derrynane, in 1836. This bereavement, coming as it did amid the stir and bustle of his active political life, sank deep into his heart. His love for his wife was not a sentiment; it formed a part of his being; it was the talisman of his success. In the most trying moments of his stormy life she proved herself worthy of being a a great man's wife—the sanctuary of his confidence. Moreover, she was the mother of his nine children, and her death created a void the repairing hand of Time never filled. Amidst the requiems and prayers offered on every Catholic altar of Ireland, his soul gave itself up to spiritual meditation, and he resolved to enter on a retreat the first opportunity that offered itself. O'Connell's duty in Parliament, and the occupations common to a representative man, left him few intervals of repose, and it was not until 1838 that he was able to carry out his intentions in this regard. In the early part of that year, accompanied by Mr. O'Neill Daunt, he set out from Dublin for Mount Melleray Abbey, in the County of Waterford. This monastery was founded by Cistercian monks from Nantes, in France, who had taken refuge in Ireland when driven from their native land. During the journey he appeared more than usually communicative, referring to the part he had taken in Catholic Emancipation, and relating anecdotes of the different points of interest along the road. At Kilkenny, where O'Connell and his friend breakfasted, he was waited on by many of the leading Repealers, who urged him to renew the agitation for Repeal. He assured them it was the darling project of his heart, but the time had not yet expired which he had decided upon allowing the Imperial Legislature for the fulfilment of a promise made to him in 1838, to render justice to Ireland.

Leaving Kilkenny, they once more resumed their journey. Ascending the rugged road that winds through the mountainous boundary line of Tipperary and Waterford, they encountered a violent storm. The scenery on all sides was most dispiriting. Acres of dreary waste stretched out for miles around, destitute of a single living object. The drive from Lismore to Mount Melleary, however, is exquisitely beautiful, and the travellers soon forget the gloom of the rain-storm in the beautiful scenery about them.

It was night when he arrived at the monastery, where he was met by a procession consisting of

twenty of the brethren in their gowns and cowls,
bearing torches, and accompanied by the abbot,
wearing a mitre and bearing a crozier. The abbot
led O'Connell by the hand, while his companion was
conducted by the sub-prior in a similar manner.
Behind them came the monks chanting a hymn.
They proceeded through the aisle of the monastery
church, of which the extent, partially revealed by the
torches borne by the brethren, seemed greater than
it really was, from the utter darkness that obscured
its farther extremity. The loud music had a grand
effect as it rolled along the lofty roof. When the
usual Vesper service had been concluded, an address of welcome was presented to O'Connell, who
made an appropriate reply. He begged permission to constitute himself counsel to the monastery,
whose inmates were at that period threatened with
litigation. The matter alluded to was shortly after
set to rights. "Two hours after midnight," says
O'Neill Daunt, "I was awakened by a violent
storm of rain and wind. Looking forth upon the
night, I saw lights in the chapel, and the chant of
hymns was heard in the fitful pauses of the gust.
The monks were celebrating the usual service of
Lauds. The hour, the darkness, the storm, the dim
lights of the chapel, and the voices streaming out
upon the lonely mountain-side — all combined to produce
duce an effect in a high degree wild, impressive, and
romantic."

O'Connell, during his stay in the monastery,
breakfasted every morning with his secretary in the
abbot's parlor. Immediately after breakfast he re-

tired to his bed-room, where he remained quite alone until dinner, which meal he. partook with his friend O'Neill Daunt, and immediately on its conclusion he would again retire, either to his dormitory or to the chapel, where he remained for an hour or two.

After a week of meditation and prayer, O'Connell left the enjoyable repose of Mount Melleray, deeply grateful to its inmates for the happiest week in his life.

During O'Connell's retreat, Villiers Stuart called upon him, but as orders had been left with the porter that no one should be admitted, he was obliged to return. A few days after, Mr. Stuart alluded to the circumstance at a public meeting in Lismore, and said, "He was happy to find that Mr. O'Connell's sojourn at Mount Mellary had not infected him with the silence of its inmates, as his adoption of the Carthusian rules would seriously injure the interests of popular liberty in Ireland."

O'Connell, speaking of the manner in which he spent his time at this period, said: "From twelve to four every day I was in regular attendance at the committees. After going home from the committees, I took a hasty dinner and proceeded to the House, and continued in it until twelve or one o'clock —I was never absent. By the time I got home and to bed, it was generally two o'clock. Then, a man at my time of life requires some sleep, although I was never fond of it—I never took over-doses of sleep; and so it was generally nine o'clock when I was dressed and ready for breakfast. It was ten when I had done breakfast and read· a small portion of the letters which I received. Then, from ten to twelve, Heaven help me! I don't exaggerate when I say that I generally got two hundred letters a day. There never was a man who had been so besieged by persons looking for places. No man asked me, to be sure, to get him a bishopric, although I have been positively asked for places in the Established Church. There is not an office, from lord high admiral down to scavenger, that I have not been asked for. Heaven help the applicants; for it is but little I can do for them. The government have been so repeatedly accused of being under my influence, that it has caused a reaction against me; and I believe there is not a single man who votes with them who has got less from them than I."

On the 1st of January, 1839, Lord Norbury was murdered at Kilbeggan, County Meath. The murdered man was not unpopular, and even to this day the assassin has not been discovered. No one could adduce a motive for this crime; but the Tories, ever ready to make capital at the expense of Ireland, at once credited it to O'Connell's agitation. The affected indignation of the aristocracy gave vent to itself in Parliament, where Mr. Shaw, the Recorder, on the 7th of March, moved for a return of the outrages committed in Ireland during the past four years. O'Connell replied in a speech worthy of himself. His sense of justice was outraged, and his noble rage was well represented in his reply.

"Speeches have been made by four gentlemen, natives of Ireland, who, it would appear, come here for the sole purpose of villifying their native land,

and endeavoring to prove that it is the worst and most criminal country on the face of the earth. (Loud cries of 'Oh!' from the Tories.) Yes; you came here to calumniate the country that gave you birth. It is said that there are some soils which produce enormous and crawling creatures — things odious and disgusting. (Loud cheers from the Tories.) Yes; you who cheer — there you are — can you deny it? Are you not calumniators? (Cries of 'Oh!' and hisses.) Oh! you hiss, but you cannot sting. I rejoice in my native land; I rejoice that I belong to it; your calumnies cannot diminish my regard for it; your malevolence cannot blacken it in my esteem; and although your vices and crimes have driven its people to outrage and murder — (order) — yes; I say your vices and crimes. (Chair, chair.) Well, then, the crimes of men like you have produced these results. . . Fourteen murders have occurred in Ireland since the 16th of November. England since that period has presented *twenty-five;* yet no English member has arisen to exclaim, 'What an abominable country is mine! What shocking people are the people of England!' To these you may add two cases of supposed murder, thirteen of personal violence, and not less than twenty incendiary fires — one of which, by the way, was at Shaw, in Berkshire."

O'Connell had waited in vain for a redress of Irish grievances. He felt, if justice was to come at all, it must come from Ireland herself. The English Reform movement for which O'Connell had labored unceasingly, and from which he hoped to derive encouragement and support, gave no signs of furthering his purpose. He accordingly determined to make a final effort for Repeal.

On the 15th of April, 1840, he founded the "Repeal Association." The meeting was held at the Corn Exchange, a site which O'Connell particularly prized.

During the days of the Catholic Association, the Trinity College boys frequently threatened to break up their meetings. "The Corn Exchange," said O'Connell, "possesses the advantage of being in the close vicinity of at least 150 coal-porters every day in the week, who would have thrown the College lads into the Liffey in case of any effort to disturb the proceedings. The circumstance was known to the intending aggressors, and the salutary knowledge effectually checked their projects of intrusion."

The meeting opened, and Mr. John O'Neil, a staunch patriot, took the chair. But, strange to say, long after the appointed hour only a mere handful of people had assembled. There was more than one reason for this. The people had not been sufficiently armed, they did not feel the meeting was a *bona fide* Repeal gathering. The young men who were then coming to the front, in their heated judgment and impatience, believed the field a surer means to obtain redress than the rostrum. They therefore held aloof. O'Connell had met with too many reverses in the long course of his experience to be daunted. He had seen Catholic meetings dissolve like the morning mist; but they had not produced emancipation? He began life by opposing the Union, he determined to end it by advocating Repeal. He felt the people were with him, the clergy were with him, and wherever he led he felt sure the nation would follow.

Finding, at length, there was no possibility of a larger gathering, O'Connell arose and addressed the meeting as if there were thousands present. After expressing his determination to enter earnestly into the great work of Repeal, and alluding to the splendid result of agitation on behalf of Emancipation, he burst forth in a noble illustration of his purpose.

"We have assembled," said he, "to take part in proceedings that will yet be memorable in the history of our country. Yes, this 15th of April will be yet memorable in the annals of Ireland. It shall be referred to as the day on which the flag of Repeal was unfurled ; and I shall fearlessly, legally, and constitutionally keep it unfurled, until the day of success shall have arrived, or the grave shall close over me, and on my tomb shall be inscribed: 'He died a Repealer!' . . . We must be up, I say, and stirring. We can do no good by quiescence; it may do us evil, but it can do us no service. We must take counsel from the French proverb, which says, 'Help yourselves, and God will help you.' We must not forget the story of the fellow who, when the wheel of his cart stuck in the mud, prayed to Jupiter to help him. 'You lazy rascal,' said his godship, 'put your shoulder to the wheel, and get along out of that.' I tell you there is nothing else for us but to help ourselves; and help ourselves, with the aid of Heaven, we shall!"

The first meeting may not have been a success in point of numbers, but its influence moved over all Ireland as the wave circles move from the contact of the dipping pebble. Young and old vied in their earnestness to promote Repeal. In a single day, at Waterford, a bishop and eighty-three of his clergy were enrolled in the Repeal Association, and thus the work went on.

The coöperation of the clergy, which proved a necessary and substantial assistance to O'Connell in enlisting the sympathies of the people, was made use of by his enemies to charge him with bigotry. The Liberator's life gives the lie to the base calumny. To show how unfounded this charge was, we need only quote a passage from a letter addressed by O'Connell himself, at this time, to the venerable Archbishop of Tuam.

In that letter he makes the following summary: "In short, if we had the Repeal, Religion would be free; education would be free; the press would be free. No sectarian control over Catholics; no Catholic control over sectarians — that is, no species of political ascendency."

Another instance will confirm his rightful sense of religious tolerance. His son Maurice married a Protestant lady, and, when she arrived at Derrynane, he thus addressed her:

"You are a Protestant, and here at Derrynane the nearest place of worship of your own persuasion is at Sneem, which is twelve miles off. Now, I have taken care that you shall not want the means of worshipping God in your own way on Sunday. You shall have a horse to ride to Sneem every Sunday during the summer, and a fresh horse, if requisite, to ride back; and if the ride should fatigue you, your carriage shall attend you." Her answer was, "I thank you, sir; but I have resolved to go to Mass." "Going to Mass is nothing," said O'Connell, "unless you believe in the doctrines of the Catholic Church. And if you do *not*, it is much better that you should continue to attend your own place of worship; I shall provide you with the necessary accommodation."

In the October of this year, we find O'Connell rising at six, and hunting across the mountains between Derrynane and Sneem. Imagine a man of five-and-sixty, after a wearing political struggle of forty years, following the chase with the enthusiasm of youth. Surely O'Connell possessed an old-fashioned constitution.

CHAPTER XVI.

Reluctantly tearing himself from his sports at Derrynane, the Liberator plunged once more, refreshed and invigorated, into the political arena, and during the years between 1840 and 1843, devoted his energies to promote the cause of Repeal.

At Cork, the people met him without the town, and, had not O'Connell protested, they would have taken the horses from his carriage, and drawn him into the town. The following day he addressed an enthusiastic meeting of over fifty thousand people. During his speech he alluded to the *London Examiner*, which had compared the Repeal movement to the cry of the Derrynane beagles. "Yes," observed O'Connell, "but he made a better hit than he intended, for my beagles never cease their cry until they catch their game."

At Limerick a still greater triumph awaited him. There the welcoming crowd numbered one hundred thousand. He was met three miles from the town by a procession of trades, conspicuous amongst whom were the ship-carpenters. They had constructed a boat, resting on wheels, on which sat Neptune, trident in hand, dressed in a suit of sea-green. The sea-god arose on the approach of O'Connell, and, in a humorous speech, gave him welcome on behalf of his marine subjects. Not to be outdone in pleasantry, and ever ready with a quick-witted reply, O'Connell declared "he felt quite refreshed by receiving an acquatic compliment on the dusty high-road," and expressed his high sense of "the condescending courtesy of the potent and illustrious monarch of the ocean."

In Kilkenny a Repeal meeting was held, at which it was calculated two hundred thousand persons were present, twenty thousand of whom were on horseback.

Aside from the patriotism of these monster gatherings, the most commendable features were their order and sobriety. Father Mathew, the Apostle of Temperance, had marshalled the nation under the banner of a moral reform, and thousands had already taken the pledge. The temperance societies were of great assistance to O'Connell in his Repeal movements. Already organized and officered, they carried out the necessary movements with precision and credit to themselves. The fact that the Liberator was able to preserve order and control the great meetings over which he presided, was, no doubt, due to this cause.

In the feverish excitement of political agitation, the imprudence of a single individual might have precipitated a collision with the government, ending only in open insurrection.

In the year 1841, the untiring energy of O'Connell was something miraculous. "I rise," said he, "every morning now by candle-light, and often go to Mass before breakfast." A list of his engagements will enable the reader to form some idea of his super-human activity at this advanced period of his life. "Mr. O'Connell," says a newspaper of that day, "stands pledged to the following engagements: To attend the Repeal Association on the 4th; to preside at an orphan charity dinner on the 5th; to agitate for Repeal in Mullingar on the 7th, in Cork on the 11th, and in Dungarvan on the 13th; to attend a Reform meeting in Dublin on the 15th, and in Belfast on the 18th; on the 19th to attend a Repeal dinner in the same town ; on the 21st and 22d, a Reform meeting and dinner at Leeds; and on the 23d, a Reform meeting at Leicester; and on the 26th, to take his seat in the House of Commons, attired in his gray frieze Repeal coat."

At Mullingar O'Connell was met by a procession of fifty thousand persons; the Bishops of Ardagh and Meath, with many of their clergy, taking part in the demonstration. Some disturbances arose in Limerick at this time, but Tom Steele, the "Head Pacificator," went down with a white flag edged with green, to make peace. On the flag were inscribed the following words of warning : "Whoever commits a crime adds strength to the enemy." No further action was necessary; the troubles ceased at once. O'Connell, at this supreme moment of his popularity, was virtually " King of Ireland," and his orders were promptly obeyed by the nation. In Cork the people met with a welcome of "Hurrah for Repeal."

Back again in Parliament, at the end of January, O'Connell opposed Lord Stanley's Bill to amend the representation in Ireland with his characteristic boldness. "You would now," said he, "refuse to Ireland equality of franchises with England. What plea do you allege for this refusal? Why, the *poverty* of Ireland. But mark your inconsistency. When I arraigned the Legislative Union as having caused poverty in Ireland, how was I met? Honorable gentlemen produced multitudinous statements and calculations to demonstrate that poverty was not general in Ireland, that my statements were exaggerated, and that the Union had created great general prosperity in that country! You then alleged the prosperity of Ireland as a reason why she should not possess legislative independence; you now allege her poverty as a reason why she should not enjoy the franchise!"

O'Connell had been repeatedly invited to address the Repealers of Belfast, but he had postponed visiting there, fearing his presence might result in bloodshed. At length he publicly accepted a pressing invitation to attend a meeting and dinner in that town. Finding that the Great Repealer was about to "invade the North," the Orangemen of Belfast determined to offer personal violence. They placarded the walls of Lisburn, calling upon all Protestants to resist this *invasion*. O'Connell was fully aware of the danger his visit would entail. "I have got so many intimations," said he, "that the Orange party meditate personal violence against me on my way to Belfast, that I really do believe there is some peril. Whatever it may be, I am now committed, and must brave it. Perhaps, after all, the peril may prove illusory; but prudence requires me to guard against the worst. I shall take loaded fire-arms in the carriage." Meantime, the Orange party were evidently preparing for hostilities, and the government, to insure order, prudently crowded Belfast with troops, and added two thousand specials to the regular police force.

O'Connell, however, resorted to a stratagem which, whilst it exhibited great ingenuity, probably saved his life. He knew the Orangemen had determined to waylay him as he approached Belfast. Accordingly, he wrote to all the inn-keepers along the route from Dublin to Belfast that he would require post-horses on Monday, the 18th of January, 1841.

The innkeepers, many of whom were Orangemen, lost no time in communicating to the "brethren" that they might expect O'Connell on that day. At the same time, these hospitable publicans received other letters, signed C. A. Charles (the name of a popular Dublin ventriloquist), bespeaking post-horses for Saturday, the 16th.

This plan succeeded admirably. The road was clear, and O'Connell, who was received by mine host as the travelling ventriloquist, made his way quietly into Belfast. The news of his arrival soon spread among the liberals of the town, who joyfully gathered around him. The Orangemen, enraged at being thus duped, crowded the streets in great numbers, but were restrained from committing violence by the presence of the troops.

Despite the exasperation of the Orangemen, the Repealers held an open-air meeting, and afterwards entertained their guest at a splendid banquet. In the evening, a grand soiree was given by nearly four hundred ladies of different religious denominations, at which O'Connell's health was proposed by the distinguished Bishop of Dromore, Dr. Blake. In his reply, O'Connell paid the following gallant compliment to the ladies :

"Yes, ladies, I thank you most heartily for the kindness you have bestowed upon me in placing me in so very honorable a position this evening. I have always respected all that is good; and you are all good in your several circumstances of life. I have ever treated with contempt, as a ribald jest, the giving to men a superiority which they do not possess or deserve, in taking from woman that power which has been given her by her Creator, of mitigating all that is harsh, all that is rough, and all that is cruel in our nature. She is man without his roughness or passions, but with all his patience and intellect!"

The rancor of the Orangemen would not suffer the occasion to pass without some disturbance. Whilst O'Connell was speaking, a shower of stones came crashing in through the windows, breaking the chandeliers and causing the greatest commotion among the ladies, one of whom is said to have been injured.

O'Connell left Belfast for London, where he once more resumed his Parliamentary duties.

A general election occurred during 1841, and O'Connell lost his seat for Dublin. The Whig ministry broke down owing to the Tory majority in the House, and Peel became Prime Minister. The Tory press, carried away by this success, became more slanderous and virulent than ever. One journal exultingly exclaimed, "Steam has given us Ireland, inextricably clutched within our grasp." O'Connell, in a speech delivered soon after, demonstrated that the new motive power was not to be used one way only. Said he: "They threaten us with troops by steam. They say that a few hours will land an army here. Steam is a powerful foe; but steam is an equally powerful friend. Whisper in your ear, John Bull — steam has brought America within ten days' sail of Ireland." And the cheering that followed these remarks attested how well they were appreciated.

The Municipal Reform Act, which had recently come into force, opened to the Catholics of Ireland the various offices of city governments. The Lord Mayors of Dublin for the preceding one hundred and fifty years had been Protestants, and now that Catholic city was about to be represented by a Catholic.

The Catholics were not long in taking advantage of this privilege, and on the 1st of November, 1841, Daniel O'Connell was elected Lord Mayor of Dublin. Who was better entitled to this, the highest honor in the gift of the nation, than the Liberator, whose manhood had been dedicated to her service, and who had torn the shackles from her feet and placed her upon the threshold of prosperity? There was some doubt whether O'Connell would not use his office to further the interests of Repeal. Being asked in relation to this subject, he replied "that no one should be able to discover from his conduct what was his religion or his politics; yet a Repealer he certainly would be until the hour of his death."

Every one was anxious to see how O'Connell would acquit himself on his first day in court, and the place was crowded to suffocation. Among the first cases to be tried was a claim for some alleged arrears of wages, made against a Catholic priest. O'Connell, finding the clergyman in the wrong, with becoming impartiality, gave judgment against him.

In another case, the following characteristic little scene occurred. It was a question of accounts, in which a person named Burke was plaintiff.

" Mr. Burke," quoth the attorney, "did you keep a book ? "

"I never kept a book," cried Burke very angrily.

"I'll tell you what you'll keep," said O'Connell, "keep your temper."

"Were you boarded in the house of your employer?" inquired the attorney.

"What has this to do with the case?" asked Burke ferociously.

"There never was a question," said O'Connell, "that required so little anger. You were asked if you got something to eat, whereupon you break out into a passion!"

The following incident amused O'Connell exceedingly: An old gentleman accused his servant, among other thefts, of having stolen his stick. The servant protested perfect innocence. "Why you know," rejoined the complainant, "that the stick could never have walked off with itself." "Certainly not," said the attorney for the defence, "unless it was a walking-stick!"

To enable the reader to understand the difficulty of O'Connell's duties, we shall cite a few of the cases investigated, taken at random from the journals of the day.

A gentleman with the strange name of "Stanley Ireland" having presented himself as a claimant for the franchise, he was objected to by Mr. Crean for non-payment of water-pipe tax.

"I did not think," said O'Connell, "that an objection to Ireland would come from your side."

"You know we do not like the name of Stanley," said Crean.

"But by admitting Stanley you extend the franchise to 'Ireland,'" said O'Connell.

It was discovered that the tax was paid, and Mr. Ireland was admitted.

"Well, this is a great day for Ireland," said O'Connell.

The next name was Henry Chinnery Justice. When the word Justice was called, Mr. Wauchob said: "Now, my Lord, you cannot but say you have justice very near Ireland."

A few days after this, O'Connell attended the dinner of the Malachean Orphan charity, at Mrs. Mahony's rooms, Patrick Street, where, alluding to the splendid gold collar of the Dublin corporation which he wore round his neck, he made a very felicitous application of a line from "Moore's Melodies." He said: "I am here, it is true, but an uncanonized Malachi; I resemble the old monarch of that name, of whom the poet sings that

'Malichi wore a collar of gold'!

He won it, we are told by the same authority, 'from the proud invader,' whereas I won *this* from the old rotten corporation of Dublin."

O'Connell's mayoralty ushered in the year 1842. In January of that year Lord Shrewsbury, then regarded as the leading lay Catholic of the British Empire, assailed O'Connell in a public letter. The Liberator's reply was probably the most brilliant effort that ever issued from his prolific pen. Alluding to his sacrifices for Ireland, he wrote thus:—

"I flung away the profession—I gave its emoluments to the winds—I closed the vista of its honors and dignities—I embraced the cause of my country—and, come weal or come woe, I have made a choice at which I have never repined, nor ever shall repent. An event occurred which I could not have foreseen. Once more high professional promotion was placed within my reach. The office of Lord Chief Baron of the Exchequer became vacant. I was offered it. Or, had I preferred the office of Master of the Rolls, the alternative was proposed to me. It was a tempting offer. Its value was enhanced by the manner in which it was made; and preëminently

so by the person through whom it was made — the
best Englishman that Ireland ever saw — the Mar-
quis of Normanby. But I dreamed again a day-
dream — was it a dream ? — and I refused the offer.
And here am I now taunted, even by you, with mean
and sordid motives. I do not think I am guilty of
the least vanity, when I assert that no man ever
made greater sacrifices to what he deemed the cause
of his country than I have done. I care not how I
may be ridiculed or maligned. I feel the proud consciousness that no public man has made greater or
more ready sacrifices. Still there lingers behind one
source of vexation and sorrow — one evil, perhaps,
greater than all the rest — one claim, I believe,
higher than any other upon the gratitude of my
countrymen. It consists in the bitter, the virulent,
the mercenary, and therefore the more envenomed
hostility towards me which my love for Ireland
and for liberty has provoked. What taunts, what
reproaches, what calumnies have I not sustained —
what modes of abuse, what vituperation and slander
have been exhausted against me — what vials of bitterness have been poured on my head — what coarse-
ness of language has not been used, abused, and
worn out in assailing me — what derogatory appellation has been spared — what treasures of malevolence have been expended — what follies have not
been imputed — in fact, what crimes have I not been
charged with ? I do not believe that I ever had, in
private life, an enemy. I know that I had and have
many, very many, warm, cordial, affectionate, attached friends. Yet here I stand, beyond contro-

versy the most and the best-abused man in the universal world! And, to cap the climax of calumny, you come with a lath at your side instead of the sword of a Talbot, and you throw Peel's scurrility along with your own into my cup of bitterness. All this have I done and suffered for Ireland. And let her be grateful or ungrateful — solvent or insolvent — he who insults me for taking her pay, wants the vulgar elements of morality which teach that the laborer is worthy of his hire; he wants the higher sensations of the soul which enable one to perceive that there are services which bear no comparison with money, and can never be recompensed by pecuniary rewards. Yes, I am — I say it proudly — I am the hired servant of Ireland; and I glory in my servitude."

O'Connell, during this year, refused his autograph to the proud Emperor of the Russias, who applied through his representative at the Court of St. James. The King of Bavaria was more successful in this regard, and expressed himself thankful and pleased.

O'Connell did not spare himself in his capacity of Mayor. During the interval of his official duties he wrote his famous "Memoir of Ireland," and performed the herculean task of revising the burgess rolls of Dublin. This obliged him to examine and determine the claims of no less than eighteen thousand persons; and he accomplished the task, contrary to the predictions of the wiseacres of the city.

CHAPTER XVII.

THE year of 1843 O'Connell determined to make *par excellence* " the Repeal year." The silent labors of the Repeal Association now began to yield fruit. Its ranks were divided into three classes, — Members, Associates, and Volunteers. The Associates paid in thirty shillings, and received a card as a means of recognition; the members paid one pound each, and the Volunteers ten pounds each. The card of membership was remarkable for its design, as will be seen from the following description:

"The names of four great battles in which the Irish defeated the Danes or English were printed conspicuously on this card — viz., "Clontarf, 1014;" "Beal-an-atha-buidhe, 1598;" "Benburb, 1645;" "Limerick, 1690." The card was adorned with pikes, banners, and columns. On the shaft of the left column was this description: "Ireland contains 32,201 geographical square miles. It is larger than Portugal by 4,649 miles; larger than Bavaria and Saxony united by 4,473 miles; larger than Naples and Sicily by 409 miles; larger than Hanover, the Papal States, and Tuscany by 1,285 miles; larger than Denmark, Hesse Darmstadt, and the Electorate of Hesse by 9,609 miles; larger than Greece and Switzerland by 5,565 miles; larger than Holland and Belgium by 13,065 miles; is in population superior to eighteen, and in extent of territory superior to fifteen, European states — and has not a parliament!" On the shaft of the right column was this inscription: "Ireland has 8,750,000 inhabitants; has a yearly revenue of £5,000,000; exports yearly £18,000,000 worth of produce; sends yearly (after paying government expenses) to England £2,500,000; remits yearly to absentees, £5,000,000; supplied, during the last great war against France, the general and two-thirds of the men and officers of the English army and navy; has a military population of 2,000,000 — and has not a parliament."

The work of Repeal now indeed began in earnest. "Monster meetings" followed each other in rapid succession. The first took place at Trim, on the 16th of March, and was rapidly followed by others of equal interest and importance. At Limerick one hundred and ten thousand persons were present, and at Kells one hundred and fifty thousand Repealers assembled.

The government was thoroughly alarmed by the increasing force of a movement which the law offered no means of destroying. Sir Robert Peel had threatened to use every means in his power to crush the Repeal movement, and he boasted that if the law as it stood could not put down O'Connell, the law should be amended so that he could.

At Mullingar O'Connell attended to this threat of the Prime Minister in a speech delivered before one of the most enthusiastic meetings yet assembled.

"We are told," said he, "that some desperate measures are to be taken for the suppression of public opinion upon the question of Repeal. I will tell Peel where he may find a suggestion for his bill: In the American Congress for the District of Columbia, they have passed a law that the House shall not receive any petitions from, nor any petitions on behalf of, slaves, even though the petitioners be freemen! I shall send for a copy of that Act of the Columbian Legislature, and send it to Peel, that he may take it as his model when he is framing his bill of coercion for the Irish people. He shall go the full length of the Coercion Bill if he stirs at all."

At Athlone, on the 18th of June, a vast concourse of people gathered to hear the Liberator. When O'Connell rose to speak, the cheers which greeted his ear were positively deafening. This was the anniversary of the battle of Waterloo, and he paid a gallant compliment to the valor of the Irish general and Irish soldiers who secured the triumphs of that battle.

O'Connell next proceeded to speak of Peel. He denied that the Queen was opposed to Repeal. Peel, in saying that she was so, had told a lie. "I wish," cried a voice in the crowd, "that a crow would come and pick Peel's eyes out." "I wish," replied O'Connell, "that a crow would come and stuff your mouth with potatoes!" Roars of laughter followed this sally.

While he yet spoke, a disturbance in the crowd threatened to end in a panic. When the excitement was at its height, O'Connell's voice was heard above the uproar, crying, "Stand still!" Instantly confidence was restored, and the meeting resumed its order and decorum. The meetings still continued. At Enniscorthy, in July, two hundred thousand men assembled; at Dundalk three hundred thousand; but these gatherings appear insignificant when compared with the great gathering at Tara, which took place August the 15th, 1843. The hill of Tara is situated some twenty miles from Dublin, and O'Connell set out from the metropolis at an early hour of the morning, attended by his staff. The citizens followed in vehicles, estimated as high as fourteen hundred in number. The roads leading to the grand rendezvous were lined with people, attended by bands of music which discoursed national airs, and cheered their hearts as they marched along. The vast concourse of people who gathered on this memorable occasion about the hill of Tara has been variously estimated, one authority placing it as high as seven hundred thousand. The *Times* said, "a *million* of people were present;" not so much of an exaggeration, when we consider that all Ireland had its heart with them.

On the summit of the hill an altar was erected, upon which, from early dawn until noon, the Holy Sacrifice of the Mass was offered. O'Connell arrived just as the officiating clergyman was giving the blessing to the multitude, who knelt to receive it. On reaching the summit of the hill, O'Connell mounted a platform which was occupied by two bishops, three vicars general, and thirty priests. When the great patriot arose to speak the people at once became silent, and the order which prevailed that day was a credit to the nation. Many years after, one of those who was fortunate enough to be present was asked if he was able to hear O'Connell's voice. "Oh, no, sir!" he replied; "only about *thirty thousand* could hear him, but we all kept as quiet and silent *as if we did.*" The speech which O'Connell delivered on this memorable occasion subsequently caused his arrest.

From the meeting at Trim, in March, to the meeting at Tara, in August, thirty monster meetings had been held. The Repeal Rent, which was collected to defray the necessary expenses of the movement, had amounted in this year to £48,421. O'Connell now felt sure of success. His plan was to assemble "a court of three hundred" in Dublin, which he thought could be easily converted into an Irish Parliament. This assembly would be contrary to law — O'Connell was a lawyer, and respected the law. Herein lay a difficulty as gigantic as the intellect of O'Connell.

The meetings which followed that of Tara were repetitions of these already enumerated. At Waterford, in July, six hundred thousand persons assembled. The last of the meetings took place in October, at Mullaghmast. On that occasion O'Connell was crowned by Hogan, the sculptor, in the presence of four hundred thousand Repealers. Placing the crown on his head, the great sculptor remarked, "Sir, my only

regret is that this is not gold." Overcome by the
ceremony, O'Connell placed his hand upon his heart,
and exclaimed, in a voice trembling with emotion, " I
shall wear this cap with the proud remembrance that
it was given to me on the Rath of Mullaghmast, and
that it was placed upon my head by one of the first
of modern sculptors in this or any other country. I
shall continue to wear it during my life, and it shall
afterwards be buried with me in the grave."

At a meeting of the Repeal Association, it was
decided to hold another monster meeting on Sunday,
October the 8th, at Clontarf, the memorable battle-
ground of an Irish victory over the Danes. The
preparations made for this meeting surpassed those
of any other ever held in Ireland. The government,
fearing that the crisis had come, determined to strike
a signal blow at Repeal. On the afternoon of Saturday, October 7th, a proclamation from the Viceroy,
Lord de Gray, appeared at the gates of the Castle,
prohibiting the intended meeting of the morrow.
Fearing bloodshed, which seemed inevitable in case
the meeting took place, O'Connell wisely issued a counter proclamation, in which he enjoined the Repealers
to abandon their purpose of assembling. Messengers
were despatched in all directions, and the quiet which
reigned in Dublin on the morrow attested the control which O'Connell possessed over the actions of
the people. The judgment of O'Connell on this
occasion merits the greatest respect. Had the Clontarf meeting taken place, the people would have
been slaughtered. Lord Cardigan had planted cannon so as to command the approaches to Clontarf,

the infantry were supplied with sixty rounds of ball cartridge each, and that *moral* aristocrat would have perpetrated a massacre on the unarmed assemblage of the people.

CHAPTER XVIII.

. ON the 12th of October, rumors were afloat in Dublin that O'Connell was to be tried for high-treason. When O'Connell learned of the danger that threatened him, his countenance fell, and he evinced great uneasiness. His advanced age led him to believe that confinement would shorten his life, and he feared the result. In conversation with a friend, he said, " I scarcely think they will attempt a prosecution for high-treason, though, indeed, there is hardly anything too desperate for them to attempt. If they do, I shall make my confession, and prepare for the result."

Finding that the charges preferred were not as serious as he had anticipated, he began to look at the matter less gloomily, and soon regained his usual buoyancy of spirits. To his son John he laughingly remarked, " I do not think two years imprisonment would kill me; I should keep constantly walking about, and take a bath every day."

"But why talk of imprisonment at all?" returned John; "surely there is, please God, no danger of it."

"I take the most discouraging view of the case," said his father, "in order to be prepared for the worst."

The terrors of the impending prosecution did not hinder O'Connell from paying his annual visit to Derrynane, from which, August 17th, he wrote to a friend a private letter so characteristic of the man, that we cannot refrain from giving an extract: "What a tasteless fellow that Attorney-General was, not to allow me another fortnight in these delightful mountains. I forgive him everything but *that*. Why, yesterday I had a most delightful day's hunting. I saw almost the entire of it — hare and hounds. We killed five hares. The day's run, without intermission, five hours and three quarters. In three minutes after each hare was killed we had another on foot, and the cry was incessant. They were never at more than a temporary check, and the cry with the echoes was splendid. I was not in such wind for walking these five years; and you will laugh at me when I tell you the fact, that I was less wearied than several of the young men, and we had a good three miles to walk home after the last hare was killed, just at the close of the day. I was not prepared for such good hunting, as the plague among my dogs had thinned the pack. It killed six couple of beautiful beagles of mine. I could almost weep for them. Yet the survivors seemed determined to indemnify me. If to-morrow be dry, I hope to have another good day's hunt."

On the 14th of October, 1844, the Crown Solicitor waited on O'Connell, and informed him that the government had instituted proceedings against himself and his son, John O'Connell, for "conspiracy, and other misdemeanors." In the afternoon of the same day he appeared before Justice Burton, and gave bail to abide his trial on the charges preferred against him. Immediately after, O'Connell addressed a letter "to the people of Ireland," in which he implored them "to observe the strictest and most perfect tranquillity." O'Connell and his son were not the only individuals charged with this "conspiracy to intimidate the government." In the indictment, which covered about ninety-seven feet of parchment, were found the names of Thomas Steele, Thomas Matthew Ray, Charles Gavan Duffy, John Gray, Richard Barrett, Rev. J. Tierney, and Rev. Mr. Tyrrell.

The trial opened on January 15th, 1844. A stranger in Dublin on that day might have mistaken O'Connell, as he rode down to the court-house side by side with the Lord Mayor, and followed by the aldermen in their official robes, for the King of Ireland. The enthusiasm of the citizens, who lined the streets on either side, manifested itself in loud and prolonged cheers as he passed along — a pledge, as it were, of their sympathy and devotion. The city swarmed with soldiers. The government was alarmed, and feared an outbreak. It was the fear of the bully, who parades his strength to conceal his lack of courage. On arriving at the court-house,

O'Connell entered amidst murmurs of friendly welcome and sympathy.

On the Bench sat Chief Justice Pennefather, and assistant judges Burton, Crampton, and Perrin. The jury was Protestant to a man. Between Tory judges and a Tory jury the traversers had small chance of acquittal. "If our Saviour himself were in the dock," said the shrewd Jack Gifford, "the Dublin Orangemen would find him guilty, if it would serve their purpose." The principal witnesses were reporters and policemen, and their evidence would have proved weak enough in any but an Irish state trial. The counsel on both sides were distinguished men. The case for the crown occupied ten days, the Attorney-General's charge alone covering "eleven mortal hours." On the eleventh day, Sheil arose to open the case for the defence. He acted as counsel for Mr. John O'Connell. His speech was in every respect worthy of his great reputation as a lawyer and orator. In defending the son, Sheil likewise defended the father. He scorned the charge of conspiracy against a man whose honest purposes courted the world's inspection, and matured best in the broad light of public scrutiny.

"Can you bring yourselves," said he, "to believe that he would blast all the laurels which it is his boast that he has won without the effusion of a single drop of human blood; that he would drench the land of his birth, of his affections, and of his redemption, in a deluge of profitless blood, and that he would lay prostrate the great moral monument which

he has raised so high that it is visible from the re-
motest region of the world?".

The other traversers were defended individually
by counsel, among whom were Fitzgibbon, White-
side, MacDonough and Henn. From the first day of
the trial, O'Connell had resolved to be his own advocate. On the the twentieth day of the trial the Liberator, who had impatiently awaited his turn, arose.
His speech on this occasion, although full of ability,
was not equal to his best efforts. This proceeded in
a great measure from a founded conviction that his
sentence was already determined upon.

In combating the charge of "conspiracy," which
the Attorney-General confidently promised to establish, O'Connell was supremely successful: "If, my
lords, I look into the dictionary for the meaning of
that word, I find that it is 'a secret agreement between several to commit a crime;' and that is the
rational, common-sense definition of it. It has been
admitted even by the crown that this secret conspiracy had no secresy at all   What a monstrous thing it
would be to hold that that was a conspiracy which
everybody knew of, everybody heard of, and three-
fifths of the people of this country were engaged in!
And what was the evidence that those conspirators
assembled? That Mr. Such-a-one attended at such
a meeting; that Mr. Barrett attended at a certain
meeting, and that Mr. Duffy attended once or twice;
that I myself attended; and this is the way the
charge of conspiracy is spelt out. Is it common
sense that that should be denominated a conspiracy?
Conspiracy! Where was it formed? When was it

formed? How was it formed? Was it formed in summer or in winter, in spring or in autumn? Tell me the hour, the week, the month, the year it was made. When and where did it take place? Should I not, at all events, have the advantage of being able to prove an *alibi?* (Laughter.) No; but you must go over nine months, and toss up which place or time you shall select. Do you not believe that if there was a conspiracy it would be proved, and that the only reason it was not proved is that it did not exist? The Attorney-General told you that it did exist — that it must have existed. But this is all imaginary, and you are called upon to find me guilty if you imagine that this agreement was entered into." O'Connell concluded his defence with the following eloquent words: "I leave the case in your hands. I deny I have done anything to stain me. I reject with contempt the appellation of conspirator. I have acted boldly in the open day, in the presence of the magistracy; there has been nothing secret or concealed. I have struggled for the restoration of the parliament of my native country. Others have succeeded before me; but succeed or fail, it was a struggle to make the fairest land in the world possess those benefits which Nature intended she should enjoy."

The combined eloquence of the United Kingdom would have been thrown away upon such a jury; the verdict had been agreed upon long before the trial began, and, as a consequence, O'Connell and his associates were found guilty.

Scarcely had the verdict issued from the jury-box,

when O'Connell addressed a "Letter to the Irish People." In that letter he tore the mask from the hypocritical designs of the government, and exposed the base trickery which had been employed throughout the trial. In conclusion, he implored the people to abstain from violence, promising if they kept the peace "for six, or, at most, for twelve months, he would guarantee them Repeal."

In Ireland the result of the trial was received with ill-assumed submission. In England, where O'Connell went immediately after the trial, the people expressed their indignation at public meetings held to protest against this wanton desecration of constitutional right. At the Covent Garden meeting, O'Connell said himself, "the scene was never exceeded, and perhaps never equalled, in any other country." When the Liberator entered the House of Commons, the Whigs, who were then "out of place," received him with cheers, and the member who was at that moment addressing the assemblage was obliged to pause. Singularly enough, the House at that time was discussing Irish affairs, and Lord John Russell took occasion to arraign the government for its unnatural treatment of Ireland, and boldly asserted that O'Connell had been tried by a packed jury. When the debate closed, O'Connell returned to Dublin.

Judge Burton did not pronounce sentence upon the condemned until the 30th of May, three months after the termination of the trial. The judge, who was a man of high principle and a great admirer of O'Connell's, became greatly affected when pronouncing judgment. He commenced with much calmness, but soon lost control of his voice, and, bursting into tears, hid his face in his hands. In a few minutes the kind-hearted judge recovered his self-possession, and concluded the formal part of the judgment.

"With respect to the principal traverser, the Court is of opinion that he must be sentenced to be imprisoned for the space of twelve calendar months; and that he is further to be fined in the sum of £2,000, and bound in his own recognizances in the sum of £5,000, and two sureties in £2,500, to keep the peace for seven years. With respect to the other traversers, they shall be imprisoned for the space of nine calendar months, each of them to pay £50 fine, and enter into their own recognizances of £1,000, and two sureties of £500, to keep the peace for seven years."

It is impossible, at this late day, to fully appreciate the outraged sentiment of the people of Ireland. Their leader, their all but kingly Liberator, was about to be deprived of his inalienable rights as a citizen, and suffer confinement in a common jail. The public pulse beat high. A single word from O'Connell would have precipitated a rebellion against the government, whose wanton disregard of justice led the people to hope little from purely *moral* force. It would have been far easier for many a man who was present at Tara to have faced the cannon at Clontarf than witness the incarceration of "the hope of Ireland." The Repeal Rent rose up to £2,000 a week.

The prisoners were allowed to choose their place of confinement, and O'Connell, in behalf of his companions, chose Richmond Bridewell. A carriage was procured for the Liberator, and covered vehicles for his fellow prisoners, and the cavalcade made a circuitous route to the jail, escorted by a strong force of mounted police. The people, who had collected in vast numbers, followed in mournful silence until the party reached Richmond, when their pent-up feelings could no longer be controlled, and they burst forth into a long and hearty cheer.

On entering, the prisoners were escorted to the office of the prison, where the warder registered their names. As it will prove of interest to our readers, we give below an extract from the Prison Registry, showing how O'Connell's name was entered.

RICHMOND BRIDEWELL.

Extract from General Registry, 1844, of the undernamed State Prisoners :—

Name, D. O'Connell ; Age, 67 ; Height, 5ft. 11 1-4 in. ; Hair, Dark ; Complexion, Good ; Born, Cahirciveen ; Occupation, Barrister ; Education, Superior. ; Committed, May 30, 1844 ; Crime, Conspiracy. By whom committed, Q. Bench ; Sentence, 12 cal. m. ; Discharged by order of Government, Sept. 6, 1844 ; Fines, £2,000 ; Sureties, Self, £5,000, and two, £2,000 each.

After the entries had been made, the prisoners remained in the outer hall, waiting to be shown their "quarters." Meanwhile, O'Connell was ushered into the presence of the Board of Superintendence, who arose and saluted him as he entered. This courtesy was recognized by the Liberator with a graceful bow. He was then informed that great privileges would be awarded, if he would, on the part of himself and his fellow prisoners, give a pledge not to use the concessions to effect an escape from prison. O'Connell, with gentlemanly consideration for his friends, replied that he would first consult them, and retired for that purpose into the outer hall. He there repeated the words of the Board to his fellow prisoners, who replied, "Your promise, sir, should be law to us;" and the Board, on receiving this assurance, immediately broke up.

"O'Connell, of course, had the first selection of rooms, and he fixed on a second floor bed-room in the deputy-governor's house, as being near the only room large enough for all the State prisoners to dine in together. John O'Connell naturally selected a room near his illustrious father. C. G. Duffy, lately Prime Minister of Victoria, selected the dining-room and adjoining bed-room in the governor's house. Dr. Gray, late Sir John Gray, M.P. for Kilkenny, selected the drawing-room and adjoining bed-room in the same department, and Steele and Ray made choice of rooms over those of Duffy and Gray, while Barrett selected rooms between the governor's and deputy-governor's chief apartments, but practically in the deputy-governor's, as he said, 'to be near O'Connell.' Mrs. John O'Connell, Mrs. Gray, Mrs. Duffy, Mrs. Barrett, and Mrs. Ray were installed as rulers in the respective 'cells' of their husbands, and great was the confusion of bandboxes and parcels, great and small, and trunks and bags, as they were tumbled into the hall of Richmond Bridewell on that day. Each was, however, soon restored to order under the gentle sway of the ladies, and as dinner hour approached and the bell rang, the prisoners, each with his wife or relative, might be seen assembling in the great dining-room in the deputy-governor's house, not in full dress, but in something nearly approaching to it. O'Connell on that day led 'Mrs. John,' as he affectionately called her, to her seat, and the first dinner in Richmond was partaken of by as joyous a family party as ever assembled. Seated at a round table, the property of the governor, now in the possession of Lady Gray, the prisoners were, on that occasion, in allusion to the great round table, called by the Liberator 'The Knights of the Round Table,' a title they bore during their stay at Richmond."

"During his imprisonment, O'Connell was as accessible to visitors, and as informal in his mode of 'giving audiences,' as the most youthful of his companions. A 'friend of the cause,' from the most distant village in Ireland, whether lay or clerical, who desired to see 'the Liberator,' was at once presented by one of his fellow-prisoners, some member of the family of a 'fellow captive,' or some one of the faithful body-guard which was always in attendance on 'the Liberator' as he took his walk in the prison-garden or sat on 'Tara' or 'Mullaghmast.'"*

"Tara" and "Mullaghmast" were two mounds in the prison-garden, which the Liberator had chosen to name after those celebrated places of meeting. The prison life, which O'Connell at first dreaded so

* From the late Sir John Gray's Narrative.

much, was not as serious a matter as he had anticipated, and in every way differed from that of the
common prisoner. He and his companions were
allowed the free use of the garden already alluded to,
which gave them ample opportunity of exercise.
"Three times round the jail garden is a mile," said
O'Connell, "and I will walk it three times a day,"
which he did. They were allowed to receive and
entertain their friends. The generous citizens of
Dublin vied with one another in seeing that the prisoners wanted nothing, and their table was constantly
supplied with the delicacies of the market. Mass was
celebrated each day in the prison; and so numerous
were the applications of those zealous to offer this
great spiritual consolation, that many clergymen
were obliged to wait days before their turn came.
The prisoners gave dinner-parties regularly twice
a week, whilst visitors without number, coming
from all parts of Ireland, were freely admitted and
cordially received.

"You are more visited here," said one of a deputation to O'Connell, who stood on "Tara," "than if
you were at large." "Yes," replied the Liberator,
"and, being a prisoner, I cannot use the excuse
'not at home.'"

Addresses of condolence were sent to O'Connell
from all parts of Europe, and among others one
from the Catholic clergy of Wurtemburg. The address from England, however, was most gratifying.
It was signed by some of the best and noblest Catholics of that country.

"Tell your friends that my heart is joyful," said

the Liberator, in reply to the bearer of one of the many addresses which were presented at this time; "my spirits are buoyant, my health is excellent, my hopes are high. My imprisonment is not irksome to me, for I feel and know that it will, under Providence, be the means of making our country a nation again. I am glad I am in prison. There wanted but this to my career. I have labored for Ireland; refused office, honor, and emolument for Ireland; I have prayed, and hoped, and watched for Ireland — there was yet one thing wanted, that I should be in jail for Ireland! That has now been added to the rest, thanks to our enemies, and I cordially rejoice at it."

CHAPTER XIX.

MEANTIME O'Connell's friends were not idle. They clamored for justice in the very halls of Parliament. An appeal for a reverse of judgment was made to the House of Lords. The matter was referred, at first, to twelve judges, who decided that the indictment was illegal, but the finding was right. Carried from the Court of Appeal to the House of Lords, it was finally placed in the hands of five law lords, a majority of whom was in favor of reversal.

O'Connell and his fellow prisoners were at last set free. On the afternoon of Thursday, the 5th of September, 1844, large crowds of people were assembled on the pier at Kingstown, patiently awaiting the arrival of the steamer *Medusa*, which was expected to bear to Ireland the glad tidings of O'Connell's release. The traversers' Solicitors had provided themselves in London with banners, on which were inscribed "*Triumph of law and justice; the judgment reversed. O'Connell is free.*" No

sooner had these gentlemen landed than the joyful
tidings were communicated to the crowd, who immediately gave utterance to their delight in cries of
"Free, free." The engineer of the train which carried
the Solicitors to Dublin placed one of the banners
on his engine, and thus the people along the way
were made acquainted with the grateful intelligence.

It is impossible to describe the joy manifested at
the prison on learning the news. Friends flocked
thither in great numbers to congratulate the re-
leased, who were obliged to write thousands of signatures before they departed for their homes. It
was determined that a triumphal procession should
be made on the morrow from Richmond Prison
to Merrion Square. Accordingly, on the following
day, Saturday, the 7th (1844), thousands were looking
for O'Connell to escort him from the prison whence
the procession was to begin. But the Liberator was
at Mass, concluding the last day of a novena in
which all the Catholic prisoners had joined. From
Merrion Square to the Richmond Bridewell, the way
was lined with one dense mass of human beings.
At twelve, the first part of the procession reached
the penitentiary, but the triumphal car did not arrive
until two hours later. This monster *cortége* was
composed of delegations from the trades and the
temperance societies, headed by Very Rev. Dr. Spratt,
bearing banners and headed by bands of music.
The Lord Mayor was there in his robes, attended by
a numerous gathering of the best citizens of Dublin.
The carriages which followed after the trades were
filled by the Repeal Wardens and members of the

Association. The climax was, however, the moment at which O'Connell, accompanied by his son John and Dr. Miley, his chaplain, was conducted from the jail by Smith O'Brien, and ascended the triumphal car. Then arose a shout so loud, so long, so enthusiastic, as to be perfectly deafening. The other prisoners, with their friends, entered carriages, and the procession moved forward. When opposite the old "Parliament House" in College Green, his car was stopped. O'Connell rose up, and, taking off his cap, pointed significantly to the building again and again. The people understood the meaning of these gestures, and loudly proclaimed their appreciation. At length the procession reached Merrion Square, where O'Connell addressed the multitude, who listened with profound attention to his words. He said: "This is a great day for Ireland (tremendous cheering) — a day of justice.· All that we ever desired was justice, and we have got an instalment of it, at any rate. The plans of the wicked and the conspiracy of the oppressor; the foul mismanagement of the jury panel; the base conspiracy against the lives, the liberties, and the constitutional rights of the public — have all, blessed be God, been defeated."

He then proceeded to prove that he in no way had transgressed the law, and assured them he was still "young enough, in law and in fact," to continue his great work. At the conclusion of his speech the immense crowd separated, delighted to feel that their beloved chieftain was once more at liberty.

On Monday, two days after the procession, O'Connell appeared at Conciliation Hall, where a dense

multitude awaited him. It is needless to remark the reception which greeted him as he arose to address the meeting. The tender bond of sympathy between O'Connell and the people had ripened into parental love. It was the very ecstacy of national confidence and national devotion. He reviewed the trial, the prejudice of the judges, the perfidy of the jury, and his sentence and confinement. He alluded to the confidence reposed in him by the Protestants of Ireland. "We were strong enough to commit violence," said he; "and nothing save the spirit of conciliation and love for each other could have brought us together in such multitudinous masses without violence." He concluded with a glowing tribute to the Catholic clergy:

"I have kept my compact; but I never could have done this without the assistance and coöperation of the Catholic clergy. They saw the jealous scrutiny with which our movements were watched by our Protestant brethren; they entered unreservedly into my views, and here is all the secret of my success. They knew me; they appreciated me. They knew that I was the first apostle and founder of that sect of politicians whose cardinal doctrine is this, — that the greatest and most desirable of political changes may be achieved by moral means alone, and that no human revolution is worth the effusion of one single drop of blood. Human blood is no cement for the temple of human liberty."

In 1843, a club had been founded in Ireland called the '82 Club, in honor of the era of Ireland's independence (1782).. On the 3d of May of this year (1845), a

festival was held under the auspices of this club, to
commemorate O'Connell's imprisonment. O'Connell
was seated on a green throne in the Round Room of
the Rotunda, surrounded by members of the club in
their green and gold uniforms. A platform twenty-
six feet in diameter supported the throne, over which
the arms of Ireland were conspicuously emblazoned.
In short, the Round Room had every appearance of
a royal court. It was, indeed, the supreme moment
of O'Connell's life. Seated in state, he received
successively the nobility, gentry, and clergy of Catholic Ireland.

The noon of O'Connell's illustrious and eventful
life had passed; already the " wing of the shadow of
death " was upon him. Troubles and disappoint-
ments so common to his stormy life, now increased
in such a degree that his advanced age and decayed
energies were no longer able to contend with them.
The " Young Ireland " party, composed of the
younger members of the Repeal Association, eager
to draw the sword, were showing themselves impatient of the Fabian policy of the Liberator. A new
element also had united itself with Repeal, which
boded no good to the cause. This consisted of influential men, large property owners, who were
wedded to the aristocracy. One of these gentlemen,
Grey Porter by name, brought forward a plan for
raising a national militia; and when he found that
he did not meet with much attention, he took to
inspecting the ledgers of the Repeal Association,
and then endeavored to cast suspicion upon O'Connell's management of its funds. To fill the cup

of bitterness, a rescript from Rome was received in Ireland, by which its Catholic clergy were in. structed to give less time to politics and more atten. tion to their religious duties.

Late in September of 1845, O'Connell visited Cashel, where over one hundred thousand people assembled to receive him. His own description of the affair will be read with interest:

"The meeting of Tipperary did not so much lie within a compass (as Tara) that it could be seen together; but it was all seen by me, who traversed it from one end to the other, who was surrounded by immense multitudes from Cashel to Thurles, a distance of ten miles, and to the place of meeting, two miles beyond it. They came in three great divisions, by the three roads that meet in Thurles; and one of those divisions, and not the largest of the three, took two hours and forty-five minutes in passing the bank. A friend of mine was stationed there. They marched eight or ten abreast, and they were two hours and forty-five minutes in passing the bank; and that was only one-third of the entire number! They were mounted upon excellent, serviceable horses. Mr. Bianconi, the mayor of Clonmel, who understands horses as well as any man living, told me he never saw such a number of excellent horses. Upwards of fifteen thousand of them rode *in one group* on horseback. In a word, it was one of the noblest sights that ever Ireland exhibited — for nothing can be finer than such a congregation of human beings. They were not confined to men alone, but consisted of women, boys, and children of all ages. I want language to describe the demonstration. It was not a military demonstration, for that means a feint, a pretended attack; but it was a political demonstration, having reality for its basis, having determination for its guidance, and the Repeal of the Union for its object."

O'Connell boasted at Cashel, that the Catholic Association, when emancipation was conceded, consisted of only fourteen thousand members, but the Repeal Association already numbered one million. " I have," said he, " the draft of a bill for the Repeal of the Union almost complete already. It is an act entitled " An act to enable Her Majesty the Queen to summon her Parliament of Ireland."

Alas! these happy anticipations were far from being realized. Early in October of 1845, the dark shadow of impending famine fell upon Ireland. No one felt this calamity more keenly than O'Connell. His voice was lifted in behalf of the suffering people, to obtain relief for whom he exerted his utmost powers. He publicly accused England of wilfully aggravating the sufferings of the Irish; for at the very moment the people were starving by thousands, Irish grain was being imported to England. O'Connell was accused, in the *Times*, of neglecting his own tenantry, but he soon exposed that lie, by showing that Cahirciveen, where his property lay, enjoyed a prosperity relatively greater than any other town in Ireland.

Early in 1846, O'Connell delivered before the Repeal Association his last speech in Ireland. He informed the meeting that he had resolved to proceed

to Parliament in order to counteract the machinations
of a party in England, who boldly asserted that there
was no suffering or misery in Ireland. The Duke
of Cambridge was the head of this party. "Ireland,". said the duke, "is not in so bad a state as has
been represented. . . . I understand," continued
his highness, "that rotten potatoes and sea-weed, or
even grass, properly mixed, afford a very wholesome
and nutritious food. We all know that Irishmen can
live upon anything, and there is plenty of grass in
the fields even if the potato crop should fail!"

Notwithstanding the duke's exalted dignity, O'Connell commented on this speech with terrible and deserved severity. "There," said he, "is the son of a
king!—the brother of a king!—the uncle of a
monarch!—there is his description of Ireland for
you! Oh, why does he think thus of the Irish people? Perhaps he has been reading Spenser, who
wrote at a time when Ireland was not put down by
the strong arm of force or defeated in battle—because she never was defeated—but when the plan
was laid down to starve the Irish nation (oh! oh!).
For three years every portion of the crop was tram-
pled down by the hoofs of the horses of mounted
soldiery; for three years the crops were destroyed,
and human creatures were found lying behind
ditches, with their mouths green by eating sorrel
and the grass of the field! (Sensation.) The Duke
of Cambridge, I suppose, wishes that we should have
such scenes again enacted in this country. And is
it possible that in the presence of some of the most
illustrious nobility of England, that royal personage

should be found to utter horrors of this description ?
I will go over to England to see what they intend to
do for the Irish — whether they are of opinion that
the Irish are to feed on grass or eat mangel-wurzel
(laughter). If that should be attempted — and may
God avert the possibility of the occurrence! — I do
not hesitate to say it would be the duty of every man
to die with arms in his hands." The moment
O'Connell uttered these words the whole assembly
róse like one man, and cheered with the utmost enthusiasm for several minutes.

CHAPTER XX.

ON January 26th, 1846, O'Connell, now rapidly declining in health, but still devoted to the cause of his beloved countrymen, set out for London to plead for their relief in Parliament,

On the journey he was accompanied by two clergymen, one Catholic, the other Protestant, but both on the same humane mission, viz. : seeking relief for their starving parishioners. Arriving in London, O'Connell exerted his waning faculties in striving to soften the English heart. He laid bare the deplorable condition of the people, and earnestly supported Lord George Bentinck's bill to empower the government to loan the Irish railways £16,000,000. · This measure would have given nearly a fifth of the population employment, and, whilst it alleviated their wants, would have advanced the interests of Ireland. The bill was not carried. This blow fell with fatal effect upon O'Connell. Meanwhile, the news from

Ireland was most discouraging. The horrors of the famine still increasing, surpassed, as Brougham said, "anything in the pages of Thucydides, or on the canvas of Poussin, or in the dismal chant of Dante." In addition to this, the Young Irelanders seceded from O'Connell's followers. Smith O'Brien, at the head of his party, marched out of Conciliation Hall, despite the noble exertions of John O'Connell to reconcile their differences. Two days after Lord George Bentincks's bill had been rejected, a rumor prevailed in London that O'Connell was dead. His friends hastened to Jermyn Street, where he resided, to ascertain his condition, and there learned that he was seriously indisposed, and intended returning to Ireland immediately. His physicians, however, opposed his return, and recommended a milder climate. They disagreed regarding the exact nature of his disease, but were all of opinion that rest, and a cessation from business and excitement, was absolutely necessary. O'Connell had long turned his eager eye on Rome. It had been his constant desire to visit the shrine of Peter, although his unremitting labors in behalf of Ireland had never yielded him an opportunity. Feeling, however, that his end was drawing near, and that his mind was no longer able to endure the strain of his political labors, he resolved to set out, before his declining health would render the journey impossible.

"His days," writes an intimate friend, "were evidently drawing to a close. His voice was broken, hollow, and occasionally quite inaudible; his person was debilitated; the vigor of his eloquence was gone,

and his appearance was that of one who, destined
soon to descend into the grave, makes the last feeble
rally of his fainting powers in performance of a duty
to his country. His indisposition now daily increased.
If his mind could have been soothed by the atten-
tions of the great, he possessed that species of consolation;. nobles and ministers of state made daily
inquiry at his hotel. Nay, even royalty once or
twice paid him a similar compliment. Prior to quit-
ting England for the Continent, he sojourned for
several days at Hastings. While he stayed there he
was visited by three of the most distinguished of the
Oxford converts. Those gentlemen stated 'that
their visit was not made for the mere purpose of
compliment or condolence; but in order that they
might have the pleasure of personally assuring him
that the religious change which they and numerous
others had made, was ascribable, under God, to *his*
political labors, which had in the first instance attracted their attention to the momentous questions at
issue between Protestants and Catholics. The inquiry
that originated thus, ended in a conviction of the truth
of Catholicity.' He was pleased at this intelligence;
his spirits rallied, and he conversed with his new
friends for nearly an hour, with the point and vivac-
ity that had characterized him in the days of his
vigor."

From Hastings O'Connell proceeded to Folke-
stone, accompanied by his sons John and Daniel, together with Father Miley, his chaplain. At Folke-
stone, he embarked for Boulogne, where he arrived
after a pleasant voyage of a few hours. Here he was

greeted with marks of public courtesy by both the English and French residents, similar to those which had attended his departure from England. From Boulogne he proceeded to Paris, where he consulted Drs. Oliffe and Chomel, who pronounced his disease "a slow congestion of the brain." During his sojourn in the French capital, Count de Montalembert presented him an address on behalf of a Catholic society. This address was worthy of its illustrious author, and was eulogistic in the highest degree of the "Catholic Liberator of Ireland." "Gentlemen," said O'Connell, in reply, "sickness and emotion close my lips. I should require the eloquence of your president (Montalembert) to express to you all my gratitude. But it is impossible for me to utter all I feel. Know, simply, that I regard this demonstration on your part as the most significant event of my life."

From Paris to Lyons the journey occupied twelve days, as the invalid was obliged to rest on the way. At Lyons he consulted Dr. Bonnet, who coincided in the opinion of the Paris physicians.

Mr. Bonnet's description of O'Connell's appearance and condition at this period, as given by Dr. Lacour, is full of melancholy interest: "His weakness was so great that he believed it incompatible with life, and he constantly had the presentiment of approaching death. The arms were slow in their movements; the right trembled continually, and the left hand was cold, and could be warmed with difficulty, although he wore very thick gloves. The left foot was habitually colder than the right. He walked with some facility, but his step was slow and faltering. His face had grown thin, and his look proclaimed an inexpressible sadness; the head hung upon the breast, and the entire person of the invalid, formerly so imposing, was greatly weighed down. 'I am but the shadow of what I was, and I can scarcely recognize myself,' said he to M. Bonnet, who regarded him with visible emotion."

During his stay in Lyons, crowds followed him along the streets whenever he ventured forth. He passed along heedless of these demonstrations, and scarcely conscious of their presence. To a gentleman who strove to cheer him with a hope of recovery, he said, "Do not deceive yourself; I may not live three days."

On the 22d of April, O'Connell left Lyons, and proceeced to Marseilles, tarrying some days at Valence and Avignon. "During this journey," wrote Dr. Lacour, "the invalid took an active part in all our conversations." On the 3d of May, at Marseilles, he conversed with a vigor and gayety that he had not displayed since his departure from England. Delusive hope! alas! too soon to be followed by death.

On the 6th, O'Connell arrived at Genoa, where his condition gradually became more alarming.

"The Liberator is not better," wrote Father Miley on the 15th. "He is worse — ill as ill can be. At two o'clock this morning I found it necessary to send for the Viaticum and the holy oil. Though it was .the dead of night, the Cardinal Archbishop (he is eighty-eight years old), attended by his clerics and several of the faithful, carried the adorable Viaticum with the solemnities customary in Catholic countries, and reposed it in the tabernacle which we had prepared in the chamber of the illustrious sufferer. Though prostrate to the last degree, he was perfectly in possession of his mind whilst receiving the last rites. The adorable name of Jesus, which he had been in the habit of invoking, was constantly on his lips with trembling fervor. His thoughts have been entirely absorbed by religion since his illness commenced. For the last forty hours he will not open his lips to speak of anything else. The doctors still say they have hope. I have none. All Genoa is praying for him. I have written to Rome. Be not surprised if I am totally silent as to our own feelings. It is poor Daniel who is to be pitied more than all."

O'Connell was haunted through his illness with the fear of being buried alive, which was, no doubt, produced by the diseased condition of his brain. "I shall have the appearance of death," said he to Rev. Dr. Miley, "before life is really departed. You must take care not to bury me until quite sure that I am dead."

About three o'clock on the afternoon of Saturday (15th), O'Connell called his faithful servant, John Duggan, to his bedside, and, taking him warmly by both hands, whispered his thanks for the rare fidelity with which he had served his master. He then sank back in his bed, and continued to repeat the holy name of Jesus, the Memorare, and verses from the Psalms. His patience and resignation in agonizing pain were remarked by those who attended him. Towards evening he grew rapidly worse. The flame of that great light, which, in its strength, had directed a nation to religious freedom, gradually flickered away, and at half-past nine expired. For years his life had been a continuous preparation for eternity, and he passed into the presence of his Creator to meet the reward which, in humble hope, he had labored to gain.

Immediately the church bells of Genoa, slowly tolling, acquainted the sorrowing citizens that the great man was dead. An imposing train of Friars moved solemnly to his bed, and, kneeling, offered their prayers for his eternal repose. In the great church of the Annunziatia, the Franciscans chanted during the night the office for the dead, concluding with a grand Requiem Mass in the morning. The whole city seemed wrapped in mourning for the departed patriot.

O'Connell had ordered that his heart should be embalmed, placed in an urn, and deposited in Rome. The request was sacredly fulfilled; and the heart was accordingly placed in an urn, upon which was inscribed, " Daniel O'Connell, natus Kerry, obiit Genuæ die 15 Maii, 1847, ætatissuæ anno 72" — (Daniel O'Connell, born in Kerry, died on the 15th May, 1847, in Genoa, in the 72d year of his age.)

Funeral torches were burning incessantly day and night round the bier on which O'Connell's body lay, before an altar in the church of *Della Vigne*, while Dr. Miley and Daniel O'Connell, Jr., were bearing the heart of the Liberator to the tomb of the apostles.

On arriving in Rome, these mourning pilgrims, bearing the palladium of Ireland's love, were ushered into the presence of His Holiness Pius IX. "Since the pleasure of seeing and embracing the hero of Catholicity was not reserved for me," said the Sovereign Pontiff, "let me have the consolation of embracing his son." He then drew young O'Connell to his breast, and embraced him with the tenderness of a friend and a father. "The death of O'Connell was blessed," added the ·benign Pontiff; "I have read with extreme consolation the letter in which his last moments were described." He then proceeded to eulogize the departed Irishman as "the great champion of the Church — the father of his country — the glory of the Christian world." Monsignor Cullen, who had introduced the visitors to the presence of the ruler of the Christian Church, observed, as they were retiring: "Had His Holiness been the bosom friend of O'Connell he could not have spoken of the illustrious deceased with greater warmth of affection."

His Holiness ordered that the obsequies of the great deceased should be solemnized with the greatest pomp and magnificence. The most skilled artists, sculptors, and artizans were employed for a week in preparing for the funeral ceremonies. The ceremonies, which lasted two days, began at four in the morning and concluded at ten. Father Ventura, justly called the Bossuet of Italy, pronounced the funeral oration, which consumed four hours in its delivery. It will be found in full at the end of this volume. This magnificent oration, which has been translated into all the languages of Europe, was described by one of the cardinals as "an event which will live in the history of the Church." It is said that some fifteen thousand persons attended these solemn rites.

O'Connell's remains were not removed to Ireland until August. Wherever they rested on the mournful journey, marked reverence was paid them. They were borne to Dublin on the steamer *Duchess of Kent.* On their arrival, the people received them with more than kingly honors. On the deck of the steamer a sea-chapel had been erected, on which, during the entire voyage, prayers were offered for the repose of his soul. On the silver plate of the coffin were inscribed the following words:

"Daniel O'Connell, Hiberniæ Liberator, ad limina apostolorum pergens die xv Maii, Anno MDCCCXLVII. Genuæ abdormit in Domino vixit annos LXXI. menses IX. dies IX.—R. I. P." Which may be translated as follows: "While proceeding to the threshold of the apostles, the Liberator of Ireland, Daniel O'Connell, fell asleep in the Lord at Genoa, on the 15th May, in the year 1847. He lived 71 years, 9 months, and 9 days. May he rest in peace."

The remains were carried solemnly to the shore, when the people, who had gathered in thousands, escorted them to the Church of the Conception, Marlboro' Street. Two days later, a solemn Requiem Mass was celebrated by the Archbishop of Dublin, the Most Rev. Dr. Murray, assisted by the venerable Dr. MacHale, and Drs. Nicholson, Keating, and Whelan. On the fourth day, the remains were carried in solemn procession to the cemetery of Glas-nevin, where, after the ceremonies for the dead were concluded, the remains were reverentially entombed. The procession which followed the dead Liberator to his final resting-place was far more imposing than had ever honored him whilst living. All Dublin, with a common impulse and a common sorrow, joined in this last tribute to the memory of a man whose life had been freely offered as a hecatomb upon the altar of his country.

Ever the same; from boyhood up to death;
　His race was crushed; his people were defamed;
He found the spark, and fanned it with his breath,
　And fed the fire, till all the Nation flamed !

He roused the farms; he made the serf a yeoman;
　He drilled his millions and he faced the foe;
But not with lead or steel he struck the foeman —
　Reason the sword, and Human Right the blow !

He fought for Home; but no land-limit bounded
　O'Connell's faith, nor curbed his sympathies;
All wrong to Liberty must be confounded,
　Till men were chainless as the winds and seas.

He fought for Faith; but with no narrow spirit;
　With ceaseless hand the bigot laws he smote;
One chart, he said, all mankind should inherit, —
　The right to worship and the right to vote.

Always the same; but yet a glinting prism :
　In wit, law, statecraft, still a master-hand;
An "uncrowned king," whose people's love was chrism;
　His title — LIBERATOR OF HIS LAND !

　　　　　　— From John Boyle O'Reilly's Centennial Ode.

APPENDIX.

PADRE VENTURA'S FUNERAL ORATION.

Simon magnus, qui liberavit gentem suam a perditione ; et in vita sua corroboravit templum. —ECCLUS. l. 1, 2.

FOR the Liberator of Ireland did not confine the benefits of liberty to Ireland alone, but he extended them to all Europe, to all the world. God does not create great men for the use of a single age and of a single people, but he gives them for the advantage of all nations and of all ages, and therefore it is that the name of genius belongs to all humanity. And more to make my ideas understood, it is necessary that I should point out to you an important doctrine, which alone can give us to understand the two principal epochs of modern history. The history of our century is written in that of the 16th. At that time men who united every infamy and every crime to unbounded talents, with the word *Reform* in their mouth, threw into confusion the whole Christian world ; and in our days men of the same character, with the word *Liberty* on their lips, have revolutionized the entire political world. But what !—is it then permitted to the genius of evil personified in man to.agitate and overturn the world at his will, and to drag it into the abysses of revolt and heresy? No, no, it is not so. The heresiarchs of the 16th century loved *reform* as little as the revolutionary spirits of our age love *liberty*. The reform, in the mouths of the former, the word liberty, in those of the latter, is only a pretext, a lie, and an imposture. With these magic words the one wished to destroy the Church, the other to annihilate liberty. All this is incontestible — proved by experience. Both have heaped up ruins on their way, and when masters of the field of battle the one showed themselves the most impious and the most debauched Christians, the others the most despotic and the most cruel statesmen. But how is it, then, and by what means have they been able to attain such a degree of power, to draw after them the half of Europe in their career of disorder and of error?

I will tell you.

As a river which at certain points of its course deposits and sweeps up mud, so time accumulates, at certain epochs, disorders and abuses. This phenomenon is common to all human societies; the best constituted, even the Church herself, so far as human elements enter into her constitution, is not exempt from it. Hence a sickliness, a weakness, a secret disturbance, seizes on the social body, which demands a prompt and efficacious remedy. Then, whoever, recommended by his daring, his knowledge, and his genius, presents himself to give the remedy, is sure to be received and listened to. Hence it was when the scandals and the abuses of the clergy, accumulated for ages past, made *reform* in the 16th century a universal want of the Church. Hence the injustice and tyranny of the politicians of past ages, transmitted to ours, made *liberty* a universal want of the State.

It is not, then, because the heresiarchs and the revolutionists had taught false doctrines that they obtained such great and fatal successes, but because they had divined the distance of the true and universal want of the Church and of the State, and that the offer to satisfy it, promising, preaching from their mouths that which they certainly had not in their hearts — the one *liberty*, the other *reform*. But in this rapid glance which I have cast over these two epochs, and on the causes of the terrible perturbations which followed them, we find indicated not only the philosophy of history, but, furthermore, the nature of their cure. How was the fearful torrent of heresy, which threatened to swallow up in its fetid waters all Europe, arrested in the 16th century? It was when the Church, taking up the very word of heresy, shouted in its tongue the cry of *reform*. Yes; hardly had the Church, by the mouth of the great Pontiff Paul III., and later in the immortal Council of Trent, articulated the great word of "*reformatio*," than that promise, that assurance of a true reform given by the Church, annihilated the false reform proclaimed and offered by heresy, and broke the redoubtable talisman with which it had deluded the nations. The Lutheran and Calvinist heresies, which already invaded the frontiers of France, for the future only existed as a political dogma in States whose constitutions and dynasties were linked with it; but as a theological doctrine, it ceased to make new ravages or fresh conquests.

In the same manner the revolution which threatened to make the circuit of the world, could not be checked in its devastating march over thrones and governments, until they themselves, adopting the same sentiment, cried out, also, "*Liberty.*" That word, I repeat it, is without doubt as lying in the mouth of demagogues, as formerly the word reform was in that of heretics ; but if, following the example given by the Church in respect to reform, the governments adopted the same policy in respect of liberty, they would make a truth of that word, which in the mouth of sedition is a lie ; if they hastened themselves to accomplish all that which they can promise without being able to give, or at least to secure ; if they showed themselves ready to satisfy a real evident want of a Christian people, and thus deliver them from the seductions of the demagogue ; if they would do with good will, and with just measure, that which they will be constrained to do without limit, and by an inexorable necessity ; if, I say, governments pursued this course, they would take away from the enemies of order the favor of the people ; and, as a wise reform undertaken by the Church disarmed heresy, so a wise liberty granted by governments will disarm revolution ; and this, let it be well understood, is the only method — the sure and infallible method — to suppress it.

Now, the first person to proclaim to put in practice this great doctrine, so simple, yet so profound, understood by few minds, professed by no party at the commencement of this century, was O'Connell.

When this great man appeared on the political scene of the United Kingdom, that is to say, on the greatest stage in the world, the best disposed were ruled by bad prejudices, but unfortunately too justifiable by the spectacles of so many thrones tottering or fallen. so many extinguished and banished dynasties, so many spoliations, such havoc, such ruin completed in the name and under the standard of liberty. That name which recalled such excesses caused all to tremble with affright. That flag, stained with so much blood, awakened no sentiments but those of horror. All the ideas of order were consequently identified with the idea of a senseless absolutism, and all notions of liberty confounded with a cruel Jacobinism. Liberty and rebellion, liberal and regicide, had become synonymous. Every attempt at political reform was considered as an attempt against the stability of the throne, and the tranquillity of the State. A fanatical despotism was regarded as the only refuge of order, the only safeguard of society.

Thus modern loyalty could not conceive order without despotism, as ancient philosophy could not comprehend society without slavery. But as soon as a man like O'Connell, the greatness of whose genius, the purity of whose intentions, whose fidelity to his principles, whose love for his people, and above all, the warmth and zeal of whose faith and the sincerity of whose belief could not be doubted —when he, in one word, the great citizen and the great Christian, was seen invoking and preaching liberty, and boldly proclaiming his liberal ideas, those words began to be less alarming to the delicate and timid ears of Catholicism, and of Irish loyalty. They soon became familiar to that people; they naturalized themselves among them, and with the ideas they represented were born the sentiments they inspired. Ultimately Ireland, under the guidance of O'Connell, became the most liberal and the most enthusiastic for liberty of any people in Europe. But for what description of liberty? Yes, the Irish nation, despite the calumnies and outrages of Anglican heresy, which, like the proud and cruel Jews, blasphemed and insulted the Victim whom they crucified, the Irish nation is a nation of heroes. Formed by the liberal and Christian theories of O'Connell, she has adopted true liberty—the daughter of religion—and has put herself on her guard against false liberty—the monstrous produce of rebellion. She has presented to the world the singular spectacle of a people bold in demanding their rights, and docile in all due and proper obedience—jealous of their independence, and the enemies of rebellion—passionately attached to their country, and faithful to their sovereign—proud enough to be above anything base or mean, and sufficiently wise not to insult power —sublime in resignation, and moderate in resistance—zealous in the acquirement and defence of their own rights, scrupulous in respecting those of others—uniting themselves with firmness and determination, but without tumult—complaining of their grievances, but without invective—crying out against injustice, but without transgressing the bounds of law.

Glory, then, and triumph to O'Connell for having thus reconciled liberty with order, independence with loyalty; for having formed into a principle of security and happiness the principle of the destruction of thrones, of the desolation and servitude of the people.

This great and powerful revolution in ideas and sentiments soon passed from Ireland into England, and from England quickly began to spread over Europe. The example of eight millions of men who, obeying the doctrines of their master—I would say of their prophet —is always agitated and always tranquil—always ready to learn their rights, and the most exact in the performance of their duties—always complaining of the injustice under which they suffer, yet always loyal —this example, I say, opened the eyes of all other people, and threw a clearer light upon the science of the government of States. Prejudices were dissipated; elevated minds then saw the possible alliance between liberty and obedience, between the most active and determined agitation and respect for the laws, between the rights of subjects and the security of princes, between the independence of the people and the stability of the throne. The word "liberty" began to be pronounced without repugnance — it was then seen that a man could be the friend of the people without being the enemy of kings, and could be liberal without being a Jacobin.

And where are to be found to-day the advocates of exclusive laws, the vile flatterers of power, the supporters of the doctrine of the ancient Pagans — the absolute supremacy of the State — a doctrine which abandons a whole Christian people to the arbitrary will or caprices of a few men who call themselves the State, and create a universal servitude? Where now are those who refuse to the fathers of families the liberty to bring up and educate their own children — who deny the right of the corporate body to regulate their own affairs — of a province to endeavor to become prosperous — of the Church to preach and conduct the people in the paths of truth and justice? Where now will you find the men whose hatred of the people is only equalled by the contempt with which they speak of them? Where, in fine, are the enemies of all liberty, the abettors of every description of servitude? They are to be found amongst the most fanatical demagogues, among the disciples of Jacobinism and rebellion. While on the other hand liberty knows no friends more sincere — no proselytes more constant, no defenders more intrepid, no advocates more generous, than among the most learned and intelligent supporters of monarchy — than among the heroes and martyrs of loyalty.

This change, so strange and so unexpected, has proceeded from Ireland — there was its cause and its principle. It was produced under the auspices and by the instruction of O'Connell. It is he who, by the example of his country, has modified or entirely altered the political ideas of a great part of Europe. It is he who has destroyed false liberty, and proved the safety and advantage of the liberty which is true. It is he who has unmasked the vile hypocrisy of the demagogues, and forever brought sedition into discredit.

It is true that this doctrine was that of the ancient apostles, of the first Christians, of the martyrs of the first times, who, in demanding their rights by their words and by their writings, by their protests before the tribunals, and their apologies to the emperors, and who, in loudly and perseveringly exclaiming against injustice, never ceased to be faithful subjects. But the fear of a worse situation — the fear of aggravating their grievances — had obscured, and, as it were, extinguished, this noble doctrine among persons who were faithful Christians, and, therefore, faithful subjects. A thought, a word of complaint against injustice, or of censure agaiust an abuse of power, appeared an offence in their eyes. But O'Connell revived this conciliatory doctrine ; he renewed it, spread it abroad, taught it by the power of his eloquence and the *eclat* of his success, and rendered it common and popular in Europe.

Yourselves, O Romans, who listen to me, you are yourselves a proof that the influence of the political apostleship of O'Connell has reached this fine portion of Europe.

It is true, and I say it with grief, there are yet perhaps among you some disciples of the revolutionary philosophy of the past century — some foolish pedants who labor to realize in Christian Rome the republican theories of Pagan Rome, and to apply to society the ideas of the college. It is true that there are some men to whom, as to the sanguinary men of '93, from whom they have descended, the words "liberty of the people" convey the dark and terrible thought of destruction, and the horrible sentiment of hatred of monarchy ; but these degenerate citizens (if the name of citizens can be given to men who meditate the ruin of their country) are very few in number. The people, the true Roman people, by their spirit of order, of obedience, of love for their sovereign, become the admiration of Europe and of the world, regard with horror these dark artisans of rebellion, and compel them to conceal themselves and their doctrines of disorder and blood. The exquisite good sense of the people will not permit them to be caught by their snares or hypocrisy. The people comprehend liberty only in connection with order ; they do not separate the desire of their own well-being from their obedience and fidelity to their sovereign. This people, so good and intelligent, have carried into perfection the doctrine that O'Connell has made to be so esteemed throughout Europe. To the most scrupulous legality they have joined the enthusiasm of love. They demand through the means of an affectionate agitation, as Ireland demanded by means of a legal agitation, the reform of abuses which, through the effect of time and of the passions, as it happens always and everywhere, have altered the nature of the ancient constitution of the States of the Church, in which order and liberty are so well reconciled. And as it is impossible that the language of a people who loves him should not be heard by a Pontiff full of affections for his people, since it is impossible that hearts which bear such sincere love towards one another should not end by fully under-

standing one another.   O Rome! what glory do you prepare for
yourself if you properly appreciate your situation, if you are not
stopped in your career, if you are not deceived, if you are not betrayed!   What a fine page you will add to your history!   A page in
which posterity will be astonished to read the conquest you made of a
wise and true liberty through the means of love alone!

I say of true liberty, for as one description of gold is true and another is false, so there is a true and a false liberty.   Oh! how beautiful is the one!   Oh! how hideous is the other!   How majestic is the
one!   How terrible is the other!   How much the one breathes of
grace and peace!   How much the other inspires fear and horror!
The one has ornamented its head with the splendid halo of order—
the other has covered it with the bloody cap of anarchy!   The one
holds in its hand the olive branch of peace—the other the torch of
discord!   The one is clothed with the white robe of innocence—the
other is enveloped in the dark mantle of crime, soiled with blood!
The one is the support of thrones—the other is their ruin!   The one
is the glory and felicity of the people—the other is its disgrace and
scourge!   The one is vomited from hell, like the poisoned breath of
the spirit of darkness—the other descends from heaven, like a sweet
incarnation of the Spirit of God!   *Ubi spiritus Domini ibi libertas!*

For this reason be well convinced of it, my dear brethren, this true
liberty never proceeds from the secret orgies of rebellion, but from
the sanctuary.   It has sprung forth, not under the doctrines of philosophy, but under those of religion.   Liberty is the peaceful radiation
of truth, as slavery is the fatal firebrand of error.   Liberty can only
be obtained pure and beneficent through the Church, in which alone
is found pure and unmixed truth.   As it is the Church which has sustained the metaphysical liberty of the soul against the pretended phil-
osophers and heretics who attacked it; as it is the Church which has
created domestic liberty, in elevating woman to the dignity of her husband, and in consecrating the rights of children; as it is the Church
which has created civil liberty in abolishing slavery and the sale of
human beings among Christians; in like manner the Church alone is
able to proclaim political liberty, in fixing the true and just limits of
obedience and of the commandment—the true and just rights—the
true and just duties of the people and of the governing powers.
Loyalty, then, obedience, confidence, love for the true religion, in imi-
tation of the great man whose loss we deplore, who not only sought
the aid of religion to obtain true liberty for his people—*liberavit gentem suam a perditione*—but employed that liberty to secure the tri-

umph of religion — *corroboravit templum.* This we shall see more fully in the Second Part of our discourse.

As there is a true greatness, the daughter of virtue and merit, there is also a false greatness, the daughter of the favor and caprice of those who bestow it, or of the prejudice and illusion which believe in it, or of the adulation, the intrigue, and the meanness which seek after it.

And as true greatness varies in its principle, it varies also in its duration. False greatness is scarcely sufficient to distinguish or raise in any degree the person who is clothed with it, as with a mantle badly adjusted. It perishes with him, and even frequently before him. True greatness, on the contrary, not only ennobles an individual, but an entire family ; like a pure light, it is reflected upon the whole of a long posterity, and the most brilliant emblems transmit the glory of it to the most distant ages.

It is, therefore, that in the magnificent device of the O'Connell family we read these fine words : The eye of O'Connell is the salvation of Ireland — *salus Hiberniæ oculus O'Connell.*

This magnificent device is not only the testimony of the past glories of that illustrious family, but it has been as a prophecy of its future glories, which has had its fulfilment in Daniel O'Connell, for the vigilant and penetrating eye of O'Connell has saved Ireland in our days. *Salus Hiberniæ oculus O'Connell.* A citizen and a Christian, he sought the aid of religion to conquer the liberty of his country, as I have already shown ; and as a Christian and a citizen he made use of liberty to effect the triumph of religion, as I shall demonstrate to you to-day. Hence he has been great from true greatness, and there can be properly applied to him the praise conveyed in the Scripture language — *Simon magnus, qui liberavit gentem suam a perditione ; et in vita sua corroboravit templum.*

I will not to-day, dear Romans, ask your attention, your kindness, or indulgence, for you have already extended them to me in the most flattering manner. I am in possession of them, and it only remains for me to profit by them, to thank you affectionately, and to begin.

PART SECOND.

Like a legitimate sovereign, Truth has need but of herself alone ; she has but to reveal herself in order to secure adhesion and homage, and reign in the world of mind and intellect. On the contrary, like a usurping tyrant, Error can only impose on the minds of men, and preserve the empire thus gained by means of violence and fraud.

For this reason, while heresy always begins by attaching itself to the great, in order to be afterwards able, through the aid of their passions and the might of their power, to govern the people, the Catholic doctrine, on the contrary, begins by announcing itself to the people alone, after which it deigns to admit the great also amongst its followers, but always on the condition that they shall come with the people to eat at the table and drink of the cup of Christian equality, clothed in garments of humility. While heresy is always on its knees at the feet of the throne, begging a rag of purple to cover itself, and a sword to defend itself, the Catholic doctrine, religiously proud of its divine origin, presents itself standing before the thrones, only to preach the utmost unwelcome truths and the hardest duties. Finally, while the heretical or schismatical churches go about everywhere craving the protection of man, the true Church asks from God only liberty. *Ut ecclesia tua secura tibi serviat libertate.*

From this it follows, as I have shown elsewhere, that liberty of conscience, which, in an absolute sense, signifies indifference, atheism, impiety, denial of all revelation, of all positive religion, of every rule of faith and conduct, yet, in its relative sense — that is, in its relation to the civil power, which has not received from God the mission to preach and to interpret the gospel — is a Catholic principle that the Church has professed, taught, defended, and which she never could renounce without abdicating her divine mission, without destroying herself — it is a necessary condition of her existence and of her propagation.

But at the end of the last century the Catholic Church saw her Pontiffs imprisoned, her ministers dispersed, her altars destroyed, her temples profaned, her holy virgins violated, her property plundered, her cloisters pulled down, her doctrines discredited and mutilated — her laws, her worship, her institutions abrogated — all in the name of, and by the apostles of, liberty — and, as at that mournful epoch liberty always went hand in hand with blasphemy and sacrilege, the Church began to consider it as the necessary and irreconcilable enemy of true religion; and the faithful could not hear its name without trembling, and thought they could not pronounce it without committing a crime.

On the other hand, as at the same epoch the altar had fallen under the blows of the same axe which had demolished the throne, the idea that they could only be raised together prevailed ; on this account the *"throne and the altar"* inspired a common interest, and were united in the minds, hearts, and mouths of all honest, well-disposed men ;

and as sad experience had proved that the throne could do nothing without the altar, the opinion began to prevail that the altar was powerless without the throne. Therefore the throne was looked upon not only as the necessary support of political order, but of religious order also.

Those ideas had become general in Europe. The faithful directed their eyes not only to Catholic thrones, but to Protestant thrones too. The Catholics of Ireland themselves expected, from the liberality of the Protestant Crown of England, the emancipation of their consciences and religion. All their hopes rested upon a throne which was constitutionally the enemy of their faith.

But that was to make of divine religion a human institution, which is able to do nothing without the support of man. That was to abandon faith, morality, worship, the Church itself, to the arbitrary will of the civil power, which, under the pretext of being their protector, would not have failed to make itself her Pontiff (it has been seen that the Church has had more cause to complain of her protectors than of her persecutors). That was to make the faith of the people depend upon the good or bad disposition of the prince — to consecrate, as politically legitimate, all the systems of error, even atheism, and to consent to the hardest and most insupportable of all servitudes, the servitude of conscience. In fine, that was to be willing to destroy even the last vestige of human dignity.

How necessary was it to make the people feel that the civil power which extends its hand to religion, apparently for the purpose of protecting it, governs it, and in governing injures and degrades it, and that true religion can exist only under the shadow and protection of liberty.

But, great God ! to destroy a prejudice that a complication of terrible circumstances had deeply engraven in the minds of the wisest — which was "that liberty is the enemy of religion;" to calm the apprehensions, the fears, the terrors, but to legitimate, which the word liberty had awakened in the hearts of the most religious, the most pious, to lead a people as Catholic as the Irish to seek in liberty the triumph of Catholicism, while in the rest of Europe that Catholicism had been destroyed or disfigured under the blows of liberty. What a task ! what an enterprise ! An entire generation of apostolic men would not have seemed sufficient to succeed, and yet a single man, a single layman, O'Connell alone, has done it ! His genius was sufficient to conceive, his courage to undertake, his constancy and power to accomplish it !

With what prudence, with what discretion, not to alarm prejudices but too reasonable, sentiments but too delicate, did he not apply himself at first in the public meetings, and at private reunions, to persuade the people and the clergy that there was nothing advantageous for the Catholic religion to be expected from the spontaneous liberality of the Protestant government; that religious emancipation could only be obtained through the means of, and in conjunction with, political emancipation; that the independence of the Catholic Church in Ireland should be a peaceable and legal conqnest made by the people, and not a gratuitous concession from the government; and that liberty was the only means which remained to them to secure the triumph of religion. He often said that he found nothing more difficult than to persuade the clergy that religion could only be victorious by the aid of liberty.

There were not wanting, at the beginning, some men of a weak piety or a malignant hypocrisy, who, on hearing language so novel in the mouth of young O'Connell, permitted themselves to entertain jealousy or mistrust, and to traduce him before the tribunal of public opinion, as being a man without discretion, led astray by the philosophy of the eighteenth century, or as a dangerous enemy, engaged to sow in Ireland the anarchial doctrines of the French revolution. But his horror of bloodshed, his love of legality, the strength of his convictions, and above all, his great and sincere zeal for religion, soon dissipated all these suspicions, all these calumnies. His pure and upright intentions were soon discovered, his doctrines understood and relished, his designs approved and applauded.

Such was the magical effect of his language, conduct, and acts, that in the space of five years he succeeded in implanting his mind entire in the heart of Ireland, in transforming Ireland into his own image. He brought over to his ideas and opinions not only the Catholics in a body, but a great number of Protestants — not only laymen, but ecclesiastics — not only the men, but even the women — not only in Ireland, but in England also; and he established the religious liberty association, in which all honest men, all noble hearts, all generous minds, of all churches and of all opinions, found themselves united and associated for the same object, to obtain by their common efforts liberty of conscience, and to effect the triumph of their own religion by means of liberty.

But the circumstance by which he exhibited, in the most striking manner, the nobleness of his Catholic liberal, and liberally Catholic, soul, was the great affair of the *Veto;* of that attempt of the Protestant government of England to interfere in the appointment of the Catholic bishops of Ireland. He displayed in that discussion the learning of a professor, the zeal of an apostle, the courage of a hero, and, in the midst of all the pain and trouble he had to undergo, the patience of a martyr.

In the eyes of some, the object of England did not seem to have a dangerous tendency. Of the three candidates for a vacant see, whom the clergy of Ireland presented, as they do still, to the Pontiff, that he might appoint from among them the new bishop, the English government wished to have the power to exclude one. The advantages that it promised for this concession was great, seducing, capable of dazzling the most clear-sighted, and deceiving the most pious. Those advantages were, the emancipation, or the religious and political liberty of all the Catholics in the United Kingdom, and the endowment of the Irish Church. The people already began to smile upon a proposition which appeared to them as the termination of three centuries of cruel persecution. A part of the clergy, anxious to see the dignity of religion maintained, were apparently not far removed from a willingness to accept a fixed and certain endowment, which would relieve them from the hard condition of a life sustained by alms and beggary. The bishops themselves, assembled in Synod, had at first unanimously rejected the present offered by the hands of these modern Ulysses (*greca manu*), as being directed against the independence and discipline of the Church, but were afterwards divided on the question. Some bishops, deceived by fallacious promises and affected adulation, had expressed their approval of the proposition of the government, an approval which they at a later period withdrew, ashamed and grieved at having ever given it. The English Catholics, seeing, in the insidious bill proposed by the government, only an important concession which would put an end to their political degradation and open the doors of the legislature to them, flung themselves into the party of the government with a zeal so deplorable that they styled the opposition of the Irish bishops as imprudent temerity, and expelled from the Catholic committee a celebrated prelate, the only member of the English Catholic clergy who, in an eloquent petition addressed to the legislature, combated the government measure with the zeal and doctrinal learning of an Athanasius. Rome, even in this great struggle, appeared to incline towards the enemies of the Irish Church; as the poor Irish said in their native simplicity — " Rome, too, it appears, is becoming *Orange*." Mgr. Quarantoleo, President of Rome during the captivity of the immortal Pius VII., had, by a rescript, given his assent to the insidious propositions of the English government, which were calculated to prove so fatal to the liberty of the Church. Orangeism, encouraged by this supposed concession from Rome, became more insolent; the country, torn by intestine divisions, abandoned by the English Catholics and its defenders in Rome, and left wholly unsupported, was no longer able to resist the compact phalanx of English heresy. The most courageous are fatigued in an unequal struggle, which offers no probable chance of success. Discouragement is in every mind, and coldness in every heart.

Oh, unfortunate Church! Behold! to all thy misfortunes is about to be added the greatest, the most humiliating of any, — the loss of that religious independence which thy generous children purchased by three centuries of sufferings, and by a bloody martyrdom! But no; fear nothing; there is O'Connell, whom Providence has raised up, like a new Judas Maccabeus, to watch over the defence of the Church. O'Connell will justify now again the truth of the words on his noble escutcheon. The eye of O'Connell is the salvation of Ireland. *Salus Hibernæ O'Connell.*

Oh, soul truly great! So many united difficulties, far from daunting thy courage, inflamed it; in the midst of the general despair, he alone despaired not; in the midst of the fears of all upon the conduct of Rome, he alone is full of confidence in the wisdom of Rome. Every means, every support in combatting a powerful enemy is wanting to him, yet he alone dares to engage in the combat, as a man certain of victory!

Behold him, then, addressing himself to the nation, and pointing out the snares that were prepared for it; he united the clergy and laity in great meetings; he demonstrated to them, with the learning and knowledge of a theologian, and the experience of a legist, how a heretical power would certainly abuse this concession demanded from the Church, as certain Catholic powers had sometimes abused similar concessions. He comments on the bill, and exposes the crafty and insidious designs of those who proposed it. He examines the promises made, and demonstrates their vanity, falseness, and futility. He unveils the intentions and objects of the ministry, and reminds the country of the treaty of Limerick, which had been so infamously and faithlessly violated by England. He speaks of the English Catholics to humiliate them; he does not forget, but stigmatizes the courtier priests.

Further, he at the same time encouraged the clergy, and animated the people; aroused the zeal and vigilance of the bishops, and sustained their courage; sent ten deputies to England, to implore the assistance and support of the society of the friends of religious liberty. He caused two bishops to set out with all speed for Rome, to lay at the feet of the Sovereign Pontiff, who had returned from a glorious exile, a memorial in the name of the Catholics of Ireland, in which he demonstrated with the irresistible force of reason, the evils which the admission of the *Veto* would bring upon the Church of Ireland. At every time, on all occasions, in public and in private, he did not cease to repeat — " We shall now, as ever, reject every favor which must be purchased by the sacrifice of our religion, and of our liberty."

What at length does he obtain by all these efforts of his eloquence, activity, and zeal ? He obtains the most complete and triumphant success. The bishops, assembled in synod, " declare that the clergy of Ireland will not cease to oppose, by every canonical and constitutional means, all interference of the temporal power in the affairs of religion." The entire nation rejects the fraudulent offers of Anglicanism ; all the public journals are filled with protests, in which the people vow " that every attempt to weaken the Church of Ireland shall be vain, and that despite of the government, the parliament, the Orangemen, and the Quarantollists, Ireland will ever maintain, in all its purity, the faith of its protector, St. Patrick." The same sentiments are officially expressed to the government, in the name of the clergy and Irish people, in the following declaration : " The political and religious liberty of Ireland being the end towards which the Catholic people direct their efforts, we believe that we would degrade ourselves, if, in return for the advantages you offer us, we agreed to a condition which would increase the power of the members of the government to the detriment of the discipline of our Church." And finally, the Sovereign Pontiff himself, justifying the confidence which O'Connell had placed in the wisdom of the Holy Apostolical See, disavows the document of Quarantollo.

In vain the cowardly and obstinate partisans of the royal concessions, — frequently more dangerous than open, declared adversaries, seeking to justify their shameful apostasy from the cause of the Church, — opposed its generous champion, and said that to expect Protestant England would grant emancipation, without concessions, was temerity and folly. O'Connell replied, " To effect a reconciliation I am ready to do anything, except to immolate the religion of my country and of my fathers." And the people, adopting his sentiments, said, " We love civil liberty, but we love our religion more. If it were necessary to die to obtain our civil liberty, we are ready to

give up our lives, but not to abandon our faith.   It is better to be
Catholics and slaves than Protestants and freemen.   Martyrdom is not
a new thing to us.   Three   hundred   years of   torture   have already
passed over our heads.   We are content that our chains shall weigh
still heavier upon us rather than consent to the smallest alteration in
the discipline of our Church."

To those who sought to weaken the firmness and constancy of the
clergy, by holding out the prospect of a rich endowment, which would
relieve them from the hard necessity of begging their bread, that noble
clergy did not hesitate to reply: "Chains, even though they are of
gold, are chains still; a poor liberty is preferable to an opulent
slavery.   Honor can exist with poverty, but infamy is the inseparable
companion of voluntary servitude.   Poor priests, we are more respected than the rich prebendaries of heresy.   The Church does not
require aid to live well, but that she be left free to do well; she does
not seek or require riches, but liberty."

Now the sentiments so noble, and, at the same time, so natural, and
so deeply felt by the clergy and the people of Ireland were due to the
preponderating influence of O'Connell, the invincible superiority of
his genius, the power of his speeches, and of his teaching, the example of his courage, of his magnanimity, and his disinterestedness; he
concentrated and gave life to these sentiments, and opened to them a
vast field where they would shine in all their magnificence, in all their
splendor, for the glory of the Catholic faith, which alone had the all-
enlivening energy to create them.   When was there ever offered to
view in a mercenary and selfish generation, in the midst of a money-
hunting nation, a more beautiful spectacle than that which this people,
whom O'Connell had imbued with his spirit — which this people,
loaded with misery, wanting everything, yet always preferring to deprive themselves of their last morsel for the support of the altar and
its ministers, rather than receive assistance from heresy, presented!
What a glorious contest between an opulent government which offers,
and a begging people which refuses, between England which promises
to give everything, and Ireland which will receive nothing, in the
dread of the slightest injury being inflicted on her religion.

Such unbounded self-denial, such noble heroism, must necessarily
triumph; as Ireland did not sacrifice her spiritual gifts for earthly advantages she must obtain terrestrial blessings whilst preserving her
heavenly gifts.   For the Incarnate Truth has solemnly promised that
the people who seek before all things the kingdom of God and his
justice, that is to say, the triumph of the true religion, shall preserve

that holy religion, and, in addition, shall obtain all temporal blessings. "*Queriti primum regnum Dei et justitiam ejus et hæc omnia adjicientur vobis*" (St. Matt.). Therefore it was the Liberator never ceased exhorting his people: Fear nothing; never relax. Patience and perseverance, and you shall have the glory of winning your liberty without sacrificing a jot of the religion of your forefathers.

Never was human prediction more literally fulfilled. When the Protestant government saw the noble firmness, the invincible perseverance of Catholic Ireland, it renounced forever the expectation of carrying the Veto, which, during six years, it had so uselessly endeavored to promote by all the threats and promises, stratagems and open violences it could use. The Church of Ireland still maintained its glorious poverty, and its still more glorious independence of the civil power as to the nomination of its bishops. For as beauty is the most charming ornament of a chaste spouse, so the true riches of a Catholic nation is its religious independence.

After six years of a new agitation, of efforts, of contests, of suffering of agony, Ireland, led by her Liberator, obtained her emancipation, her civil liberty, without any humiliating conditions, and, as O'Connell had prophecied, *without the sacrifice of an atom of religious principle.*

O, you of childish ignorance and of little faith, who, governed by a fatal prejudice, following a worldly policy in the affairs of religion, require of the sentinels of Israel to become as dumb dogs who bark not at the approach of the wolf — ye who impose on the noble combatants of the faith a silence so agreeable to those who exercise an usurping and destructive policy towards the Church which ye ought yourselves to condemn — ye who call remonstrances imprudent; protestations impertinent, the zeal of defenders of the Church, which you ought to encourage, sustain, and recompence, fanaticism; and all this is to obtain some temporal advantage, some temporal support for the Church, of which it has no need; ah! reflect that God owes it to Himself to baffle your Jewish calculations! Of you it will be said as was said of the Jews: Because they have preferred temporal advantages to their eternal welfare, they shall löse both — "*Temporalia amittere timuerunt et vitam æternam non cogitaverunt; et sic utramque amisserunt*" (St. Augustine). Learn ye from the noble and generous policy which O'Connell made use of for the triumph of the Irish Church, that it is not by the sacrifice of ecclesiastical independence that you conquer and restrain the civil power within due limits, but by resisting with firmness, and in a legal manner, its unjust pretentions; know this, and let your hearts be inaccessible to fear.

These victories which O'Connell secured by the means of liberty to the true Church were not confined to Ireland ; they had a powerful echo, they produced wonderful effects in the rest of the world. In order to make you understand this vast whole, it is necessary for me to raise your thoughts to the sanctuary of the designs of God, in so far as it is given to us, wretched mortals, to penetrate them.

The greatest, the most wonderful, the most providential history of the modern world was not the separation of the States of America from their dependence on Europe, nor the French Revolution, nor the Empire, but the use which God has made, in His sovereign rule, of the most inscrutable means and the most opposing causes for the propagation of the Gospel and the glory of His Church.

Now the chief of these means, visibly co-ordained by God for so sublime and so holy an end, is the mercantile enterprise of England. She seems to extend the limits of the globe in searching for an outlet for her manufactures ; but God makes use of this indefatigable activity of the devouring avarice of this people to spread over the world these celestial gifts of His mercy, grace, and truth. England has occupied all the important positions of the earth with the view of enlarging and establishing everywhere the empire of the British Lion. But God, by this means, provides an easy access for the ministers of His Gospel, who are everywhere to establish the empire of the cross. Already the afflicted sons of Erin, whom intolerance and heretical tyranny have obliged to emigrate, spread over, dispersed on all points of the globe, in every English colony, on the immense continent of Oceanica, have everywhere carried the precious seeds and the glorious confession of their faith ; and thus, by these unexpected means, the persecuting spirit, the cruel bigotry of heresy has, in opposition to its own wishes, lent its hand to the foundation of more new bishoprics in the world, than had heretofore existed in Europe.

But the Irish Catholic, prostrated and groaning under the brutal yoke which kept him in a state of slavery, a serf, he was scarcely able to achieve victory for the truth of his religion in the face of the reigning religion of cruel masters. It was then necessary, for the completion of the designs for which Providence seemed to have destined the Irish nation, that it should burst the fetters of its political slavery, and by that means secure the liberty and religious independence of its faith.

Now, it was precisely this which the penetrating genius of O'Connell saw and understood. For, very different from other men known to fame, and who only hold their position from the idle prejudices and adulation of the day, and who are doomed to their original nothingness when their day has passed, O'Connell is always greater than he appears. His intentions, his objects, are more sublime and more astonishing than his acts. It is only through some fugitive expressions of O'Connell, through his unheard-of zeal, and the perseverance unrivalled in the history of true patriotism, which he displayed to achieve the liberty of his country, that it has begun to be understood that he regarded the people of Ireland as a missionary people, a chosen people, selected by God for the eternal salvation of a number of nations. We can now comprehend that O'Connell, in struggling for the emancipation of Ireland, did not regard it as an ordinary question of human policy, but as a measure of co-operation with one of the greatest designs of the mercy of God, that he did not look upon himself simply as an Irishman, but as the servant and instrument of God in His Church.

In proportion, then, as the proofs of the noble destiny of Ireland, from the glory of religion throughout the universe, developed themselves and became manifest, O'Connell was more and more impressed with the religious character of the mission he had received from God to enfranchise and elevate his country. His acts became more daring, his intentions more holy. He considered the *Isle of Saints* as *saintly*, not only because it was covered with the bones, and moistened with the blood, of millions of martyrs, but still more, because it was destined to carry the mission of holiness over the entire globe. Ah! when he called it " the gem of the sea, the flower of the earth " — when he apostrophized it with the most tender epithets, the most loving expressions, it was not for the salubrity of its climate, the fertility of its soil, the charms of its picturesque landscapes, the strength, the beauty, the high-mindedness of its inhabitants, it was because he looked on that noble nation, which had been stigmatized as barbarous and turbulent, as the depository of the treasures of God, of truth and of grace ; as clothed with the dignity of the mission of God ; called to give proof of its fruitfulness, which had been acquired, like that of the ancient Roman Church, by three centuries of martyrdom and of blood, and to multiply the generation of the children of God over the world. Hence it was he disciplined the people with such patience, hence he defended it with such courage, hence he gave himself up, he immolated himself for it with such eagerness, with such joy ; hence it was he thought no effort, no sacrifice, too great for Ireland ; as a mother rears with the greatest care, watches over with the most jealous anxiiety, cherishes and caresses with a tenderness mixed with respect, the son whom she knows is destined one day to reign.

The benediction of God awaited on these noble designs, these holy transports, which his grace had caused to spring up in the bosom of his servant.   O'Connell saw the civil liberty which he had predicted and conquered for his country, become a means of triumph for religion all over the universe.

Thanks to the heroic efforts of Ireland, civil and religious liberty were granted to all the Catholic subjects of the Crown of England. From that moment the Catholic religion, hitherto regarded by England with supreme contempt, as the religion of slaves, and, under the name of *Popery*, delivered over to every species of insult, acquired importance, strength, and dignity.   Full of a holy pride, it mounts the palaces of the great, it penetrates into parliament, enters the court, sits in the secret councils of royalty, and compels the haughty policy, which heretofore scarcely acknowledged its existence, to treat with it on equal terms, nay almost to acknowledge its superiority.   See further how that religion, heretofore looked upon as the religion of the igno-rant, of the feeble-minded, of the populace, and of woman, enters the Universities of Oxford and Cambridge, makes proselytes amongst their most distinguished members by these Catholic traditions which heresy could not entirely destroy, and counts amongst its humble dis-ciples the noblest minds, men the most educated and most profoundly acquainted with the knowledge of religion, the most exalted souls, the most distinguished characters.

Yes, the time is passed for insulting a religion which, without any assistance from human power, and despite of its efforts, strong by its liberty and divine charms alone, attracts great souls by the ardor of its sanctity, causes them to attach themselves to it, even by the sacrifice of the most lucrative and brilliant positions, and to embrace poverty, from the desire to possess the truth.

Admirable circumstance !   The Catholic religion, which, deprived of its civil rights, appeared but as a slave, when made free by the genius of O'Connell, appeared as a Queen.   Liberty has caused its virtue and truth to be better known and appreciated.   To become a Catholic is no longer, even in the eyes of English Protestants, to de-grade one's self; it is, on the contrary, to elevate and honor a man in the general opinion.   The conquests which the Catholic faith never ceases to make in the most distinguished classes of society provoke a sentiment of envy, not of contempt.   Those who still remain in the ranks of heresy look upon themselves with shame and chagrin ; but they no longer exhibit their wrath against those who leave them. They no longer dare to blame the Anglican who becomes a Papist; they rather grieve that they have not the courage to follow his example.

If sarcasms, invectives, and slander yet sometimes issue from the mouths of bigoted fanatics, as vile by their sentiments as by their birth, the high aristocracy, true knowledge, good faith, the philosophy which reflects, the statesman who respects himself, use towards the Catholic Church and its august chief only expressions of respect, admiration and praise. The roofs of Westminster resound each day with the generous accents which render homage to Catholic truth, and treat as they deserve the worn out and henceforth insupportable insolences of the old sectaries. Now, in considering the progress of these things, how can we doubt the truth of a prophecy which a great genius (Count de Maistre) made at the commencement of this century: " That before it was ended, Mass would be celebrated in St. Paul's, London." But whenever the Mass is celebrated in St. Paul's, who can say in how many other churches of the vast dominions of England it will be celebrated on the same day? The British Crown rules over about eighty millions of subjects in different parts of the world. It is to that enormous mass of men that O'Connell has opened the doors of the true Church, and to whom he has forever insured liberty and safety, in becoming Catholics, by demanding and obtaining liberty for Ireland! Who can measure the extent of the importance of such success? Had O'Connell never done anything else, this alone would suffice to insure him an eminent place, a particular glory in the annals of Catholic apostleship.

See the precious results that the Catholic faith, emancipated in the mother country, produces in all the dependencies of that vast empire. Wherever the flag of Great Britain floats, the faith of Ireland, under the protection of liberty, displays a force and a majesty that nothing can resist. The Irish soldier, the priest, the Irish missionary, are the objects of particular respect from those who command in those places in the name of England. The Catholic has no longer any enemies but the Methodists, a sect in which are united and concentrated all the mean sentiments, all the cruel instincts of heresy. The other sects feel the superiority of the Catholic faith in converting and civilizing the nations, and render it the homage which is justly due to it. The Church becomes free, continually fortifies and strengthens itself in these regions, extends itself, and triumphs there.

This revolution, the greatest effected in the world, next to that wrought by Christianity—this revolution, so precious by its princi-ples, its means and results, God has brought about by the hand of a single man. Daniel O'Connell is, after God, the man to whom be-longs this glory!

What shall I say of the effects the emancipation of Ireland has pro-duced upon English Protestantism? A prediction was made by the most profound politicians of Great Britain, while the cause of eman-cipation was being pleaded, and that was, that the emancipation of the Catholic Church would be the destruction of Protestantism. This prophecy tends to its accomplishment with astonishing rapidity. Protestantism exists only by exclusive laws; it feels itself in safety only under the shadow of intolerance and tyranny. Deprived of these frightful auxiliaries, abandoned to its own weakness, vitiated by error, it can no longer sustain itself.

It is on that account that expiring Orangeism, in the convulsive throes of its agony, turns its uneasy looks to the throne, and with loud cries implores the repeal of the emancipation bill; it is there-fore that bigoted Anglicanism fears to grant to Ireland the comple-ment of her liberty; it is therefore that the Protestant Universities, those citadels of error, founded, as it is said, to save and protect the principle of free inquiry, the first basis of Protestanism, punish, by ex-clusion and ostracism, the noble courage of him who, by the aid of free inquiry, is convinced, believes, and confesses that the Catholic is the only true religion. O'Connell, then, by emancipating the Cath-olic Church in Great Britian, has, by that act alone, given to English Protestantism a blow from which it cannot recover. This horrible scandal of Christian royalty, this monstrous produce of the spirit of luxury, united to the spirit of cupidity and pride, is upon the point of expiring, and it is the powerful arm of O'Connell which has pierced it to the heart with the sword of liberty.

But English Protestantism is united by secret bonds to Swiss and German Protestantism; it is this alliance that constitutes their strength, their authority, and their hope. England is at the head of Protestantism, as France is at the head of Catholicism, in the whole universe. When, therefore, our apostle has given Protestantism its death-blow in England, he has prepared its fall in the world.

These triumphs, however, are not the only ones that O'Connell has given the Church through the means of liberty. The principle of the independence of religion in regard to the civil power has been, in our days, proclaimed for the first time by the irreligious philosophy of the last century, with the infernal intention of injuring the true Church.

This philosophy, entertaining the fatal idea that the Catholic Church is an institution purely human, which has neither life nor strength of itself, and which maintains itself only by the aid of thrones, believes that if the doctrine of the independence of religion, or of the separation of the Church from the State, came to prevail, the Church, deprived of the assistance of the State, and attacked by knowledge, and all the human passions, must infallibly fall. But, O! calculations as foolish as impious! O! admirable economy of the Providence of God over His Church! Behold the eighteen centuries during which the Church has declared to the civil power that it had no jurisdiction over conscience of faith; behold the eighteen centuries which it has struggled against power for its independence and liberty. Unbelief, then, in preaching the same doctrine, has spoken the language of the Church, has employed its eloquence in defending her, while it foolishly thought it was attacking her; it has been divinely inspired; it has, without comprehending them, forwarded the designs of God relative to the Church. Balaam's ass has spoken the language of intelligence; the imposter filled with the spirit of hell, has raised his voice for the interests of heaven; Caiphas has prophesied; Judas has preached the Gospel; the enemies of the Church have proved themselves the true necessity of the Church, the true principle to which is attached the success of her regenerating power, her propagation, her triumph!

It is known, however, in what manner the unbelieving philosophy, when it was able to do it, put in practice this doctrine of the liberty of conscience that it had itself proclaimed. It is known how, under its power, it was permitted to each to be a Jansenist, schismatic, heretic, atheist, or deist; but misfortune to him who, considering this liberty of conscience seriously, resolved to become a Catholic; the guillotine was permanently erected, the executioner was always at his post, to do justice to that man! See, then, the reason why the doctrine of liberty of conscience excited the horror of some, the suspicions of others, and counted among its partisans only the unbelieving and the indifferent. But when O Connell had taken it under his patronage; when he converted it into truth, where it was but a horrible falsehood; when he had proclaimed it with his powerful voice, and encircled with the *prestige* of his authority; when he professed it with so much sincerity, carried it into practice with such success, and purified it in a manner from the stains with which the lips of impiety had profaned it, in pronouncing its name; when, in fine, he had baptized it, sanctified it, and made it serve to secure the triumph of the true religion in his country, soon his doctrine, which up to that had remained hidden in some obscure corners of France and Germany, resounded, like a sonorous echo, throughout the whole of Europe; it has gained the universities, it has entered into the cabinets, it has penetrated the sanctuary, and, sad intelligence for heresy and error alone, it has produced or prepared the most brilliant triumphs for the truth.

In effect, in presence of this doctrine, and conseqnently of free discussion in matters of religion, in the country where true religion finds itself surrounded by erroneous sects, all the new religious sects, born of pride and voluptuousness, like the worms of corruption, die, so to speak, in being born; and whilst heresy and unbelief from day to day see their ranks thinned, Catholic truth, coming out of the struggle stronger and more free of life, each day sees the number of her disciples doubled. She alone profits by liberty, under whose assaults it was feared she would fall. It can, therefore, with more reason, be said of liberty what was said of knowledge, — that it is a dissolvent which decomposes all metals except gold. So, in effect, liberty dissolves and pulverizes all religions except the true one. And if that was not certain, if that was not evident, if liberty, which is one of the greatest attributes of God, did not agree with the religion of God, you would not hear me speak its praise with so much confidence from this sacred pulpit, which should only defend what is true, holy, and divine.

It is with this weapon in his hand that German rationalism boldly refuses to submit to the official worship in Prussia, and that, denying to the civil powers the right to impose symbols and interpret them, it destroys the last ramparts of Luther's edifice, and labors for the entire liberty of the Catholics. It is with this weapon that the democracy of Geneva, combatting the intolerant pretensions, the doctrinal jurisdiction of the ministers of heresy, overthrow the impiety of Calvin in the metropolis of its empire, and prepares the liberty of Catholicism. It is with this weapon that European diplomacy saps Mussulman intolerance at Constantinople — gloomy Paganism in China, and opens the doors of these countries to the preaching of the Gospel. It is with this weapon, in fine, that the faithful are strong, and to which the bishops and priests of the Catholic Church have recourse in Spain, Portugal, France, Belgium, Holland, and. many parts of Germany. It is this weapon that they wield to-day, with a confidence equal to the fear it inspired at first to obtain the liberty which the Church requires, and which a hypocritical liberalism refuses it. They stop the civil power in its career, attempting to forge new chains for the Church, and fearing to break the old. Yes; the cause of true religion, placed by O'Connell upon the soil of liberty, agitated in the open day of publicity, cannot perish; its rights cannot be contested; its legitimate progress, its conquests, can no longer be limited or hindered.

It is therefore in vain that certain governments flatter themselves that they will be still allowed to rule the Church, or in the Church. Since the great apostleship of O'Connell has made the independence of religion in regard to the civil power a universal dogma; since he has implanted it in all minds, imprinted it on all hearts, and made it be adopted and relished by the zealous and pious among the pastors of the Church, this principle can no longer perish or fall into oblivion. It will acquire strength even from resistance; it will triumph over all obstacles, and secure the triumph of religion.

And misfortune — misfortune to the governments which imagine that they will be able to practise religious despotism in the nineteenth century, after the great revolution that has been wrought in men's ideas! The emperors who, in professing Christianity, did not desire to comprehend Christianity, and attempted to continue to exercise Pagan despotism over the Christian Church, were abandoned by the Church. They fell into that state of meanness which has caused their reigns to be called the history of the Lower Empire, and they disappeared from the political stage of the world without inheritors and without successors. The Church, which disdains not, but which seeks out, which despises not, but welcomes and sanctifies all that has force and life, turned towards the barbarians, and made them a miracle of a Christian monarchy. If one day the successors of the barbarian chiefs, permitting themselves to be led into the errors of Paganism, essentially despotic, renounce the Christian doctrine, essentially liberal, because it is all charity, and no longer wish to recognize the doctrine of religious liberty of the people and the independence of the Church, which constituted the glory and security of their ancestors, the Church can bestow her care upon others; she will turn towards the democracy; she will baptize this savage heroine; she will make a Christian of her, as she has already made Christians of the Barbarians; she will impress upon her brow the seal of her divine consecration, and will say to her, — Reign! and she will reign. Yes, governments have no support, no safety, no defence, no probability of duration, but by giving to the Church the liberty which belongs to her, and treating and respecting the people as children of God!

What was the pure joy of O'Connell's heart, when with his own eyes he saw the signal advantages, the glorious triumphs, assurances of still more glorious triumphs to come, which his intelligent zeal, his doctrines, his generous sentiments, had secured to the true religion ? But how much greater was his religious joy, when he saw the hand of God raise and place in the Chair of St. Peter the beloved and adored Pius IX., that great soul, capable of comprehending all the instincts, all the necessities of this religious age — that noble heart so desirous to satisfy them.   For O'Connell was well convinced that the lofty and privileged genius of Pius IX. would walk with a sure and firm step in the path that O'Connell had opened — that he would seize, and wield with equal intelligence and courage, the powerful weapon that O'Connell had resuscitated ; that he would accomplish upon a vast plan, with greater success, because he possesses a divine authority, that which O'Connell had only commenced : the triumph of the Catholic faith and of the Catholic Church, by means of liberty !

Thus could he say, with the good old man, Simeon — " Now, Lord, send me to enjoy the peace of the tomb ; I die willingly this day. My eyes have seen what my heart desired, but what I believed myself unworthy to see ; they have seen your promise accomplished, to prepare great succor in great necessity ; they have seen the Church confided by you to able and enlightened heads, capable of governing it — the world to a great soul capable of saving it."   " *Nunc dimittis servum tuum domine, secundum verbum tuum in pace. Quia viderant occouli mei salutare tuum.*"   Oh ! great luminary which has begun to shine over the Vatican.   Oh ! great ligh tfrom God, which He will continue to brighten and cause to shine upon the nations !   Oh ! to what a light of glory have you commenced to raise your people, the true Israel, your holy Church !   " *Lumen ad revolutionem gentium et gloriam tuæ Israel.*"

It was therefore that, desirous to bow himseif before this divine light, feeling his end approaching, he wished to come and lay his mortal remains at the feet of this great representative of God. Ah ! the soul of an O'Connell appeared very worthy of being transmitted by the hands of Pius IX. to the gates of heaven, and deposited in the bosom of the mercy of God ! It was therefore that he made a vow to accomplish a pilgrimage to this holy city, the metropolis of the empire of Jesus Christ upon the earth, the source of the consolations of the heart, the universal country, the place of repose here below for all those who have had the happiness to be born again by baptism ! . . . . Death came to surprise him at Genoa, upon the way to

Rome. But no, I deceive myself, he was not surprised by death. I have myself seen, I have had in my hands the precious copy of the work of St. Alphonso de Ligouri, entitled PREPARATION FOR DEATH, which he used, with notes made by his own hand; an evident proof that in the midst of the greatest agitations of his life he was always preparing himself for death, and that he regulated his actions in life by the unerring light of the maxims of eternity. For this reason, full of that courage, of that holy sincerity which a true Christian feels as the effort of a life passed in the faithful discharge of the duties, and in zeal for the glory of Christianity, he saw the approach of death without fear; he bent his head to its decree without repugnance. SPIRITU MAGNO VIDIT ULTIMA. He asked and received the last Sacraments with the humility of a child and the fervor of a saint. It was in frequently repeating the prayer of St. Bernard, MEMORARE OPIISSIMA VIRGO, in reciting the Psalms, in renewing in each instant acts of contrition, of hope and of love, in pronouncing the blessed names of Jesus and Mary, that died away the voice which had shaken the world, that left its earthly tenement the great soul which had excited the admiration of the earth! And as it was not granted him to come in person to Rome, he at least came here in spirit, and he died here in heart. For his last directions were—"My body to Ireland, my heart to Rome, my soul to Heaven."

O admirable disposition! O precious gift! Can we imagine anything more sublime, and at the same time more pious, than such a testament? Ireland, it is his country; Rome, it is the Church, Heaven, it is God. God, then, the Church, his country—that is to say, the glory of God, the liberty of the Church, the happiness of his country. Behold the great ends and objects of all his actions; behold the noble objects, the only objects of his love! He loved his country, therefore he bequeathed to it his body; but he loved the Church still more, and therefore he leaves his heart to her; but he loved God even more than the Church, and for that reason to God he gives his soul. He loved God for himself; the Church in relation to God, because she is divine; his country in relation to the Church, because she is Catholic. Behold the order of his love, the foundation of his being, the character of his soul, the economy of all his conduct, the history of his life. O'Connell faithfully depicted by O'Connell himself! Behold the testament of the truly great man, of the true philosopher, of the true citizen, of the true Christian! Happy the man who, in dying, can thus dispose of himself, with as much reason, as much confidence, as much truth!

But observe again, that country is liberty, the Church is religion, God is the hand that unites together country, the Church, religion and liberty.   Then Daniel O'Connell, in bequeathing his body to his country, his heart to the Church, his soul to God, has demonstrated that in that great genius the love of country and of liberty were united to the love of religion, but through God, in God, and with God.

Let us profit, then, by this great lesson, given in such a magnanimous example, by so great a man, who has deserved so well of the Church, of his country, and of humanity.   And since O'Connell, a Christian citizen, has given liberty to his country by the aid of religion, and since he has secured the triumph of religion by means of liberty, let us no more separate that which is united by God and in God — true liberty and true religion.   .

Besides, such is at present the state of the opinions and of the sentiments of the people in Europe, that liberty can effect nothing without religion, no more than religion can effect anything without liberty, and that the enemies of religion are the real enemies of liberty, as the enemies of liberty are the real enemies of religion. Whoever speaks of religion without liberty, speaks of a human institution; whoever speaks of liberty without religion, utters an infernal sentiment.   Religion without liberty, loses its dignity; liberty without religion, loses all its charms; religion without liberty, falls into contempt; liberty without religion, becomes anarchy.   Liberty takes away from religion whatever might be humiliating to the conscience; religion takes from liberty whatever there is savage about it.   Liberty renders religion more beautiful, as beauty makes virtue be more prized; religion preserves liberty as salt hinders corruption.

But yes, dear Romans, you have these ideas and these sentiments in the thoughts of your hearts.   The day before yesterday you heard me combat all the errors, and proclaim all the truths, of social science. You heard me plead the cause of order and condemn sedition, speak in favor of the throne a language the less suspected as it was the more free and the farther removed from adulation, praise liberty, but that liberty which has religion for its foundation and support.   You have applauded me as much as your respect for this sacred place would permit.   You are thus confessed in public; you have demonstrated, in the clearest and most solemn manner, that you are not such as a calumniating voice would make you appear.   No, you are not the enemies of the pontifical throne, of the ecclesiastics, and of order; you love true liberty, but you also love the sovereignty of the head of the Church and religion. Yes, as the great Pontiff who governs us is incapable of trifling with you, you are incapable of forgetting the loyalty that you owe him. Duplicity and revolt are things too vile to be found in noble and generous hearts, such as those of Pius IX. and the Roman people.

It only, then, remains for me to exhort you to remain in your present disposition, and to say to you — let us show ourselves the faithful disciples of religion, in loving true liberty, and let us prove ourselves worthy of liberty by the sincere practice of true religion. Let us make liberty the auxiliary of religion, and take religion as the guardian of liberty. Let us leave a servile religion to obscurantism, and an unbelieving religion to anarchy. Let us be Christian citizens, and citizen Christians; let us unite with love of the people love of the Church, and love of liberty with love of religion; and thus walking in the safe path of the great Christian and the great citizen, for whose soul we pray to-day, and whose memory we honor, we will be partakers of the eternal reward which he will enjoy in heaven; we will on earth have the glory of deserving well of our country and of religion, and it will be said of us also — *Liberavit gentem suam a perditione ; et in diclens suis corroboravit templum.*" Amen.

FATHER BURKE'S ORATION.

THE following Oration in praise of O'Connell was delivered by the eminent Irish orator, Father Thomas Burke, of the Order of Friars Preachers, on the occasion of the removal of the remains of Ireland's Liberator to their final resting-place in Glasnevin: —

" Wisdom conducted the just man through the right ways, and showed him the Kingdom of God, made him honorable in his labors and accomplished his works. She kept him safe from his enemies, and gave him a strong conflict that he might overcome ; and in bondage she left him not till she brought him the sceptre of the kingdom and power against those that oppressed him, and gave him everlasting glory." — WISDOM X.

These striking words of the inspired writer tell us the glorious history of a great man of old, the father and founder of a great people. They also point out the true source of his greatness and the secret of his success. He was a just man, and the spirit of wisdom was upon him. He was led by this spirit through the right ways, — that is to say, the ways of truth and justice, the straightforward paths of reason and obedience ; and the ends of his ways, the object ever before his eyes, was the "kingdom of God," the independence, the glory, the spiritual freedom of the children of his race. A high and holy object was this, a grand and a noble purpose, which wisdom held out to him as the aim of his life and the crown of his days. And as the end for which a man labors determines all things either unto shame or unto glory, so he who labored for so great an end, "the kingdom of God," was made "honorable in his labors," and the source of this honor was also the secret of success, for he "accomplished his works." But in the midst of these "honorable labors" the inspired writer tells us that the just man's path was beset by enemies, but the spirit of wisdom which guided him "kept him safe from his enemies," enabled him to meet their violence and their wiles, their open hatred and their subtle cunning, to overcome them and to baffle them. The contest was long; it was a "strong conflict," which was given to him only that he might overcome, and so be worthy to be crowned. He was made to taste of sorrow; his enemies seemed to prevail; but in bands the spirit of wisdom, truth and justice forsook him not, "till she brought him the sceptre of the kingdom," the love and veneration of his brethren and of his people; "and power against those that oppressed him;" the power of principle and of justice, and so changed his sorrow into joy, "and gave him everlasting glory" — glory on the earth in the history and traditions of his people, where his name was in honor and benediction, and his memory enshrined in their love, and the higher glory, the everlasting glory "of the kingdom of God," for which he had labored so honorably, so successfully, and so long. Now, all this honor, triumph and everlasting glory came to the great Israelite through the spirit of wisdom, the same spirit of which it is written elsewhere, "that it can do all things . . . . that it reneweth all things . . . . and through nations conveyeth itself into holy souls, and maketh the friends of God and the prophets"—"the friends of God," that is to say, the defenders of His Church and of His faith; and "prophets," that is, the leaders of His people.

The destinies of nations are in the hands of God, and when the hour of His mercy comes, and a nation is to regain the first of its rights, the free exercise of its faith and religion, God, who is never wanting to His own designs, ever provides for that hour a leader for His people, such a one as my text describes — wise, high-minded, seeking the kingdom of God, honorable in his labors, strong in conflict with his enemies, triumphant in the issue, and crowned with glory. Nor was Ireland forgotten in the designs of God. Centuries of patient endurance brought at length the dawn of a better day. God's hour came, and it brought with it Ireland's greatest son, Daniel O'Connell. We surround his grave to-day, to pay him a last tribute of love, to speak words of praise, of suffrage, and of prayer. For two-and-twenty years has he silently slept in the midst of us. His generation is passing away, and the light of history already dawns upon his grave, and she speaks his name with cold, unimpassioned voice. In this age of ours a few years are as a century of times gone by. Great changes and startling events follow each other in such quick succession, that the greatest names are forgotten almost as soon as those who bore them disappear, and the world itself is surprised to find how short-lived is the fame which promised to be immortal. He who is inscribed even in the golden book of the world's annals, finds that he has but written his name upon water. The Church alone is the true shrine of immortality — the temple of fame which perisheth not; and that man only whose name and memory is preserved in her sanctuaries, receives on this earth a reflection of that glory which is eternal in heaven. But before the Church will crown any one of her children, she carefully examines his claims to the immortality of her praise and gratitude — she asks, What has he done for God and for man? This great question am I come here to answer to-day for him whose tongue, once so eloquent, is now stilled in the silence of the grave, and over whose tomb a grateful country has raised a monument of its ancient faith and a record of its past glories; and I claim for him the meed of our gratitude and love, in that he was a man of faith, whom wisdom guided in "the right ways," who loved and sought "the kingdom of God," who was most "honorable in his labors," and who accomplished his "great works;" the liberator of his race, the father of his people, the conqueror in "the undefiled conflict" of principle, truth and justice. No man of our day denies that Ireland has been a most afflicted country; but seldom was her dark hour darker, or her affliction greater, than toward the close of the last century. The nation's heart seemed broken, and all her hopes extinguished. The Catholics of Ireland were barely allowed to live, and were expected to be grateful even for the boon of existence; but the profession of the Catholic faith was a complete bar and an insurmountable obstacle to all advancement in the path of worldly advantage, honor, dignity, and even wealth. The fetters of conscience hung heavily also upon genius, and every prize to which lawful ambition might aspire was beyond the reach of those who refused to deny the religion of their fathers, and to forget their country. Amongst the victims of this religious and intellectual slavery was one who was marked amongst the youth of his time. Of birth which in other lands would be called noble, gifted with a powerful and comprehensive intelligence, a prodigious memory, a most fertile imagination, pouring forth its images in a vein of richest oratory, a generous spirit, a most tender heart, enriched with stores of varied learning and genius of the highest kind, graced with every form of manly beauty, strength and vigor, of powerful frame — nothing seemed wanting to him —

> "A combination and a form indeed
> Where every god did seem to set his seal,
> To give the world assurance of a man"—

yet all seemed to be lost in him, for he was born a Catholic and an Irishman. Before him now stretched, full and broad, the two ways of life, and he must choose between them; the way which led to all that the world prized — wealth, power, distinction, title, glory, and fame; the way of genius, the noble rivalry of intellect, the association with all that was most refined and refining — the way which led up to the council chambers of the nation, to all places of jurisdiction and of honor, to the temples wherein were enshrined historic names and glorious memories, to share in all blessings of privilege and freedom. The stirrings of genius, the promptings of youthful ambition, the consciousness of vast intellectual power, which placed within his easy grasp the highest prizes to which "the last infirmity of noble minds" could aspire — all this impelled him to enter upon the bright and golden path. But before him opened another way. No gleam of sunshine illumined this way; it was wet with tears — it was overshadowed with misfortune — *it was pointed out to the young traveller of life by the sign of the Cross*, and he who entered it was bidden to leave all hope behind him, for it led through the valley of humiliation into the heart of a fallen race and an enslaved and afflicted people. I claim for O'Connell the glory of having chosen the latter path, and this claim no man can gainsay, for it is the argument of the apostle in favor of the great lawgiver of old — "By faith Moses denied himself to be the son of Pharaoh's daughter; rather choosing to be afflicted with the people of God than to have the pleasure of sin for a time — esteeming the reproach of Christ greater riches than the treasure of the Egyptians." Into this way was he led, by his love for his religion and for his country. He firmly believed in that religion in which he was born. He had that faith which is common to all Catholics, and which is not merely a strong opinion, or even a conviction, but an absolute and most certain knowledge that the Catholic Church is the one and only true messenger and witness of God upon earth; that to belong to her communion and to possess her faith is the first and greatest of all endowments and privileges, before which everything else sinks into absolute nothing. He believed and knew that it was not enough for him to "believe in his heart unto justice," but that he must "confess with his mouth unto salvation," and the strength of his faith left him no alternative but to proclaim loudly his religion, and to cast in his lot with his people. That religion was this people's only inheritance.   They had clung to it and preserved it with a love and fidelity altogether superhuman, and which was the wonder of the world.   The teaching of the Catholic Church was accepted cheerfully by the Irish people when it was first preached to them.   They took it kindly and at once from the lips of their apostle, and Ireland was a grand exception to all the nations where the seed of Christianity has ever been the martyrs' blood.   The faith thus delivered to them they so illustrated by their sanctity, that for a thousand years Catholic Ireland was the glory of Christendom, and received amongst the nations the singular title of the " Island of Saints."

Our national history begins with our faith, and is so interwoven with our holy religion, that if you separate these our country's name disappears from the world's annals ; whilst, on the other hand, Ireland Christian and Catholic, which means Ireland holy, Ireland evangelizing, Ireland teaching the nations of Europe, Ireland upholding in every land the Cross and Crown, Ireland suffering for her faith as people never suffered, has her name written in letters of gold upon the proudest page of history.   Ireland and her religion were so singularly bound together, that in the days of prosperity and peace they shone together ; in days of sorrow and shame they sustained one another. When the ancient religion was driven from her sanctuaries, she still found a temple in every cabin in the land, an altar and a home in the heart of every Irishman.   When the war of conquest degenerated into a war of extermination, the faith, and the faith alone, became to the Irish race the principle of their vitality and national existence, the only element of freedom and of hope.   To their Church, suffering and proscribed, they remained faithful as in the days of her glory.   The Catholic religion became the strongest passion of their lives, and in their love for their great suffering Mother they said to her : —

" Through grief and through danger thy smile hath cheered my way,
　Till hope seem'd to bud from each thorn that round me lay ;
　The darker our fortune the brighter our pure love burned,
　Till shame into glory, till fear into zeal was turned ;
　Yes, slave as I was, in thy arms my spirit felt free,
　And blessed even the sorrows that made me more dear to thee."

All this O'Connell felt and knew.   He was Irish of the Irish, and Catholic of the Catholic.   His love for religion and country was as the breath of his nostrils, the blood of his veins ; and when he brought to the service of both the strength of his faith and the power of his genius, with the instinct of a true Irishman his first thought was to lift up the nation by striking the chains off the National Church.

And here again, my brethren, two ways opened before him. One was a way in which many had trodden in former times, many pure, and high-minded, noble and patriotic men; it was a way of danger and of blood, and the history of his country told him that it ever ended in defeat and in greater evil. The sad events which he himself witnessed, and which took place around him, warned him off that way; for he saw that the effort to walk in it had swept away the last vestige of Ireland's national legislature and independence. But another path was still open to him, and wisdom pointed it out as "the right way." Another battle-field lay before him on which he could "fight the good fight," and vindicate all the rights of his religion and of his country. The armory was furnished by the inspired apostle when he said:—"Brethren, our wrestling is not against flesh and blood, but against principalities and powers. . . . Therefore take unto you the armor of God. . . . Having your loins girt about with truth, and having on the breast-plate of justice, and your feet shod with the preparation of the Gospel of Peace, in all things taking the shield of faith. . . . And take unto you the sword of the Spirit, which is the Word." O'Connell knew well that such weapons in such a hand as his were irresistible — that, girt round with the truth and justice of his cause, he was clad in the armor of the Eternal God ; that with words of peace and order on his lips, with the strong shield of faith before him and the sword of eloquent speech in his hand, with the war-cry of obedience, principle, and law, no power on earth could resist him. Such a battle once begun,

> "Though baffled oft, is ever won ; "

for it is the battle of God, and nothing can resist the Most High. Accordingly, he raised the standard of the new war, and unfurled the banner on which was written, — Freedom to be achieved by the power of truth, the cry of justice, the assertion of right, and the omnipotence of the law. Religious liberty and perfect legal equality was his first demand. The new apostle of freedom went through the length and breadth of Ireland. His eloquent words revived the hopes and stirred up the energies of the nation ; the people and the priesthood rallied round him as one man ; they became most formidable to their enemies by the might of justice and reason, and they showed themselves worthy of liberty by their respect for the law. Never was Ireland more excited, yet never was Ireland more peaceful. The people were determined on gaining their religious freedom. Irishmen from 1822 to 1829 were as fiercely determined on their new battle-field as

they had been in the breaches of Limerick or on the slopes of Fonte-
noy.   They were marshalled by a leader as brave as Sarsfield and as
daring as Red Hugh.   He led them against the strongest citadel in
the world ; and even as the walls of the city of old crumbled to dust
at the sound of Israel's trumpet, so, at the sound of his mighty voice,
who spoke in the name of a united people, "the lintels of the doors
were moved," and the gates were opened which three hundred years
of prejudice and pride had closed and barred against our people.   The
first decree of our liberation went forth — on the 13th of April, 1829,
Catholic Emancipation was proclaimed, and seven millions of Catholic Irishmen entered the nation's legislature in the person of O'Connell.   It was the first and the greatest victory of peaceful principle
which our age has witnessed, the grandest triumph of justice and of
truth, the most glorious victory of the genius of one man, and the first
great act of homage which Ireland's rulers paid to the religion of the
people, and which Ireland's people paid to the great principle of
peaceful agitation.

O'Connell's first and greatest triumph was the result of his strong
faith and his ardent zeal for his religion and his Church.   The Church
was to him, as it is to us, "the kingdom of God," and in his labors
for it "he was made honorable," and received from a grateful people
the grandest title ever given to man.   Ireland called him the " Liberator."   He was "honorable in his labors," when we consider the end
which he proposed to himself.   It was no selfish, nor even purely
human, end which he put before him.   He devoted himself, his time,
his talents, his energies, his power, to the glory of God, to the liberation of God's Church, to the emancipation of His people.   This was
the glorious end ; nor were the means less honorable.   Fair, open,
manly self-assertion ; high, solemn appeal to eternal principle ; noble
and unceasing proclamation of rights founded in justice and in the constitution ; peaceful but most powerful pressure of a people united by his
genius, inflamed by his eloquence, and guided by his vast knowledge
and wisdom — these were the honorable means by which he accomplished his great work, and this great work was the achievement which
gained for him not only the title of the Liberator of Ireland, but even
the œcumenical title of the Liberator of Christ's Church.   " Were it
only to Ireland," says the great Lacordaire, "that Emancipation has
been profitable, where is the man in the Church who has freed at once
seven millions of souls?   Challenge your recollection, search history
from that first and famous edict which granted to the Christians liberty
of conscience, and see if there are to be found many such acts com-

23*

parable, by the extent of their effects, with that of Catholic Emancipation. Seven millions of souls are now free to serve and love God even to the end of time; and each time that this people, advancing in their existence and their liberty, shall recall to memory the aspect of the man who studied the secret of their ways, they will ever find inscribed the name of O'Connell, both on the latest pages of their servitude and on the first of their regeneration." His glorious victory did honor even to those whom he vanquished. He honored them by appealing to their sense of justice and of right; and, in the act of Catholic Emancipation in England, acknowledged the power of a people, not asking for mercy, but clamoring for the liberty of the soul, the blessing which was born with Christ, and which is the inheritance of the nations that embrace the Cross. Catholic Emancipation was but the herald and the beginning of victories. He who was the Church's liberator and most true son, was also the first of Ireland's statesmen and patriots. Our people remember well, as their future historian will faithfully record, the many trials borne for them, the many victories gained in their cause, the great life devoted to them by O'Connell. Lying, however, at the foot of the altar, as he is to-day, whilst the Church hallows his grave with prayer and sacrifice, it is more especially as the Catholic Emancipator of his people that we place a garland on his tomb. It is as a child of the Church that we honor him, and recall with tears of sorrow our recollections of the aged man, revered, beloved, whom all the glory of the world's admiration and the nation's love had never lifted up in soul out of the holy atmosphere of Christian humility and simplicity. Obedience to the Church's laws, quick zeal for her honor and the dignity of her worship; a spirit of penance refining whilst it expiated, chastening whilst it ennobled, all that was natural in the man; constant and frequent use of the Church's Holy Sacraments, which shed the halo of grace round his venerated head — these were the last grand lessons which he left to his people, and thus did the sun of his life set in the glory of Christian holiness. For Ireland he lived, for Ireland did he die. The people whom he had so faithfully served, whom he loved with a love second only to his love for God, were decimated by a visitation the most terrible that the world ever witnessed; the nations of the earth trembled, and men grew pale at the sight of Ireland's desolation. Her tale of famine, of misery, of death, was told in every land. Her people fled affrighted from the soil which had forgotten its ancient bounty, or died, their white lips uttering the last faint cry for bread. All this the aged father of his country beheld. Neither his genius, nor his eloquence, nor his love, could now save his people, and the spirit was crushed which had borne him triumphantly through all dangers and toil; the heart broke within him, —that brave and generous heart which had never known fear, and whose ruling passion was his love for Ireland. The martyred spirit, the broken heart of the great Irishman, led him to the holiest spot of earth, and with tottering steps he turned to Rome. The man whose terrible voice in life shook the highest tribunals of earth in imperious demand for justice to Ireland, now sought the Apostles' tomb, that, from that threshold of Heaven he might put up a cry for mercy to his country and his people, and offer up his life for his native land. Like the Prophet King, he would fain stand between the people and the angel who smote them, and offer himself a victim and a holocaust for the land which he loved. But on the shores of the Mediterranean the weary traveller lay down to die. At that last moment his profound knowledge of his country's history may have given him that prophetic glimpse of the future which is sometimes vouchsafed to great minds. He had led a mighty nation to the opening of "the right way," and directed her first and doubtful steps in the path of conciliation and justice to Ireland. Time, which ever works out the designs of God, has carried that nation forward in the glorious way. With firmer step, with undaunted soul, with high resolve of justice, peace and conciliation, the work begun by Ireland's Liberator progresses in our day. Chains are being forged for our country, but they are chains of gold, to bind up all discordant elements in the empire, so that all men shall dwell together as brothers in the land. If we cannot have the blessings of religious unity so as "to be all of one mind," we shall have "the next dearest blessing that Heaven can give," the peace that springs from perfect religious liberty and equality. All this do we owe to the man whose memory we recall to-day, to the principles which he taught us, which illustrate his life, and which, in the triumph of Catholic Emancipation, pointed out to the Irish people the true secret of their strength, the true way of progress, and the sure road to victory. The seed which his hand has sown it was not given to him to reap in its fulness. Catholic Emancipation was but the first instalment of liberty. The edifice of religious freedom was to be crowned when the wise architect, who had laid its foundations and built up the walls, was in his grave. Let us hope that his dying eyes were cheered, and the burden of his last hour lightened by the sight of the perfect grandeur of his work—that, like the Prophet lawgiver, he beheld "all the land;" that he saw it with his eyes, though he did not "pass over to it;" and that it was given to him to "salute from afar off" the brightness of the day which he was never to enjoy. The dream of his life is being realized to-day. He had ever sighed to be able to extend to his Protestant fellow-countrymen the hand of perfect friendship, which only exists where there is perfect equality, and to enter with them into the compact of the true peace which is found in justice. Time, which buries in utter oblivion so many names and so many memories, will exalt him in his work. The day has already dawned, and is ripening to its perfect noon, when Irishmen of every creed will remember O'Connell, and celebrate him as the common friend and greatest benefactor of their country. What man is there, even of those whom our age has called great, whose name, so many years after his death, could summon so many loving hearts around his tomb? We, to-day, are the representatives not only of a nation, but of a race. "*Quænam regia in terris nostri non plena laboris?*"

Where is the land that has not seen the face of our people and heard their voice? and wherever, even to the ends of the earth, an Irishman is found to-day, his spirit and his sympathy are here. The millions of America are with us — the Irish Catholic soldier on India's plains is present amongst us by the magic of love — the Irish sailor, standing by the wheel this moment in far-off silent seas, where it is night, and the southern stars are shining, joins his prayer with ours, and recalls the glorious image and the venerated name of O'Connell.

> "He is gone who seemed so great —
> Gone; but nothing can bereave him
> Of the force he made his own,
> Being here, and we believe him
> Something far advanced in state,
> And that he wears a truer crown
> Than any wreath that man can weave him."

He is gone, but his fame shall live forever on the earth as a lover of God and of His people. Adversities, political and religious, he had many, and, like a

> "Tower of strength
> Which stood full square to all the winds that blew,"

the Hercules of justice and liberty stood up against them. Time, which touches all things with mellowing hands, has softened the recollections of past contests; and they who once looked upon him as a foe, now only remember the glory of the fight, and the mighty genius of him who stood forth the representative man of his race, and the champion of his people. They acknowledge his greatness, and they join hands with us to weave the garland of his fame. But far other, higher, and holier are the feelings of Irish Catholics all the world over to-day. They recognize, in the dust which we are assembled to honor, the powerful arm which promoted them, the eloquent tongue which proclaimed their rights and asserted their freedom, the strong hand which, like that of the Maccabee of old, first struck off their chains and then built up their holy altars. They, mingling the supplication of prayer and the gratitude of suffrage with their tears, recall — oh, with how much love ! — the memory of him who was a Joseph to Israel — their tower of strength, their buckler, and their shield — who shed around their homes, their altars and their graves the sacred right of religious liberty, and the glory of unfettered worship. " His praise is in the Church," and this is the surest pledge of the immortality of his glory. " A people's voice " may be " the proof and echoes of all human fame," but the voice of the undying Church is the echo of " everlasting glory ; " and when those who surround his grave to-day shall have passed away, all future generations of Irishmen, to the end of time, will be reminded of his name and of his glory.

CENTENNIAL ORATION ON O'CONNELL,
BY WENDELL PHILLIPS.

THE following Oration was delivered by the Hon.
Wendell Phillips in the Music Hall, Boston, Mass.,
on the centenary celebration of O'Connell's birth,
Aug. 6th, 1875, before an audience of over four
thousand people.   It has been justly regarded as one
of the most eloquent tributes ever offered to the
memory of the great Liberator; and as Mr. Phillips
was personally acquainted with O'Connell, he has
been able to clothe his subject with an interest which
few have ever approached:

A hundred years ago, to-day, Daniel O'Connell was born. The
Irish race, wherever scattered over the globe, assembles to-night to pay
fitting tribute to his memory; one of the most eloquent men, one of
the most devoted patriots, and the most successful statesman, that
your race has given to history. We of other races may well join you
in that tribute, since the cause of constitutional government owes
more to O'Connell than to any other political leader of the last two
centuries. The English-speaking race, to find his equal among its
statesmen, must pass by Chatham and Walpole and go back to Oliver
Cromwell, or the able men who held up the throne of Queen Eliza-
beth. If to put the civil and social elements of your day into successful action and plant the seeds of continued strength and progress for
coming times, if this is to be a statesman, then most emphatically was
O'Connell one. To exert this control and secure this progress while
and because ample means lie ready for use under your hand, does not
rob Walpole and Colbert, Chatham and Richelieu of their title to be
considered statesmen. To do it, as Martin Luther did,* when one

* Mr. Phillips' allusion to Martin Luther is from his own standpoint as a Protestant.

must ingeniously discover or invent his tools, and while the mightiest forces that influence human affairs are arrayed against him, — that is what ranks O'Connell with the few masterly statesmen the English-speaking race has ever had. When Napoleon's soldiers bore the negro chief, Toussaint L'Ouverture, into exile, he said, pointing back to San Domingo, " You think you have rooted up the tree of liberty. But I am only a branch. I have planted the tree itself so deep that ages will never root it up." And whatever may be said of the social or industrial condition of Hayti during the last seventy years, its *nationality* has never been successfully assailed.

O'Connell is the only Irishman who can say as much of Ireland. From the peace of Utrecht, 1713, till the fall of Napoleon, Great Britain was the leading State in Europe, while Ireland, a comparatively insignificant island, lay at its feet. She weighed next to nothing in the scale of British politics. The continent pitied and England despised her. O'Connell found her a mass of quarrelling races and sects, divided, dispirited, broken-hearted, and servile. He made her a NATION, whose first word broke in pieces the iron obstinacy of Wellington, tossed Peel from the cabinet, and gave the government to the Whigs; whose colossal figure, like the helmet in Walpole's romance, has filled the political sky ever since; whose generous aid thrown into the scale of the three great British reforms — the Ballot, the Corn laws, and Slavery — secured their success; a nation whose continued discontent has dragged Great Britain down to be a second-rate power on the chess-board of Europe. I know other causes have helped in producing this result. But the nationality which O'Connell created has been the main cause of this change in England's importance. Dean Swift, Molyneux, and Henry Flood thrust Ireland for a moment into the arena of British politics, a sturdy suppliant clamoring for justice; and Grattan held her there an equal, and, as he thought, a nation, for a few years. But Pitt's unscrupulous hand brushed away in an hour all Grattan's work. Well might he say of the Irish Parliament which he brought to life, " I sat by its cradle, I followed its hearse;" since after that infamous union, which Byron called a "union of the shark with its prey," Ireland sank back plundered and helpless. O'Connell lifted her to a fixed and permanent place in English affairs — no suppliant, but a conqueror dictating her terms.

This is the proper standpoint from which to look at O'Connell's work. This is the consideration that ranks him, not with founders of States, like Alexander, Cæsar, Bismarck, Napoleon, and William the Silent, but with men who, without arms, by force of reason, have revolutionized their times, — with Luther, Jefferson, Mazzini, Samuel Adams, Garrison, and Franklin. I know some men will sneer at this claim; those who have never looked at him except through the spectacles of English critics, who despised him as an Irishman and a Catholic, until they came to hate him as a conqueror. As Grattan said of Kirwan, "The curse of Swift was upon him, to have been born an Irishman and a man of genius, and to have used his gifts for his country's good." Mark what measure of success attended the able men who preceded him, in circumstances as favorable as his, perhaps even better; then measure him by comparison.

An island soaked with the blood of countless rebellions; oppression such as would turn cowards into heroes; a race whose disciplined valor had been proved on almost every battle-field in Europe, and whose reckless daring lifted it, any time, in arms against England, with hope or without. What inspired them? Devotion, eloquence, and patriotism seldom paralleled in history. Who led them? Dean Swift, according to Addison, "the greatest genius of his age"— called by Pope "the incomparable;" a man fertile in resources, of stubborn courage and tireless energy, master of an English style unequalled, perhaps, for its purpose then or since; a man who had twice faced England in her angriest mood, and by that masterly pen subdued her to his will; Henry Flood, eloquent even for an Irishman, and sagacious as he was eloquent; the eclipse of that brilliant life is one of the saddest pictures in Irish biography; Grattan, with all the courage, and more than the eloquence, of his race — a statesman's eye, quick to see every opportunity, boundless devotion, unspotted integrity, recognized as an equal by the world's leaders, and welcomed by Fox to the House of Commons as the "Demosthenes of Ireland;" Emmet in the field, Sheridan in the senate, Curran at the bar; and, above all, Edmund Burke, whose name makes eulogy superfluous, more than Cicero in the Senate, almost Plato in the Academy, — all these gave their lives to Ireland; and when the present century opened where was she? Sold like a slave in the market-place by her perjured master, William Pitt. It was then that O'Connell flung himself into the struggle, gave fifty years to the service of his country, and where is she to-day?

Not only redeemed, but her independence put beyond doubt or peril. Grattan and his predecessors could get no guarantees for what rights they gained. That sagacious, watchful, and almost omnipotent *public opinion*, which O'Connell created, is an all-sufficient guarantee of Ireland's future. Look at her; almost every shackle has fallen from her limbs; all that human wisdom has as

yet devised to remedy the evils of bigotry and misrule has been done.
O'Connell found Ireland a "hissing and a byword" in Edinburgh
and London. He made her the pivot of British politics; she rules
them, directly or indirectly, with as absolute a sway as the slave
question did the United States from 1850 to 1865. Look into Earl
Russell's book and the history of the Reform bill of 1832, and see
with how much truth it may be claimed that O'Connell and his fellows gave Englishmen the ballot under that act. It is by no means certain that the Corn laws could have been abolished without their aid.
In the anti-slavery struggle O'Connell stands, in influence and ability,
equal with the best. I know the credit all those measures do to English leaders. But, in my opinion, the next generation will test the
statesmanship of Peel, Palmerston, Russell, and Gladstone almost
entirely by their conduct of the Irish question. All the laurels they
have hitherto won in that field are rooted in ideas which Grattan and
O'Connell urged on reluctant hearers for half a century. Why do
Bismarck and Alexander look with such contemptuous indifference
on every attempt of England to mingle in European affairs? Because they know they have but to lift a finger, and Ireland stabs her
in the back. Where was the statesmanship of English leaders when
they allowed such an evil to grow so formidable? This is Ireland
to-day. What was she when O'Connell undertook her cause? The
saddest of Irish poets has described her, in 1798 : —

"O Ireland! my country, the hour of thy pride and thy splendor hath
    passed,
And the chain that was spurned in thy moments of power hangs
    heavy around thee at last ;
There are marks in the fate of each clime, there are turns in the for-
    tunes of men,
But the changes of realms or the chances of time shall never restore
    thee again.
Thou art chained to the wheel of the foe by links which a world can-
    not sever ;
With thy tyrant through storm and through calm thou shalt go, and
    thy sentence is bondage forever ;
Thou art doomed for the thankless to toil, thou art left for the proud
    to disdain,
And the blood of thy sons and the wealth of thy soil shall be lavished,
    and lavished in vain.
Thy riches with taunts shall be taken, thy valor with coldness be paid,
And of millions who see thee thus sunk and forsaken, not one shall
    stand forth in thine aid.
In the nations thy place is left void, thou art lost in the list of the free,
Even realms by the plague and the earthquake destroyed may revive,
    but no hope is for thee."

It was a community impoverished by five centuries of oppression —
four millions of Catholics robbed of every acre of their native land;
it was an island torn by race-hatred and religious bigotry, her priests
indifferent, and her nobles hopeless or traitors. The wiliest of her
enemies, a Protestant Irishman, ruled the British Senate; the sternest
of her tyrants, a Protestant Irishman, led the armies of Europe;
Puritan hate, which had grown blinder and more bitter since the days
of Cromwell, gave them weapons. Ireland herself lay bound in the
iron links of a code which Montesquieu said could have been "made
only by devils, and should be registered only in hell." Her millions
were beyond the reach of the great reform engine of modern times,
since they could neither read nor write.

In this mass of ignorance, weakness, and quarrel, one keen eye saw
hidden the elements of union and strength. With rarest skill he
called them forth and marshalled them into rank. Then this one
man, without birth, wealth, or office, in a land ruled by birth, wealth
and office, moulded from those unsuspected elements a power which,
overawing king, Senate and people, wrote his single will on the
statute book of the most obstinate nation in Europe! Safely to
emancipate the Irish Catholics, and in spite of Saxon, Protestant
hate, to lift all Ireland to the level of British citizenship — this was
the problem which statesmanship and patriotism had been seeking
for two centuries to solve. For this, blood had been poured out like
water. On this, the genius of Swift, the learning of Molyneux, and
the eloquence of Bushe, Grattan, and Burke, had been wasted.
English leaders, ever since Fox, had studied this problem anxiously.
They saw that the safety of the empire was compromised. At one
or two critical moments in the reign of George the Third, one signal
from an Irish leader would have snapped the chain that bound Ireland to his throne. His ministers recognized it, and they tried every
expedient, exhausted every device, dared every peril, kept oaths, or
broke them, in order to succeed. All failed; and not only failed,
but acknowledged they could see no way in which success could ever
be achieved.

O'Connell achieved it! Out of this darkness he called forth light.
Out of this most abject, weak and pitiable of kingdoms he made a
power, and, dying, he left in Parliament a spectre which, unless ap-
peased, pushes Whig and Tory ministers alike from their stools!

But Brougham says he was a demagogue! Fie on Wellington,
Derby, Peel, Palmerston, Liverpool, Russell, and Brougham, to be
fooled and ruled by a demagogue! What must they, the subjects be,

if O'Connell, their king, be only a bigot and a demagogue? A demagogue rides the storm. He has never really the ability to create one. He uses it narrowly, ignorantly, and for selfish ends. If not crushed by the force which, without his will, has flung him into power, he leads it with ridiculous miscalculation against some insurmountable obstacle that scatters it forever. Dying, he leaves no mark on the elements with which he has been mixed. Robespierre will serve for an illustration. It took O'Connell thirty years of patient and sagacious labor to mould elements whose existence no man, however wise, had ever discerned before. He used them unselfishly, only to break the yoke of his race. Nearly fifty years have passed since his triumph, but his impress still stands forth clear and sharp on the empire's policy. Ireland is wholly indebted to him for her political education. Responsibility educates. He lifted her to broader responsibilities. Her possession of power makes it the keen interest of other classes to see she is well informed. He associated her with all the reform movements of Great Britain. This is the education of affairs, broader, deeper, and more real than what school or college can ever give. This and power — his gifts — are the lever which lifts her to every other right and privilege. How much England owes him we can never know, since how great a danger and curse Ireland would have been to the empire had she continued the cancer Pitt and Castlereagh left her, is a chapter of history which, fortunately, can never be written. No demagogue ever walked through the streets of Dublin, as O'Connell and Grattan did more than once, hooted and mobbed because they opposed themselves to the mad purpose of the people and crushed it by a stern resistance. No demagogue would have offered himself to a race like the Irish as the apostle of peace; pledging himself to the British government that, in the long agitation before him, with brave millions behind him, spoiling for a fight, he would never draw a sword.

I have purposely dwelt long on this view, because the extent and the far-reaching effects of O'Connell's work, without regard to the motives which inspired him, or the methods he used, have never been fully recognized.

Briefly stated, he *did* what the ablest and bravest of his forerunners had tried to do and failed. He created a public opinion and a unity of purpose (no matter what be now the dispute about methods) which make Ireland a *Nation*; he gave her British citizenship and a place in the Imperial Parliament; he gave her a *Press* and a *Public*; with these tools her destiny is in her own hands. When the abolitionists got for the negro, schools and the vote, they settled the slave question, for they planted the sure seeds of civil equality. O'Connell did this for Ireland — this, which no Irishman before had ever dreamed of attempting. Swift and Molyneux were able; Grattan, Bushe, Saurin, Burrowes, Plunket, Curran, Burke, were eloquent; throughout the island, courage was a drug; they gained now one point, now another, but after all they left the helm of Ireland's destiny in foreign and hostile hands. O'Connell was brave, sagacious, eloquent, but, more than all, he was a statesman; for he gave to Ireland's own keeping the key of her future. As Lord Bacon marches down the centuries he may lay one hand on the telegraph and the other on the steam engine and say, "These are mine, for I taught you how to study nature." In a similar sense, as shackle after shackle falls from Irish limbs, O'Connell may say, "This victory is mine, for I taught you the method, and I gave you the arms."

I have hitherto been speaking of his ability and success; by and by we will look at his character, motives, and methods. This unique ability even his enemies have been forced to confess. Harriet Martineau, in her incomparable history of the "Thirty Years' Peace," has, with Tory hate, misconstrued every action of O'Connell, and invented a bad motive for each one. But even she confesses that "he rose in power, influence and notoriety to an eminence such as no other individual citizen has attained in modern times" in the British Empire. And one of his by no means partial biographers, Lecky, has well said: "Any man who turns over the magazines and newspapers of that period will easily perceive how grandly O'Connell's figure dominated in politics, how completely he had dispelled the indifference that had so long prevailed on Irish questions, how clearly his agitation stands forth as the great fact of the time. . . . The truth is, his position, so far from being a common one, is absolutely unique in history. We may search in vain through the records of the past for any man who, without the effusion of a drop of blood, or the advantages of office or rank, succeeded in governing a people so absolutely and so long, and in creating so entirely the elements of his power. . . . There was no rival to his supremacy, there was no restriction to his authority. He played with the fierce enthusiasm he had aroused with the negligent ease of a master; he governed the complicated organization he had created with a sagacity that never failed. He made himself the focus of the attention of other lands and the centre around which the rising intellect of his own revolved. He had transformed the whole social system of Ireland; almost reversed the relative positions of Protestants and Catholics; remodelled, by his influence, the representative, ecclesiastical, and educational institutions, and created a public opinion that surpassed the wildest dreams of his predecessors. Can we wonder at the proud exultation with which he exclaimed, 'Grattan sat by the cradle of his country and followed her hearse; it was left for me to sound the resurrection trumpet, and to show she was not dead, but sleeping'?"

But the method by which he achieved this success is perhaps more remarkable than even the success itself. An Irish poet, one of his bitterest assailants thirty years ago, has just laid a chaplet of atonement on his altar, and one verse runs:—

> "O great World-Leader of a mighty age!
> Praise unto thee let all the people give;
> By thy great name of LIBERATOR live
> In golden letters upon history's page.
> And this thy epitaph while Time shall be:
> *He found his country chained, but left her free.*"

It is natural that Ireland should remember him as her LIBERATOR. But, strange as it may seem to you, I think Europe and America will rembember him by a higher title. I said, in opening, that the cause of constitutional government is more indebted to O'Connell than to any other political leader of the last two centuries. What I mean is, that he invented the great method of constitutional agitation. AGITATOR is a title which will last longer, which suggests a broader and more permanent influence, and entitles him to the gratitude of more millions than the name Ireland loves to give him. The first great *agitator* is his proudest title to gratitude and fame. Agitation is the method that puts the school by the side of the ballot-box. The Fremont canvass was the nation's best school. Agitation prevents rebellion, keeps the peace, and secures progress. Every step she gains is gained forever. Muskets are the weapons of animals. Agitation is the atmosphere of brains. The old Hindoo saw, in his dream, the human race led out to its various fortunes. First, men were in chains which went back to an iron hand. Then he saw them led by threads from the brain which went upward to an unseen hand. The first was despotism, iron and ruling by force. The last was civilization, ruling by ideas.

Agitation is an old word with a new meaning. Sir Robert Peel, the first English leader who felt he was its tool, defined it to be "the marshalling of the conscience of a nation to mould its laws." O'Connell was the first to show and use its power, to lay down its principles, to analyze its elements, and mark out its metes and bounds. It is voluntary, public, and above board ; no oath-bound secret societies, like those of old time in Ireland and of the continent to-day. Its means are reason and argument; no appeal to arms. Wait patiently for the slow growth of public opinion. The Frenchman is angry with his government ; he throws up barricades and shots his guns to the lips. A week's fury drags the nation ahead a hand's breadth ; reaction lets its settle half-way back again. As Lord Chesterfield said a hundred years ago : " You Frenchmen erect barricades, but never any barriers." An Englishman is dissatisfied with public affairs. He brings his charges, offers his proof, waits for prejudice to relax, for public opinion to inform itself. Then every step taken is taken forever; an abuse once removed never reappears in history. Where did he learn this method? Practically speaking, from O'Connell. It was he who planted its corner-stone. Argument, no violence : *No political change is worth a drop of human blood.* His other motto was, "tell the whole truth ;" no concealing half of one's convictions to make the other half more acceptable. No denial of one truth to gain hearing for another. No compromise ; or, as he phrased it, "nothing is politically right which is morally wrong."

Above all, plant yourself on the millions ; the sympathy of every human being, no matter how ignorant or how humble, adds weight to public opinion. At the outset of his career, the clergy turned a deaf ear to his appeal. They had seen their flocks led up to useless slaughter for centuries, and counselled submission. The nobility repudiated him ; they were either traitors or hopeless. Protestants had touched their *ultima Thule* with Grattan, and seemed settling down in despair. English Catholics advised waiting till the tyrant grew merciful. O'Connell, left alone, said, " I will forge these four million of Irish hearts into a thunderbolt which shall suffice to dash this despotism to pieces." And he did it ! Living under an aristocratic government, himself of the higher class, he anticipated Lincoln's wisdom, and framed his movements, "of the people, by the people, for the people." It is a singular fact, that the freer a nation becomes, the more utterly democratic the form of its institutions, this outside agitation, this pressure of public opinion to direct political action, becomes more and more necessary. The general judgment is that the freest possible government produces the freest possible men and women ; the most individual, the least servile to the judgment of others. But a moment's reflection will show any man that this is an unreasonable expectation, and that, on the contrary, entire equality and freedom in political forms almost inevitably tend to make the individual subside into the mass, and lose his identity in the general whole. Suppose we stood in England to-night. There is the nobility, and here is the Church. There is the trading class, and here is the literary. A broad gulf separates the four, and provided a member of either conciliate his own section, he can afford, in a very large measure, to despise the judgment of the other three. He has, to some extent, a refuge and a breakwater against the tyranny of what we call public opinion. But in a country like ours, of absolute democratic equality, public opinion is not only omnipotent — it is omnipresent. There is no refuge from its tyranny; there is no hiding from its reach; and the result is, that if you take the old Greek lantern, and go about to search, you will find that ninety-nine Americans out of every hundred really have, or fancy they have, something to gain or to lose in ambition, social life, or business, from the good opinion and the votes of those about them. And the consequence is, that instead of being a mass of individuals, each one fearlessly blurting out his own convictions, as a nation, compared with other nations, we are a mass of cowards. More than all other people, we are afraid of each other. If you were a caucus to-night, Democratic or Republican, and I were your orator, none of you could get beyond the necessary and timid limitations of party. You not only would not demand, you would not allow me to utter one word of what you really thought and what I thought. You would demand of me — and my value as a caucus speaker would depend entirely on the adroitness and the vigilance with which I met the demand — that I should not utter one single word which would compromise the vote of next week. That is politics. So with the press. Seemingly independent, and sometimes really so, the press can afford only to mount the cresting wave, not create or go beyond it. The editor might as well shoot his reader with a bullet as with a new idea. He must hit the exact line of the opinion of the day. I am not finding fault with him. I am only describing him. Some ten years ago I took to one of the freest of the Boston journals a letter, and by appropriate consideration induced its editor to print it. As we glanced along its contents, and came to the concluding statement, he said, "Couldn't you omit that?" I said, "No, I wrote it for that; it is the gist of the statement." "Well," said he, "it is true; there is not a boy in the streets that does not know it is true; but I wish you could omit it."

I insisted, and the next morning, fairly and justly, he printed the whole; side by side he put an article of his own, in which he said: "We copy in the next column an article from Mr. Phillips, and we only regret the absurd and unfounded statement with which he concludes it." He had kept his promise by printing the article; he saved his reputation by printing the comment. And that again is the inevitable, the essential limitation of the press in a républican community. Our institutions, floating unanchored on the shifting surface of popular opinion, cannot afford to draw forward a hated question and compel a reluctant public to look at it and to consider it. Hence, as you see at once, the moment a large issue, twenty years ahead of its age, presents itself to the consideration of an empire, or of a republic, just in proportion to the freedom of its institutions is the necessity of a platform outside of the press, of politics, and of the church, whereon stand men with no candidate to elect, with no plan to carry, with no reputation at stake, with no object but the truth, no purpose but to tear the question open and riddle it with light. So much in explanation of a word infinitely hated — agitation and agitators — but an element which the progress of modern government has developed more and more every day. However unpleasant and fretting such an element may be, it seems, in constitutional governments, indispensable to peace and progress. If the Alps, piled in still and solemn magnificence, are an emblem of despotism, the ever-changing ocean is ours, only pure because never still. Fisher Ames said, "A monarchy is a man-of-war, staunch, iron-ribbed and resistless when under full sail; yet a single hidden rock sends her to the bottom. Our republic is a raft hard to steer, your feet always wet, — but nothing can sink her."

This great invention we trace in its twilight and seed, to the days of the Long Parliament. Defoe and Le Strange, later down, were the first prominent Englishmen to fling pamphlets at the House of Commons. Swift ruled England by pamphlets. Wilberforce summoned the Church and sought the alliance of influential classes. But O'Connell first showed a profound faith in the human tongue — he descried afar off the coming omnipotence of the press. He called the millions to his side, appreciated the infinite weight of the simple human heart and conscience, and grafted democracy into the British Empire. The later abolitionists, Buxton, Sturge and Thompson, borrowed his method. Cobden flung it in the face of the almost omnipotent landholders of England, and broke the Tory party forever. They only haunt upper air now in the stolen garments of the Whigs. The English administration recognizes this new partner in the government, and waits to be moved on. Garrison brought the novel weapon to our shores. The only wholly useful and thoroughly defensible war Christendom has seen in this century, the greatest civil and social change the English race ever saw, are the result.

This great servant and weapon peace and constitutional government owe to O'Connell. Who has given progress a greater boon? What single agent has done as much to bless and improve the world for the last fifty years?

O'Connell has been charged with coarse, violent, and intemperate language. The criticism is of little importance. Stupor and palsy never understand life. White-livered indifference is always disgusted and annoyed by earnest conviction. Protestants criticised Luther in the same way. It took three centuries to carry us far off enough to appreciate his colossal proportions. It is a hundred years to-day since O'Connell was born. It will take another hundred to put us at such an angle as will enable us correctly to measure his stature. Premising that it would be folly to find fault with a man struggling for life because his attitudes were ungraceful; remembering the Scythian king's answer to Alexander, criticising his strange weapon, " If you knew how precious freedom was, you would defend it with axes,"—we must allow that O'Connell's own explanation is evidently sincere and true. He found the Irish heart so cowed, and Englishmen so arrogant, that he saw it needed an independence verging on insolence, a defiance that touched extremest limits, to breathe self-respect into his own race, teach the aggressor manners, and sober him into respectful attention. It was the same with us abolitionists. Webster had taught the North the 'bated breath and crouching of a slave. It needed, with us, an attitude of independence that was almost insolent, it needed that we should exhaust even the Saxon vocabulary of scorn, to fitly utter the righteous and haughty contempt that honest men had for men-stealers. Only in that way could we wake the North to self-respect, or teach the South that, at length, she had met her equal, if not her master. On a broad canvas, meant for the public square, the tiny lines of a Dutch interior would be invisible. " You can never make a revolution with rose-water." The world has hardly yet learned how deep a philosophy lies hid in Hamlet's

> " Nay, an thou'lt mouth,
> I'll rant as well as thou."

O'Connell has been charged with insincerity in urging repeal; and those who defended his sincerity have leaned toward allowing that it proved his lack of common sense. I think both critics mistaken. His earliest speeches point to Repeal as his ultimate object — indeed, he valued Emancipation largely as a means to that end. No fair view of his whole life will leave the slightest ground to doubt his sincerity. As for the reasonableness and necessity of the measure, I think every year proves them. Considering O'Connell's position, I wholly sympathize in his profound and unshaken loyalty to the empire. Its share in the British empire makes Ireland's strength and importance. Standing alone among the vast and massive sovereignties of Europe, she would be weak, insignificant and helpless. Were I an Irishman, I should cling to the empire.

Fifty or sixty years hence, when scorn of race has vanished and bigotry is lessened, it may be possible for Ireland to be safe and free while holding the relation to England that Scotland does. But during this generation and the next, O'Connell was wise in claiming that Ireland's rights would never be safe without "home rule." A substantial repeal of the Union should be every Irishman's earnest aim. Were I their adviser, I should constantly repeat what Grattan said in 1810: "The best advice, gentlemen, I can give on all occasions is, 'Keep knocking at the Union.'"

We imagine an Irishman to be only a zealot on fire. We fancy Irish spirit and·eloquence to be only blind, reckless, headlong enthusiasm. But, in truth, Grattan was the soberest leader of his day; holding scrupulously back the disorderly elements which fretted under his curb. There was one hour at least when a word from him would have lighted a democratic revolt throughout the empire. The most remarkable of O'Connell's gifts was neither his eloquence nor his sagacity; it was his patience — "patience, all the passion of great souls," — the tireless patience which, from 1800 to 1820, went from town to town, little aided by the press, to plant the seeds of an intelligent and united, as well as hot, patriotism. Then, after many years and long toil, waiting for rivals to be just, for prejudice to wear out and for narrowness to grow wise, using British folly and oppression as his wand, he moulded the enthusiasm of the most excitable of races — the just and inevitable indignation of four millions of Catholics, the hate of plundered poverty — priest, noble and peasant, into one fierce, though harmonious, mass. He held it in careful check, with sober moderation, watching every opportunity, attracting ally after ally, never forfeiting any possible friendship; allowing no provocation to stir him to anything that would not help his cause, — compelling each hottest and most ignorant of his followers to remember that "he who commits a crime helps the enemy." At last, when the hour struck, this power was made to achieve justice for itself and to put him in London — him, this despised Irishman, this hated Catholic, this mere demagogue, and man of words; *him* to hold the Tory party in one hand and the Whig party in the other — all this without shedding a drop of blood, or disturbing for a moment the peace of the empire. While O'Connell held Ireland in his hand, her people were more orderly, law-abiding and peaceful than for a century before or during any year since. The strength of this marvellous control passes comprehension. Out West I met an Irishman whose father held him up to *see* O'Connell address the two hundred thousand men at Tara; literally to *see*, not to hear him. I said, "But you could not all hear even his voice." "Oh, no, sir! only about thirty thousand could hear him. But we all kept as still and silent *as if we did!*" With magnanimous frankness O'Connell once said, "I never could have held those monster meetings without a crime, without disorder, tumult or quarrel, except for Father Mathew's aid." Any man can build a furnace and turn water into steam, — yes, if careless, let it rend his dwelling in pieces. Genius builds the locomotive, harnesses this terrible power in iron traces, holds it with master-hand in useful limits, and gives it to the peaceable service of man. The Irish people were O'Connell's locomotive, sagacious patience and moderation the genius that built it, Parliament and justice the station he reached.

Every one who has studied O'Connell's life sees his marked likeness to Luther; the unity of both their lives, their wit, the same massive strength, even if coarse-grained; the ease with which each reached the masses, the power with which they wielded them; the same unrivalled eloquence, fit for any audience, the same instinct of genius that led them constantly to acts which, as Voltaire said, "Foolish men call rash, but Wisdom sees to be brave;" the same broad success. But O'Connell had one great element which Luther lacked — the universality of his sympathy; the far-reaching sagacity which discerned truth afar off, just struggling above the horizon; the loyal, brave and frank spirit which acknowledged and served it; the profound and rare faith which believed that "the whole of truth can never do harm to the whole of virtue." From the serene height of intellect and judgment to which God's gifts had lifted him, he saw clearly that no one right was ever in the way of another, that injustice harms the wrongdoer even more than the victim, that whoever puts a chain on another fastens it also on himself. Confident that the truth is always safe and justice always expedient, he saw that intolerance is only want of faith.

He who stifles free discussion secretly doubts whether what he professes to believe is really true. Coleridge says, "See how triumphant in debate and action O'Connell is! Why? Because he asserts a broad principle, acts up to it, rests his body on it, and has faith in it."

Co-worker with Father Mathew — champion of the Dissenters — advocating the substantial principles of the Charter, though not a Chartist — foe to the corn-laws — battling against slavery, whether in India or the Carolinas — ready, as early as 1840, to welcome woman's action in civil affairs — the great democrat, who in Europe seventy years ago called the people to his side; starting a movement of the people by the people, for the people, — show me another record as broad and brave as this in the European history of our century? Where is the English statesman, where the Irish leader, who can claim one? No wonder every Englishman hated and feared him. He wounded their prejudices at every point. Whig and Tory, timid Liberal, narrow Dissenter, bitter Radical — all feared and hated this broad, brave soul, who dared to follow Truth wherever he saw her — whose toleration was as broad as human nature and his sympathy as boundless as the sea.

To show you that he never took a leaf from our American gospel of compromise; that he never filed his tongue to silence on one truth, fancying so to help another; that he never sacrificed any race to save even Ireland — let me compare him with Kossuth, whose only merits were his eloquence and his patriotism. When Kossuth was in Faneuil Hall he exclaimed, "Here is a flag without a stain — a nation without a crime!" We abolitionists appealed to him : "Oh, eloquent son of the Magyar, come to break chains, have you no word, no pulse-beat, for four millions of negroes bending under a yoke ten times heavier than that of Hungary?" He answered, "I would forget anybody, I would praise anything to help Hungary."

O'Connell never said anything like that. When I was in Naples I asked Sir Thomas Foxwell Buxton, "Is Daniel O'Connell an honest man?" "As honest a man as ever breathed," said he, and then told me this story: "When, in 1830, O'Connell entered Parliament, the Anti-slavery cause was so weak that it had only Lushington and myself to speak for it, and we agreed that when he spoke I should cheer him, and when I spoke he should cheer me; and these were the only cheers we ever got. O'Connell came, with one Irish member, to support him. A large number of members (I think Buxton said twenty-seven), whom we called the West India interest — the Bristol party, the slave party — went to him, saying, 'O'Connell, at last you are in the House, with one helper. If you will never go down to Freemason's

Hall with Buxton and Brougham, here are twenty-seven votes for you on every Irish question. If you work with those abolitionists, count us always against you.'"

It was a terrible temptation. How many a so-called statesman would have yielded! O'Connell said, "Gentlemen, God knows I speak for the saddest people the sun sees; but may my right hand forget its cunning and my tongue cleave to the roof of my mouth if to help Ireland—even Ireland—I forget the negro one single hour." "From that day," said Buxton, "Lushington and I never went into the lobby that O'Connell did not follow us."

And right in this connection let me read the following telegram:—

CINCINNATI, O., August 6.

Wendell Phillips, Boston:—

The national conference of colored newspaper men to the O'Connell celebration, greeting:—

Resolved, That it is befitting a convention of colored men assembled on the centennial anniversary of the birth of the Liberator of Ireland and friend of humanity, Daniel O'Connell, to recall with gratitude his eloquent and effective pleas for the freedom of our race, and we earnestly commend his example to our countrymen.

J. C. JACKSON, Secretary.
PETER. H. CLARK, President.
GEORGE T. RUBY.
LEWIS D. EASTON.

Learn of O'Connell, friends, the hardest lesson we ever have set us, that of toleration. The foremost Catholic of his age, the most stalwart champion of the Church, he was also broadly and sincerely tolerant of every faith. His toleration had no limit and no qualification.

I scorn and scout the word "toleration." It is an insolent term. No man, properly speaking, *tolerates* another. I do not tolerate a Catholic—neither does he tolerate me. We are equal, and acknowledge each other's rights; that is the correct statement.

That every man should be allowed freely to worship God according to his conscience—that no man's civil rights should be affected by his religious creed—were both cardinal principles of O'Connell. He had no fear that any doctrine of his faith could be endangered by the freest possible discussion.

Learn of him also sympathy with every race and every form of oppression. No matter who was the sufferer, or what the form of the injustice, starving Yorkshire peasant, imprisoned Chartist, persecuted

Protestant, or negro slave; no matter of what right, personal or civil, the victim had been robbed; "no matter what complexion, incompatible with freedom, an African or an Indian sun had burnt upon him; " no matter what religious pretext or political juggle alleged "necessity" as an excuse for his oppression; "no matter with what solemnities he had been devoted on the altar of slavery"—the moment O'Connell saw him, the altar and the God sank together in the dust — the victim was acknowledged a man and a brother — equal in all rights, and entitled to all the aid the great Irishman could give him.

I have no time to speak of the executive ability with which he worked the machines — Unions, Committees, Associations — that his skill had created. I have no time to speak of his marvellous success at the bar; of that profound skill in the law which enabled him to conduct such an agitation, always on the verge of illegality and violence, without once subjecting himself or his followers to legal penalty; an agitation beneath a code of which Brougham said, "No Catholic could lift his hand under it without breaking the law." I have no time to speak of his still more remarkable success in the House of Commons. Of Flood's failure there Grattan had said: "He was an oak of the forest, too old and too great to be transplanted at fifty." Grattan's own success there was but moderate. The power O'Connell wielded against varied, bitter, and unscrupulous opposition, was marvellous. I have no time to speak of his personal independence, his deliberate courage, moral and physical, his unspotted private character, his unfailing hope, the versatility of his talent, his power of tireless work, his ingenuity and boundless resource, his matchless self-possession in every emergency, his ready and inexhaustible wit. But any reference to O'Connell that omitted his eloquence would be painting Wellington in the House of Lords without mention of Torres Vedras, or Waterloo.

Broadly considered, his eloquence has never been equalled in modern times, certainly not in English speech. Do you think I am partial? I will vouch John Randolph, of Roanoke, the Virginia slaveholder, who hated an Irishman almost as much as he hated a Yankee — himself an orator of no mean level. Hearing O'Connell, he exclaimed, "This is the man, these are the lips, the most eloquent that speak English in my day." I think he was right. I remember the solemnity of Webster, the grace of Everett, the rhetoric of Choate; I know the eloquence that lay hid in the iron logic of Calhoun; I have melted beneath the magnetism of Henry Clay; Prentiss, of Mississippi, wielded a power few men ever had. It has been my fortune to sit at the feet of the great speakers of the English tongue on the other side of the ocean. But I think all of them together never surpassed, and no one of them ever equalled, O'Connell. Nature intended him for our Demosthenes. Never since the great Greek has she sent forth .any one so lavishly gifted for his work as a tribune of the people. In the first place, he had a magnificent presence, impressive in bearing — massive, like that of Jupiter. Webster himself hardly outdid him in the majesty of his proportions. To be sure, he had not Webster's craggy face and precipice of brow; nor his eyes glowing like anthracite coal. Nor had he the lion roar of Mirabeau. But his presence filled the eye. A small O'Connell would hardly have been an O'Connell at all. These physical advantages are half the battle. I remem-member Russell Lowell telling us that Mr. Webster came home from Washington at the time the Whig party thought of dissolving, a few years before his death, and went down to Faneuil Hall to protest; drawing himself up to the loftiest proportion, his brow clothed with thunder, before the listening thousands, he said : — " Well, gentlemen, I am a Whig, a Massachusetts Whig, a Faneuil Hall Whig, a revolutionary Whig, a constitutional Whig. If you break the Whig party, sir, where am I to go ? " And says Lowell : — " We held our breath, thinking where he *could* go." If he had been five feet three we should have said, " Who cares where you go ? " So it was with O'Connell. There was majesty in his presence before he spoke, and he added to it what Webster had not, what Clay might have lent him — grace. Lithe as a boy at 65, every attitude a picture, every gesture grace, he was still all nature; nothing but nature seemed to speak all over him. Then he had a voice that covered the gamut. The majesty of his indignation, fitly uttered in tones of superhuman power, made him able to "indict" a nation, in spite of Burke's protest.

I heard him once say, "I send my voice careering like the thunder-storm across the Atlantic to tell Carolina that God's thunderbolts are hot, and to remind the negro that the dawn of his redemption is breaking." You seemed to hear the tones come echoing back to London from the Rocky Mountains. Then, with the slightest possible Irish brogue, he would tell a story, which shook Exeter Hall with fun. The next moment, tears in his voice, like a Scotch song, five thousand men wept. And all the while no effort. He seemed only breathing —

" As effortless as woodland nooks
Send violets up and paint them blue."

We used to say of Webster, This is a great effort; of Everett, It is a beautiful effort; but you never used the word "effort" in speaking of O'Connell. It provoked you that he would not make an effort. And this wonderful power, it was not a thunder-storm; he flanked you with his wit, he surprised you out of yourself, you were conquered before you knew it. His marvellous voice, its almost incredible power and sweetness, Bulwer has well described: —

> "Once to my sight that giant form was given,
>   Walled by wide air and roofed by boundless heaven;
>   Beneath his feet the human ocean lay,
>   And wave on wave rolled into space away.
>   Methought no clarion could have sent its sound
>   Even to the centre of the hosts around;
>   And as I thought, rose the sonorous swell,
>   As from some church-tower swings the silvery bell;
>   Aloft and clear, from airy tide to tide,
>   It glided, easy as a bird may glide.
>   Even to the verge of that vast audience sent,
>   It played with each wild passion as it went;
>   Now stirred the uproar, now the murmur stilled,
>   And sobs or laughter answered as it willed."

Webster could awe a senate, Everett could charm a college, and Choate cheat a jury; Clay could magnetize the million, and Corwin lead them captive. O'Connell was Clay, Corwin, Choate, Everett and Webster in one. Before the courts, logic; at the bar of the senate, unanswerable and dignified; on the platform, grace, wit and pathos; before the masses, a whole man. Carlyle says: "He is God's own anointed king whose single word melts all wills into his." This describes O'Connell. Emerson says: "There is no true eloquence unless there is a man behind the speech." O'Connell was listened to because all England and all Ireland knew that there was a man behind the speech — one who could be neither bought, bullied nor cheated. He held the masses, free but willing subjects in his hands.

He owed this power to the courage that met every new question frankly, and concealed none of his convictions; to an entireness of devotion that made the people feel he was all their own; to a masterly brain that made them sure they were always safe in his hands. Behind them were ages of bloodshed; every rising had ended at the scaffold; even Grattan brought them to 1798. O'Connell said: "Follow me; put your feet where mine have trod, and a sheriff shall never lay hand on your shoulder." And the great lawyer kept his pledge.

This unmatched, long-continued power almost passes belief. You can only appreciate it by comparison. Let me carry you back to the mob-year of 1835, in this country, when the Abolitionists were hunted, when the streets roared with riot, when from Boston to Baltimore, from St. Louis to Philadelphia, a mob took possession of every city; when private houses were invaded and public halls were burned, press after press was thrown into the river, and Lovejoy baptized Freedom with his blood — you remember it. Respectable journals warned the mob that they were playing into the hands of the Abolitionists. Webster and Clay, and the staff of Whig statesmen, told the people that the truth floated further on the shouts of a mob than the most eloquent lips could carry it. But law-abiding, Protestant, educated America could not be held back. Neither Whig chiefs nor respectable journals could keep these people quiet. Go to England. When the Reform Bill of '31 was thrown out from the House of Lords, the people were tumultuous, and Melbourne and Grey, Russell and Brougham, Landsdowne, Holland, and Macaulay, the Whig chiefs, cried out, "Don't violate the law, you help the Tories! Riot puts back the bill." But quiet, sober John Bull, law-abiding, could not do without it. Birmingham was three days in the hands of a mob. Castles were burnt, Wellington ordered the Scotch Greys to rough-grind their swords as at Waterloo. This was the Whig aristocracy of England. O'Connell had neither office nor title. Behind him were 3,000,000 people steeped in utter wretchedness, sore with the oppression of centuries. For thirty restless and turbulent years he stood in front of them, and said : " Remember, he that commits a crime helps the enemy." And during that long and fearful struggle, I do not remember one of his followers ever being convicted of a political offence, and during this period crimes of violence were very rare. There is no such record in our history. Neither in classic nor in modern times can the man be produced who held a million of people in his right hand so passive. It was due to the consistency and unity of a character that had hardly a flaw.

I do not forget your soldiers, orators or poets — any of your leaders. But when I consider O'Connell's personal disinterestedness ; his rare, brave fidelity to every cause his principles covered, no matter how unpopular or how embarrassing to his main purpose ; that clear, far-reaching vision and true heart, which, on most moral and political questions, set him so much ahead of his times ; his eloquence, almost equally effective in the courts, in the senate, and before the masses ; that sagacity, which set at naught the malignant vigilance of the whole Imperial Bar, watching thirty years for a misstep ; when I remember that he invented his tools, and then measure his limited means with his vast success, bearing in mind its nature ; when I see the sobriety and moderation with which he used his measureless power, and the lofty, generous purpose of his whole life, I am ready to affirm that he was, all things considered, the greatest man your Irish race has given to history.